D1276469

BISON
BOOKS

THE YEAR

30

Bison Frontiers of Imagination

UNIVERSITY OF NEBRASKA PRESS | LINCOLN AND LONDON

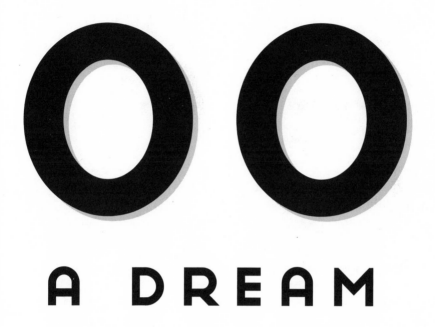

A DREAM

Paolo Mantegazza

WITHDRAWN

PROPERTY OF
SENECA COLLEGE
LIBRARIES
KING CAMPUS

EDITED AND WITH AN INTRODUCTION BY NICOLETTA PIREDDU

TRANSLATED BY DAVID JACOBSON

WITHDRAWN

JAN 2 5 2011

Translation and critical materials
  © 2010 by the Board of Regents of
the University of Nebraska.
  Originally published in Italian as
L'anno 3000: Sogno, 1897.

All rights reserved. Manufactured
  in the United States of America. ∞

  Library of Congress Cataloging-
in-Publication Data
  Mantegazza, Paolo, 1831–1910.
[Anno 3000. English]
  The year 3000 : a dream / Paolo
Mantegazza ; edited and with an
  introduction by Nicoletta Pireddu ;
translated by David Jacobson.
  p. cm. —
(Bison frontiers of imagination)
  Originally published in Italian as
L'anno 3000: sogno, 1897.
  Includes bibliographical references.
ISBN 978-0-8032-3032-3
  (paperback : alkaline paper)
1. Utopias—Fiction. I. Pireddu,
  Nicoletta. II. Jacobson, David, 1955–
III. Title. IV. Title: Year three thousand.
  PQ4712.M8A6613 2010
853'.7—dc22
  2010006790

  Set in Fournier by Bob Reitz.
Designed by Nathan Putens.

A Giovanna,

per 3000 ragioni

Contents

Acknowledgments

Each time Paolo Mantegazza was informed about an upcoming translation of one of his books, he would experience—he claimed—three different forms of pleasure: satisfaction of his own vanity, pride in the widening of his audience, and elation at realizing how the accelerated dissemination of one's work throughout the five continents could make ideas more universal and hence more human.

This project took Mantegazza verbatim at least on his last point, since it involved many people from different corners of the world, to whom I am very much indebted. Professor Arthur B. Evans read an earlier and abridged version of my manuscript and provided valuable suggestions about science fiction topoi and intertextual connections, while Professors Giuseppe Mazzotta and Luigi Ballerini generously endorsed the final product. My dear colleagues Jingyuan Zhang and Philip Kafalas kindly corroborated the totally fictional nature of Mantegazza's Chinese references. Dalila Benachenhou providentially alerted me to the recent French translation of *L'anno 3000*. An engaging and productive conversation with Lorenzo Flabbi on Mercier and Souvestre gave me new food for thought. Adriana Gualdieri, from the Biblioteca Civica "G.Canna" of Casale Monferrato, and Laura Luna were the two indispensible Italian vertices of the Alessandria-Treviso-Washington triangle, thanks to which much-needed proto–science fiction material successfully completed an interregional and intercontinental voyage that seemed more complex than the interplanetary expeditions narrated in the texts themselves. Upon shamefully short notice Elena Denisina, Natalia Malysheva, and Philip Philipovich provided Polish and Russian translations and transliterations, while Lindsay Reimschussel and Donna Scott mercifully rescued me in the midst of copier and postal breakdowns.

ACKNOWLEDGMENTS

I am delighted to have been able to undertake a second Mantegazzian editorial journey in the excellent company of David Jacobson with the aid of communication technologies that—confirming ahead of time Mantegazza's forecasts and hopes for the fourth millennium—allowed us, via ether, to cross the equator separating our respective hemispheres. To be sure, however, we would not have reached our destination without the vital support of the Interlibrary Loan Department of Lauinger Library at Georgetown University, to whose staff I wish to express once again (and certainly not for the last time!) all my appreciation.

Working with the University of Nebraska Press has been a great joy. Tom Swanson's prompt and enthusiastic response to my project was an even more powerful thrust than the propulsion of Mantegazza's spaceships. The warmth, efficiency, and professionalism of Alicia Christensen, Tish Fobben, Acacia Gentrup, Cara Pesek, Alison Rold, Carol Sickman-Garner, and Sabrina Stellrecht at all stages of the publication process have made this editorial experience truly rewarding.

And, finally, my heartfelt *grazie* to Professor Giovanna Lombardi, with deep affection and admiration, because all my exciting travels into the literature of the past, present, and future millennia started under her loving and inspiring guidance and are still progressing along the paths she continues to trace with grace and intelligence.

In recognition of all the support I have received for the production of this volume, I can only appropriate Mantegazza's desire for a global circulation of his translated works and hence hope that this English version of *L'anno 3000* will engage and amuse readers worldwide even before the diffusion of the Cosmic language.

Nicoletta Pireddu

THE YEAR 3000

INTRODUCTION

Paolo Mantegazza,
Fabulator of the Future

Nicoletta Pireddu

FOR SOMEBODY WHO, IN 1854, LEFT ITALY
for South America at the age of twenty-three with the ultimate project of creating an agricultural colony formed by Northern Italian
émigrés, the prospect of imagining human communities in the fourth
millennium must not have seemed particularly daring. And it must
have been even less problematic to put aside, at least temporarily,
the role of anthropologist and scientist to wear the hat of the literary writer.

Actually, it is impossible to talk about Paolo Mantegazza without
resorting to overly hyphenated identitarian labels like those that, one
century ago, introduced this captivating Italian intellectual to the
American audience: "Physician-surgeon, Laboratory-experimenter,

Author-editor, Traveller-anthropologist, Professor, Sanitarian, Senator."[1] By then, indeed, Mantegazza was already very popular in all these capacities in the Western world at large—read and reprinted profusely and quoted by such leading scientific figures as Charles Darwin, Sigmund Freud, Richard von Krafft-Ebing, Max Bartels and Paul Bartels, and Havelock Ellis.

Born in 1831 in the Northern Italian town of Monza, near Milan, this veritable Renaissance man whose versatility would fully satisfy any "biographer in search of six characters" (Robinson ix) began his career as a pathologist but soon combined his medical interests with a desire for travel, which led him first to Argentina and later to Lapland and India. The contact with cultural otherness turned him into an anthropologist, a profession that, in addition to winning him the first Italian chair in that discipline (Florence, 1870), would inspire over one hundred works, from his travelogues *Rio de la Plata e Tenerife*, *Un viaggio in Lapponia* (*A Voyage to Lapland*), and *India*, to his famous four-volume collection *Fisiologia del piacere* (The Physiology of Pleasure), *Fisiologia dell'amore* (*The Physiology of Love*), *Fisiologia dell'odio* (The Physiology of Hate), and *Fisiologia del dolore* (The Physiology of Pain).

However, his scientific interests always went hand in hand with a commitment to sanitary, political, pedagogical, and aesthetic matters. In all these fields Mantegazza made innovative contributions, experimenting with artificial insemination and grafting on animals, inventing the *globulimeter* to measure the number of red cells in blood, founding the National Museum of Anthropology and Ethnology and the journal *Archivio per l'antropologia e l'etnologia* (still the official Italian publication in the discipline), promoting photography for anthropological research, creating the serial *Hygienic Almanacs* as an outreach measure for the improvement of people's sanitary conditions, and inaugurating the fashion of seaside holidays with an emphasis on the therapeutic and leisure potential of beach resorts.

In the domain of literature Mantegazza showed no less variety in his choice of genres and topics, ranging from the epistolary sentimental novel *Un giorno a Madera* (*One Day in Madeira*, 1868), which brings together physiology, love, and hygiene, to the Epicurean and exotic tones of the autobiographical fiction *Il Dio ignoto* (The Unknown God, 1886), to the futuristic story of a journey to an imaginary elsewhere in *L'anno 3000. Sogno* (*The Year 3000: A Dream*, 1897). Here this provocative popularizer of knowledge transferred to a utopian fourth millennium the controversial scientific, moral, social, and political issues that he had broached over his long and productive lifetime, hence offering Italy a niche in the realm of early science fiction, a genre that had already gained ground in other European countries.[2]

The Literature of Tomorrow: The Year 3000 *and Its Foreign Models*

The Year 3000—the story of Paolo and Maria's journey to the futuristic capital city of the United Planetary States to get married—effectively represents the kaleidoscopic mentality and worldview of Mantegazza as an exponent of an epoch at the crossroads between the certainties of positivism and the anxieties of the turn of the nineteenth century. Arguably the most original of Mantegazza's fictional texts, it is equally pioneering in the wider context of Italian literature of the 1800s. With his representation of an allegedly better life in a fourth millennium transformed by scientific discoveries, technical developments, and institutional accomplishments, Mantegazza contributed to a utopian genre that, from Thomas More's seminal work *Utopia* (1515) and Tommaso Campanella's *City of the Sun* (1602), through Francis Bacon's *New Atlantis* (1627) and Cyrano de Bergerac's *Comical History of the States and Empires of the Moon* (1656), now received new impetus from a nineteenth-century futuristic imagination nourished and substantiated by the principles of burgeoning scientific and technological progress.

From the works of Félix Bodin and Émile Souvestre to those of Camille Flammarion, Jules Verne, Edward Bellamy, and H. G. Wells, among many others, literary narratives launch readers on adventurous tours de force in space and time in which ferments for the advancement of rational knowledge often merge with tensions between contrasting social ideologies—the culture of monopolies and capitalism, on the one hand, and, on the other, socialist and communist ideals. The common denominator of these works is what Darko Suvin defines as *"the narrative dominance or hegemony of a fictional 'novum' (novelty, innovation) validated by cognitive logic"* and "totalizing" in nature (63). The novelty of science fiction, in other words, "entails a change of the whole universe of the tale" (Suvin 64) or at least of its pivotal aspects, and relies upon "methodically systematic cognition" (65) to justify its difference with respect to the empirical norms of the reader's reality.

The international cultural and professional relations that Mantegazza cultivated through his numerous collaborations with foreign intellectuals, his voracious reading (of French texts in particular, as his unpublished journals confirm), and his frequent travels abroad unquestionably also allowed him to become acquainted early with the literary fashions developing beyond the Italian border, especially in France, where he lived in 1854 while completing his volume *Fisiologia del piacere*. While it is unclear precisely how much Mantegazza knew of foreign science fiction production, his formal choices in *The Year 3000* suggest that he was at least aware of the properties of this new genre and of the topoi that several earlier and contemporary authors had adopted. As a committed promoter of culture and of himself, attracted by innovation and particularly attentive to strategies and stylistic formulas that might grant him success, Mantegazza seemed to understand the impact that science fiction could have upon a wide audience and hence was eager to leave his personal imprint on this new literary realm, just as he had on other fictional and nonfictional forms, from the epistolary novel and the travelogue to the scientific and cultural essay and biography and personal memoirs.

If Louis Sébastien Mercier's 1771 utopia *L'an 2440. Rêve s'il en fut jamais* is considered the first novel with a specifically futuristic setting, Félix Bodin was the first to make critical and theoretical statements on what would take shape as a new genre, for which Bodin coined the expression *littérature futuriste* (futurist literature) (Bodin, Preface 37).[3] In the preface to his 1834 novel *Le Roman de l'avenir* (*The Novel of the Future*) Bodin emphasized the difference between, on the one hand, the lack of depth and action in traditional utopian or apocalyptic literature (32)—whose undeveloped setting, plot, and characterization were for him merely in the service of a specific moral, religious, or political agenda that does not elicit the reader's participation—and, on the other, the blend of marvelous and verisimilar elements through which futuristic fiction could fulfill both emotional and rational needs in a century that was increasingly scientific yet not ready to sacrifice the fantastic and marvelous for the sake of mere speculation. Imagining a future of plausible marvels through literature, for Bodin, would encourage hope and hasten "the progress of humanity" (34). Nevertheless, as he discussed the potential and the effects of futurist literature, Bodin highlighted one main challenge facing this "future genre" (40)—namely, its inability "to satisfy everyone" (37). Being, understandably, "more airy-fairy" (37–38) than the past, the future, for Bodin, could be constructed according to individual fantasies ("every sect and system has its own" [38]); hence its depictions would run a higher risk of disappointing an audience with very diverse mindsets and expectations.

The plot of *The Novel of the Future* seems to substantiate this apparently inevitable weakness, since, although Bodin's story is set "somewhere in the 20th century of our Christian era" (54) and allegedly intends to fulfill readers' desire "to find every appearance of reality therein" (44), it does not prioritize the display of sensational inventions as a hallmark of future life, contrary to the works of most subsequent writers. *The Novel of the Future* does introduce steamships, birdlike aerostats propelled by artificial wing power, and underwater cities, but its main concern, as Paul Alkon observes, is "the phenomenology of possible futures, not technological forecast" (265). Bodin founds his future world upon the tension between emotional and rational forces, represented, respectively, by the "Poetic" or "Anti-Prosaic Association" and by a world federation governed by a utilitarian "Universal Association of Civilization" whose parliament meets once a year in diverse cities such as Vienna, Athens, and the fictional Centropolis in the South American republic of

Benthamia. The poetic side of Bodin's fragmented and incomplete story is the patina of a vanished past that colors the wonders of his imaginary future, characterized by heroic ideals and an epic and mythic grandeur, evoked by Greek-sounding archaic names like Philirène, Philomaque, Eudoxie, and Politée and materialized by an exotic ambience, ancient ruins, emperors, pharaohs, and amazons fighting against the dehumanized and standardized life brought about by industrialization and mechanization.

Significantly, despite the idiosyncratic nature of representations of the future and their authors' personal agendas, what in fact can be observed in the "novels of the future" evolving and proliferating after Bodin's is precisely the recurrence of particular stock situations and narrative patterns. For instance, the topos of the dream and/or sleep as a literary technique to justify the leap from the present to the future is found quite often in early European science fiction, albeit for different purposes and with different outcomes. In his "preface" to *The Novel of the Future*, for instance, Bodin claims his story is a synthesis of numerous manuscripts owned by an Italian refugee and visionary he met in London, Fabio Mummio, who had an "invincible inclination to acquire knowledge of the future" (47) through forensic astrology, chiromancy, necromancy, and mesmerism. Bodin's novel is allegedly built upon the notebooks recording Mummio's hallucinations, somnambulisms, and "magnetic interrogations" (49) of women from all over the world, from whom he had gathered "visions, anticipations, and prophecies" (52) of the time to come.

But the oneiric dimension was already the main vehicle to the future in *L'an 2440*, by Mercier, whom Bodin acknowledges as a predecessor in the very act of parodying him with his dedication "To the Past" (Bodin 27)—a response to Mercier's celebration of the future of the third millennium.[4] After discussing the injustices of his time with a philosopher friend, Mercier's anonymous protagonist falls asleep only to wake up in a futuristic Paris that, even more than Bodin's civilization, stands out less for its scientific and technological innovations than for its moral, social, and institutional transformations. Touching upon issues that would be equally crucial to Mantegazza's year

3000, in Mercier's 2440 nations live in harmony and are only rarely upset by war. Standing armies, slavery, priests, and taxes have been abolished, and, thanks to a thorough reorganization of public space, safety and sanitary conditions have dramatically improved.

Indeed, the topoi, situations, and structural elements of these foundational literary constructions of the future recur, with variations, in the works of the many science fiction writers who dot the nineteenth century. Paul Alkon warns us against the temptation to extrapolate from either authors or readers a collective consciousness of futuristic literature as a monolithic genre able to encompass and systematize such diverse narrative forms as accounts of journeys through fantastic universes, epic marvels, utopias, and philosophical tales. Rather, he approaches these literary achievements as independent manifestations (11, 246). Nevertheless, a look at Mantegazza's novel substantiates the fact that many formulas of the futuristic imagination first seen in Mercier and Bodin began, just a few decades later, to fertilize the literary panorama of various countries, Italy included. Indeed, *L'anno 3000* seems to synthesize and reelaborate very specific elements belonging to what was developing, especially abroad, as the distinct literary convention of forward temporal displacement, by then characterized by a wider geographical setting, less and less confined to the authors' own nations, and by the importance of science and technology for social transformation.

Starting from a peritextual component like the book title, we could argue that in *L'anno 3000. Sogno* there resonates *L'an 2440. Rêve s'il en fut jamais*. But Mantegazza also modified the work of his established forerunner Mercier (whose novel went through twenty-five editions after its first appearance in 1771, including an Italian translation in 1798) in a way that reflects his personal *Weltanschauung*. With the overachieving attitude he displayed in most of his accomplishments, Mantegazza further stretched Mercier's temporal displacement in order to reach the fourth millennium and, eliminating the doubtful apposition in Mercier's title, stated more assertively the factualness of the oneiric dimension. Unlike in Mercier's plot, where the protagonists fall asleep in order to reach the third millennium, characters and readers in *The Year 3000* access the future naturally. The futuristic experience is conceived and presented as thoroughly verisimilar, without the mediation of a frame. Neither the narrator nor the plot justifies the role that the allusion to a dream plays in the title, apart from an indirect reference to the author's personal fantasy, which can be further substantiated by Paolo's reference to the imagination of a nineteenth-century writer who authored a book on life in the fourth millennium (58). What could be considered a structural weakness in the novel, however, is all the more intriguing precisely because it is unmotivated and not integrated in the plot, reinforcing the possibility of an element borrowed from some other source and incorporated in a mechanical way.

However, Mantegazza was not the first writer whose imagination traversed the threshold of the fourth millennium. In 1846 Émile Souvestre had published *Le monde tel qu'il sera* (*The World as It Shall Be*), an account of the adventures of Maurice and Marthe, who, after "a profound and death-like sleep" (8), are transported to the year 3000 in their coffins by the curious allegorical figure of John Progrès — "a cross between a banker and a notary" (6) and a surrogate of the fairy godmother whom Marthe wishes to have as a chaperone to the future.[5] They wake up in a future Tahiti, which, from a captivating exotic island, has turned into a center for greedy entrepreneurs, and from there they set out for a worldwide tour that discloses extravagant technological and scientific conquests, from air-conditioning, televisions, telephones, hot-air balloons, and underwater transportation, to new materials, engineered giant fruits and vegetables, and genetic manipulation of the human race. Broadly recognized in France but also widely translated in Europe and the United States, the novel must not have escaped Mantegazza.[6] Both authors transcended Mercier's limited French setting by describing a couple's worldwide journeys, touching upon a rich variety of geographical, institutional, and urban spaces with allegorical toponyms that make up part of a universal political system (the Republic of United Interests for Souvestre and the United Planetary States for Mantegazza), each with an exotic capital city located in a geographically recognizable area (Tahiti for Souvestre and the Indian town of Darjeeling for Mantegazza's Andropolis). Mantegazza's novel also seems to reproduce certain elements of *The World as It Shall Be*, including the detailed summaries at the opening of each chapter and several specific plot components. For instance, the distribution of prizes for virtue among the Academicians of the Institute of Sans-Pair in Souvestre (139) is echoed in the final chapter of *The Year 3000*, where the Andropolis Academy of Science awards the cosmic prize to the individual who has made the greatest discovery in the last decade. Likewise, the section on the evolution of the dramatic genre and the status of theater performances in Souvestre's chapter 19 (169–90) raises topics that are reelaborated in chapter 10 of *The Year 3000*, where Mantegazza explores the theaters of Andropolis and their spectacles.

Yet precisely such points of great similarity between the two novels also allow us to see that, beyond structural analogies, Souvestre and Mantegazza have different styles and priorities. Richer in narrative and descriptive details, *The World as It Shall Be* is concerned above all with the moral underpinnings of its characters' futuristic journey, whereas the more concise and linear approach of *The Year 3000* reflects its author's scientific mentality and priorities. Both authors are daring in their visions of technology's future potential, even though Souvestre's solutions, albeit ingenious, are less advanced, as in the case of catapults allowing people to move between different places. However, Souvestre and Mantegazza in fact attribute quite different values to the conquests of progress. Not accidentally, *The World as It Shall Be* is considered the first futuristic dystopia, which, in a comic and hyperbolic tone, presents implausible fourth-millennium scenarios precisely to annihilate hope in what Maurice anticipates as "all its splendid promise" (Souvestre 7). The idealistic, loving, principled couple who initially wishes to "leapfrog the centuries" (7) in order to find themselves in a "perfect future" (7), instead of living "in the present with all its strife and uncertainty" (7), in fact transport the reader to a dysfunctional, corrupt future at the mercy of capitalism and covetousness. Mantegazza's Paolo and Maria belong to the year 3000 and consistently act as spokespersons for its utopian social and political context, although, as we will see, this future milieu also reveals ambivalences and problematic contradictions.

While Souvestre's protagonists travel to the year 3000 as newly-weds, the fact that Mantegazza's Paolo and Maria are merely affianced probably stems from the work of Albert Robida, another popular French novelist and a forerunner of science fiction and fantasy illustration, chronologically closer to Mantegazza and renowned for his pioneering literary and visual technological imagination. Robida was the author, among many futuristic works (some of them parodies of Jules Verne's novels and characters), of the 1892 novel *Voyage de fiançailles au XXème siecle* (Engagement Trip to the Twentieth Century), the story of Estelle Lacombe and the young Georges Lorris, a member of a prominent family of scientists. The two young lovers, in a long-distance relationship that began by "telephonoscope"—and hence under the aegis of electricity—go on a honeymoon in 1954, before getting married, in order to get to know each other better and verify their compatibility before their wedding. More moderate than Souvestre in his temporal projection (making "only" a sixty-year leap from his book's publication, probably insufficient for Mantegazza) but bolder in terms of moral and social standards, Robida seems to speak to Mantegazza's sensitivity, especially considering Mantegazza's insistent emphasis on the need for an authentic union of souls between man and woman, as opposed to a hypocritical, self-interested, and passionless arrangement.[7] In an interesting anticipation of Paolo and Maria's departure aboard the aerotach at the opening of *The Year 3000*, Robida's Georges and Estelle leave with the "aeronef" (aeroship) that Georges's father prepares for them, together with a detailed itinerary for a journey that will take them, instead of to stereotypical romantic and touristic places like Venice, Naples, Constantinople, and Tunis, to electric furnaces and hydroelectric central stations (Robida 14).

Electricity, which supplants the steam-propelled machines of most early science fiction and is almost omnipresent in Mantegazza's *The Year 3000*, finds in Robida an enthusiastic supporter, as we can see in many of his other books, including *Le vingtième siècle. La vie électrique* (The Twentieth Century: Electric Life, 1890). Already in the previous decade, however, Camille Flammarion—visionary astronomer, science popularizer, and prolific author of space novels—had undertaken several aerostat flights to study atmospheric electricity and transposed the results in his many fictional works. Moreover, Jules Verne, who would become the father of French science fiction and who was already enjoying considerable popularity in Italy, had already narrated abundant sky, land, and underwater adventures made possible by complex instruments and means of transportation, imaginatively rendering both existing and emerging technologies, particularly electricity. After Joseph Deleuil's 1844 demonstration of the arc lamp in the Parisian Place de la Concorde, France had to wait for over four decades before the light bulb replaced candles, paraffin, oil, and gas in domestic use. Unquestionably, however, the potential of this new form of energy was immediately evident, and Verne proved a passionate fabulist celebrating its multiple uses.[8]

We may think, for instance, of *Journey to the Centre of the Earth* (originally published in 1864 and translated into Italian by Treves in 1874) with "Mr. Ruhmkorff's apparatus"(54)—that is, a "Bunsen pile," the early electrical battery that had appeared the year before in *Five Weeks in a Balloon*, here part of a more complex device leading to a portable electric lantern: "An induction coil communicates the electricity produced by the pile to a lantern of peculiar shape. In this lantern there is a spiral tube where a vacuum has been made, and in which nothing remains but a residuum of carbonic acid gas, or of azote. When the apparatus is put in motion this gas becomes luminous, producing a steady white light" (54–55). Or even more relevant is *20,000 Leagues under the Sea*, where electricity is ubiquitous although the novel was published in 1870, over a decade before the electric light bulb became a reality, thanks to the experiments of Sir Joseph Swan in England, Thomas Edison in the United States, and Alessandro Cruto in Italy. For instance, in chapter 12, "All by Electricity," Captain Nemo describes to Professor Aronnax the various instruments aboard the *Nautilus* and the boat's electric power source, extolling that "powerful agent, obedient, rapid, easy, which conforms to every use, and reigns supreme on board my vessel. Everything is done by means of it. It lights, heats, and is the soul of my mechanical apparatus" (Verne, *Complete* 177).

Interestingly, on the first page of Mantegazza's *The Year 3000* a simple switch on the wall of the aerotach "turns the electricity into heat, light, movement, whatever your pleasure" (57), a probable debt to Verne as much as an effect of the technical advances that were also gaining ground in Italy. The city of Milan, for instance, hosted the first demonstration of public electric lighting on March 18, 1877, followed, in June 1881, by the lighting of the Vittorio Emanuele Gallery by arc light bulbs on the occasion of the National Exposition. Milan would thus soon become one of the first European cities providing electric public lighting, thanks to commercial agreements to buy equipment from the international company that managed Thomas Edison's interests in Europe.[9] A speedy industrialization process allowed Northern Italy to catch up with the rest of Europe, and in 1898, one year after the publication of *L'anno 3000*, Turin hosted the General Italian and International Exposition of Electricity. By 1890 the first electric railway in Europe had begun operating between Florence and Fiesole.

The presence of electricity in Verne's novels attests to the widespread awe people felt for this new technology, seen as a powerful mark of progress that could modify all aspects of nature. Significantly, however, Verne's vague and incomplete explanations of electricity reveal that this phenomenon was still partially obscure to him. Furthermore, unlike Robida and Mantegazza, whose works integrate scientific discoveries and technological innovations into everyday life, Verne tends to present the social developments of his own inventions as the creations of mad scientists or of anomalous individuals who often act in the past or in contemporary settings—sometimes geographically "other," but only rarely in the future.

Still, among Verne's more neglected examples of futuristic fiction, *Paris in the Twentieth Century* and the novella *In the Year 2889* deserve attention, along with *Une ville idéale* (An Ideal City), a story that Verne presented as a lecture in 1875 at the Academy of Sciences,

Letters, and Arts in Amiens.[10] Whether twentieth-century Paris, the Amiens of the year 2000 that Verne declares he dreamed of, or a New York rebaptized as Centropolis in 2889, Verne's cities exhibit not just architectural innovations, but above all electrically operated machinery available to the population at large. An electric connection in *Une ville idéale* allows the Emperor's pianist to hold a concert in Paris and make his notes resonate on keyboards in London, Vienna, Rome, St. Petersburg, and Peking (*Ville* 29).[11] *In the Year 2889* features electric calculators, along with accumulators and transformers that, at the touch of a button, produce energy without batteries or dynamos and the powerful electric sparks of deadly weapons. Yet Verne was also increasingly obsessed with the risks posed by technology in the life of the future, leading, for instance, to the extremes of efficiency found in *Paris in the Twentieth Century* or to the excessive power of the press in *In the Year 2889*. Verne unquestionably preferred mysterious and exotic islands to futuristic urban spaces (and, unlike Mantegazza, did not attempt to reconcile these two milieus), as attested to by the collapse of the dejected Michael Dufrenoy in a hollow city possessed by the "demon of electricity" at the end of *Paris in the Twentieth Century* (199).

But if transalpine literary culture was certainly the most meaningful reference point for Mantegazza, the international literary panorama to which *The Year 3000* belongs must also include seminal British and American futuristic utopian authors like H. G. Wells and Edward Bellamy, whose works had begun to circulate in Italy. For instance, Bellamy's *Looking Backward: 2000–1887*, published by Treves in 1890 as *Nell'anno 2000*, soon reached its thirteenth Italian edition. It is once again a resort to induced sleep, through hypnosis, that allows Bellamy's protagonist, Julian West, to wake up at the outset of the third millennium. The abundant, efficient, and harmonious future that welcomes him makes the nineteenth century, by comparison, look appalling in its poverty, degradation, and lack of solidarity. Bellamy's twenty-first century has its share of high-tech solutions—fully electrified homes, cable telephones for home delivery of sermons, and credit cards—but above all it stands out for its commitment to equality, attained not so much through unrest and struggle as through a shift in people's intellectual and moral attitudes.

Improvements in the education and health systems, hospital treatment for the criminally inclined, and the overcoming of lying, for instance, would certainly have met with Mantegazza's approval, yet the author of *The Year 3000* could not be further from Bellamy's utopia's socialist orientation—precisely the ideology that Mantegazza most aggressively debunks in his own futuristic novel.[12] The prospect of Bellamy's future had already met with the resistance of William Morris, who, although not rejecting socialism tout court, took issue in his 1891 *News from Nowhere* with the loss of creativity and pleasure entailed by the excessively authoritarian perspective of *Looking Backward*. In any case, while both Bellamy and Morris joined the already long line of writers who could witness the future through the trick of sleep or dreams—actually a two-directional trick in Bellamy's case, toward both the future and the past—it was not until 1895, with H. G. Wells's *The Time Machine*, that an authentic journey backward and forward through time could take place with the more realistic aid of technology, rather than the intervention of oneiric or other obscure forces.

For Mantegazza, however, just as there is no time or reason for backward glances, neither fantastic machinations nor technological gadgets are necessary to justify the leap into future centuries. A belief in science and the writer's realistic imagination suffice to allow the reader to fly on the wings of progress without ever inverting the arrow of time.

Yesterday's Future: The Culture of Italian Proto—Science Fiction

If Mantegazza deserves to be considered a prominent interlocutor in the European panorama of utopian, futuristic literature, his contribution to the genre is all the more relevant in the Italian context, where the tradition of early science fiction is less visible and solid than its foreign equivalents and still little studied, even less from a comparative perspective.

Along with the popularity of the sentimental tones of the *feuilleton*, the Italy of Mantegazza's time saw the rise of two different literary movements. On the one hand, readers turned to truthful, nonidealistic accounts of reality—a trend that came to be known as *verismo* in the works of such novelists as Giovanni Verga and Luigi Capuana, similar to what had already gained ground in other European cultures as realism and naturalism. On the other hand, authors like Gabriele D'Annunzio and Giovanni Pascoli, the Italian equivalents of Charles Baudelaire, Joris-Karl Huysmans, and Oscar Wilde, penned decadent, symbolist works that celebrated the predominance of sensations, the cult of beauty, and the autonomy of art.

To be sure, these groups of writers were not themselves totally insensitive to the appeal of fantastic elements. Often, authors best known for their realist aesthetics (Verga, Capuana, De Roberto, and Serao, among others) also explored irrational and disquieting situations dealing with occultism, alchemy, magic, and superstition—phenomena that a few decades earlier had been central to the "Scapigliatura" movement. More specifically, however, in the early nineteenth century Italian culture had already experienced an intriguing although short-lived fad of marvelous literary travels in space. This trend bloomed in conjunction with the astronomer William Herschel's construction of a powerful reflecting telescope—with a 40-foot focal length and a 49.5-inch aperture—that on August 28, 1789, led to the discovery of two new moons around Saturn, then many other celestial objects, including the planet Uranus. Herschel's technological and scientific accomplishments, coupled with his belief in extraterrestrial life, nourished much public debate and many popular fantasies throughout Europe. In Italian literature and iconography this proto-science-fictional imaginary ranged from winged lunar inhabitants and hot-air-balloon journeys to the moon featuring the Neapolitan character Pulcinella, to works like Francesco Bruni's *Lettera su la ipotesi degli abitanti de' pianeti* (Letter on the Hypothesis of Planet Inhabitants, 1836) and Francesco Viganò's *Il Viaggio nell'Universo. Visioni del tempo e dello spazio* (The Journey into the Universe: Visions of Time and Space, 1838) (see Valla).

An interest in scientific and futuristic topics reemerged in Italy a few decades later, when, under the influence of leading foreign contributors to the genre, two distinct fantastic trends took shape—extraordinary voyages inspired by the marvels of Jules Verne and futuristic wars of the kind portrayed in George Tomkyns Chesney's 1871 *The Battle of Dorking*. It is hence possible to debunk the myth that slower Italian industrialization, compared to other European nations, also delayed the development of a scientific and technological imagination in Italian literature. Indeed, by the turn of the nineteenth century Italy was seeing a substantial output of fantastical works both as complete volumes and as short fiction published in serials such as *Il Giornale Illustrato dei Viaggi* (1878) (the first magazine in the field, published by Sonzogno after it acquired the rights to the French *Journal des Voyages* [Turris x]), *La Tribuna Illustrata* (1890), and *La Domenica del Corriere* (1899). Translations and adaptations of French and Anglo American authors, both established and less known, proliferated—from Poe and Verne (the Italian translations of the latter almost contemporary with the publication of the French originals), to Wells, Flammarion, and Robida, among many others. The Italian audience's tastes were further shaped by editorial choices, as, for example, Verne's and Wells's works were published as youth and popular literature, while Bellamy's and Morris's were aimed toward more engaged, adult readers.

A few works published before Mantegazza's *The Year 3000* adopted the topos of spatial and/or temporal displacement combined with utopian themes, variously expressing either optimism or anxiety and skepticism toward scientific and material progress, often transposing into the future the political and social issues that dominated public debate in Italy (e.g., socialism, matters of justice). For instance, the very successful *La colonia felice. Utopia* (The Happy Colony: A Utopia, 1874), by Carlo Dossi, addresses the question of human perfectibility through the utopian story of a group of convicts who, instead of being given a death sentence, are confined to a remote island where, by negotiating a peaceful coexistence, they learn to abide by the social contract. Although they are very diverse, several

Italian novels can in fact be inserted into the narrower category of science fiction and futuristic literature, including Guglielmo Folliero De Luna's *I Misteri Politici della Luna* (The Political Mysteries of the Moon, 1863), Agostino Della Sala Spada's *Nel 2073! Sogni d'uno stravagante* (In 2073! Dreams of an Odd Man, 1874), Antonio Ghislanzoni's *Abrakadabra. Storia dell'avvenire* (Abracadabra: The Story of the Future, 1884), Ulisse Grifoni's *Dalla terra alle stelle. Viaggio meraviglioso di due italiani e un francese* (From the Earth to the Moon: The Marvelous Journey of Two Italians and a Frenchman, 1887), and F. Bianchi's *Da Terra a Marte* (From Earth to Mars, 1895).[13] Nevertheless, although the genre was quite vital at the local level, Italian proto–science fiction, particularly futuristic works, did not enjoy the same resonance as its foreign counterparts, its practitioners developing practically no relationship with the more renowned European writers to whom they often owed a great deal. Several of these Italian authors have now fallen into oblivion, their biographies extremely difficult to reconstruct.

For his part, except general topics such as technological devices and a displacement into the future, whether into space or just to an imaginary earthly place, Mantegazza does not seem to have shared much with the visions of his immediate Italian predecessors. For instance, Grifoni's *Dalla terra alle stelle* tells, in flashback, the story of Alberto, a college student from Florence, who, accidentally mixing various chemicals, produces a paint that nullifies gravity. With his friend Professor Sandrelli, Alberto builds a ship called *Flying House* with which the two travel around the world and into space, land on Mars where they find tiny human-looking inhabitants, and fly back to Earth, until the ship sinks near the North Pole. With its adventurous interplanetary journey, its many digressions on scientific issues, and its fascinating illustrations, *Dalla terra alle stelle* recalls the work of Jules Verne, whom Grifoni, not incidentally, acknowledges as his model in the preface to his fifth edition in 1890, proudly reporting his publisher's earlier comments about the Vernian quality of this pioneering "fantastic-scientific novel."[14] Yet Grifoni's novel also intriguingly anticipates Professor Cavor's attempts to create an antigravity substance in H. G. Wells's 1901 scientific romance *The First Men in the Moon*, which would be translated into Italian only in 1910.

Despite the many innovative and captivating narrative solutions that make *Dalla terra alle stelle* a milestone in the domain of science fiction, Grifoni's novel does not introduce the scientific, social, and political issues soon to emerge in *L'anno 3000*. Ghislanzoni's *Abrakadabra. Storia dell'avvenire* and Della Sala Spada's *Nel 2073! Sogni d'uno stravagante*, however, allow us to map an intertextual background for Mantegazza's novel. First partially published in installments between 1864 and 1865, twenty years before its more complete and revised version, Ghislanzoni's *Abrakadabra* is a hallucinatory and convoluted story told by a mysterious nobleman interested in occultism and the cabala, who projects himself into a highly technologized and apparently emancipated and pacified 1977, which in fact turns out to be an era of extreme fanaticism and liberticide. Against the backdrop of complex philosophical and moralizing debates, a mystic and tragic love story develops between Albani and Fidelia, before an apocalyptic destruction and rebirth of the world by angel-like creatures that strongly recall the ending of Souvestre's *The World as It Shall Be*. Further, although it is far removed from the vision and tone of *The Year 3000*, *Abrakadabra* also provides Mantegazza with a specific political setting and key institutional elements for his adventures in the fourth millennium—namely, the idea of a federative European union whose geographical and cultural boundaries can be overcome thanks to flying gondolas and other futuristic means of transportation, supranational governments, and a "Cosmic" language. These details, which appear for the first time in Italian literature in Ghislanzoni's work, reflect important and often neglected debates on Europeanism and federalism that developed in Italy simultaneously with the Risorgimento's myth of national identity.

But before he provided food for thought to Mantegazza, proverbially avid for knowledge and intriguing ideas, Ghislanzoni was very probably the source of inspiration for Della Sala Spada's *Nel 2073! Sogni d'uno stravagante*, which, evoking Mercier's well-known title *L'an*

2440. Rêve s'il en fut jamais, might also have worked as a *trait-d'union* between the French initiator of futuristic utopias and Mantegazza's *L'anno 3000. Sogno.* Yearning to stop living and be born again in the future, Della Sala's protagonist, Saturnino Saturnini, asks the scientist Professor Rokroktwen to put him to sleep for two hundred years with the aid of magnetism, then wakes up in a virtuous and peaceful society, in which people are gathered in a confederation and unified by Latin as a universal language. They live under simple laws, with no need for lawyers, and enjoy highly improved hygienic conditions thanks to the discovery of connections between physical well-being and the earth's electromagnetic currents. All areas of life are marked by imaginative innovations, from unfolding balconies, pipes that distribute wine into each household, homes built in four days, and speedy underground shuttles, to various homages to electricity and its Vernian renditions, such as the "elettrofono" (82–83), which diffuses music as though from one hundred orchestras; the "elettrografia" (98), an electric stenographer that records and transcribes words; and a network (a sort of Internet *ante litteram*) that makes communication circulate worldwide through electric wires in each speaker's mouth (158).

Della Sala's debt to those portions of Ghislanzoni's novel already published at the time allows us to appreciate Mantegazza's penchant for reworking his predecessors' material. Beyond specific elements such as artificial storms, a universal language, moralizing emblems, and mystic women, Della Sala shares with Ghislanzoni an overall archaic, religious, and almost mythologizing atmosphere. Both authors devote lengthy digressions to their own time and milieu, solidly anchoring their work in the values of the present and the past instead of using it as a springboard to explore a truly new life in the fourth millennium, able to transcend the here and now. This conservatism also explains the local settings—respectively Turin and Milan—these authors choose for their futuristic worlds and the canonical, traditional languages designated as having attained "cosmic" or "universal" status—French in *Abrakadabra* and Latin in *Nel 2073!*[15] The universal idiom in *The Year 3000*, on the other hand, is defined simply as "cosmic," without endorsing any existing national language (and actually declaring these languages dead). For the same reason Mantegazza's fourth millennium transcends real and narrowly Italian spaces to exhibit a more global and creative interest. At the same time, however, *The Year 3000* also demonstrates concern with more verisimilar innovations, unlike the implausible and extravagant visions of Ghislanzoni and, even more so, Della Sala Spada, which do not fit into a cogent overall intellectual design. Therefore, even if they inspired Mantegazza's novel, *Abrakadabra* and *Nel 2073!* exhibit many more of the elements belonging to the category of "uchronia," namely, depicting a happy future time yet not fully localizable as a specific and plausible geographical elsewhere (Alkon 115–16). *The Year 3000*, in contrast, displays a more coherent connection between uchronia and utopia, the alterity of its setting playing a crucial role in the definition of its alternative future.

Still largely unknown to the general public, these novels have also been almost totally ignored by critics, who continue to situate the official development of Italian science fiction as a self-conscious and consistent genre right after World War II and to identify as its precursors the two major Italian names of the outset of the twentieth century, namely Emilio Salgari and Enrico de' Conti Novelli da Bertinoro, who wrote under the pen name Yambo. To be sure, by the early 1900s Italian weekly magazines focused on adventures and voyages proliferated, often imitating French titles, such as *Per terra e per mare* (By Land and by Sea), edited by Emilio Salgari himself, and *Viaggi e avventure di terra e di mare* (Journeys and Adventures by Land and by Sea), edited by Antonio Garibaldi Quattrini—both launched in 1904 and both based upon the French *Sur Terre et sur Mer*—and *L'oceano* (The Ocean), edited by Luigi Motta (1906). The interest in fantasy, both exotic and technological, hence truly became a mass cultural phenomenon, thanks not only to numerous translations of foreign works published in magazine installments but also to a growing number of young Italian authors eager to experiment with the genre.

This burgeoning of literary anticipations of the future was further encouraged by important scientific events that exerted a powerful influence upon the Italian audience. For instance, the astronomer Giovanni Schiaparelli's 1877 observation of what he called "Mars channels," and his subsequent publications on the topic in 1893, 1895, and 1909, generated creative speculations about alien forms of life on the Red Planet.[16] Indeed, Bianchi and Grifoni referred to these topics directly in their novels. Mantegazza would follow suit, as usual by overdoing things: the physicists and astronomers who in his year 3000 are "perfecting the telescope" (170) hope to be able to see not only the inhabitants of Mars but also those of Venus, Mercury, "and the other planets closest to Earth" (170). Likewise, 1885 research on the rotary magnetic field by the Italian physicist and electric engineer Galileo Ferraris led to the creation of an alternating-current motor. And on the basis of Heinrich Hertz's 1888 demonstration of the production and detection of electromagnetic radiation, Guglielmo Marconi successfully used Hertzian waves to create a system of wireless telegraphy that he employed in 1901 and 1902 to carry out the first transatlantic transmissions. Marconi thus perfected a telegraph technology that already existed not only in real life but also, as we have already seen, in several science fiction novels. The importance of technological progress was further extolled through the intense and rapid industrialization that, especially in Northern Italy, soon led to a thriving automotive production but also had crucial cultural repercussions, such as the development of a mechanically reproducible art form like cinema.

In this cultural climate, and only one year after Mantegazza's *The Year 3000*, Yambo published the parascientific adventures of *La guerra del XX secolo* (The War of the Twentieth Century), followed, among others, by *Gli esploratori dell'infinito* (The Explorers of the Infinite, 1906). Emilio Salgari—christened during his lifetime the "Italian Verne" and best known for his numerous adventures among the jungles and corsairs of the Southern Seas—also took a stab at futuristic fiction with *I figli dell'aria* (The Sons of the Air, 1904) and *Le meraviglie del Duemila* (The Marvels of Two Thousand, 1907). In the latter work James Brandok, a young American millionaire, and his scientist friend Toby Holker—thanks to the powers of an ancient exotic plant, the flower of resurrection—manage to suspend life and awaken in 2003, after one hundred years' sleep. They find themselves in a highly technological world, featuring electric ships, flying machines, underground trains, tramways passing through ice tunnels, television news, a sort of radar (*eofono*), interplanetary journeys, and contact with Martians (Salgari, too, paid homage to the Schiaparelli fad). In fact, however, Salgari's third-millennium world is not totally futuristic: machines fly by beating mechanical wings (as in Bodin's *The Novel of the Future*); the speed of trains and aircrafts is rather modest for the time; much of the visual technology had already appeared in the works of earlier writers like Robida, set in nearer epochs; and, above all, contact with the omnipresent electricity is highly destabilizing for the two protagonists, who, despite their curiosity about the future, define themselves as "uomini d'altri tempi" (men of the Old World) (168).

Ten years after the publication of Mantegazza's novel and with one less millennium to cover in its plot, *Le meraviglie del Duemila* hence makes a nod (even if not explicitly declared) to the author of *The Year 3000*, who cannot possibly have escaped Salgari's attention. At the same time, however, *Le meraviglie del Duemila* exhibits typically Vernian literary situations and solutions that highlight Salgari's different attitude toward progress. As at the ending of Verne's *Paris in the Twentieth Century*, where the protagonist chooses death at the Père Lachaise cemetery rather than yielding to the principles of the new way of life, electricity ultimately turns out to be fatal to the mental equilibrium of Salgari's equally unprepared James and Toby, who go crazy in the ultramodern, future society.

In this tug of war between the lure of the future and nostalgia for the past, which characterizes much of Italian literature and culture between the two centuries, Filippo Tommaso Marinetti, one year before *Le meraviglie del Duemila*, had published the first Futurist Manifesto. The innovations made possible by speed and technology were now no longer an imaginative projection, but, in the theory and practice of Marinetti and his fellow futurists, a reality, the new face of the present in the arts and in everyday life. But above all this reality was a *total* one, encompassing not only the content but also the form of representation. Neither *The Year 3000* nor any other novel belonging to the corpus of Italian proto–science fiction seemed to reach that milestone, despite the works' unanimous recognition of the role of technology, electricity above all, in promoting increasingly faster worldwide communication. Bold technological projections like the distribution of energy "without need of conductor tubes" (87) in *The Year 3000* do not go hand in hand with equally radical innovations in the technology of the word. These novels lack what, according to Marinetti, is the ability to abandon the musty style and static syntax of the passé nineteenth century to embrace the expressive dynamism and simultaneity of the "wireless imagination" and "words in freedom."[17]

To be sure, however, before Marinetti decided to murder the moonshine—that is, to get rid of languid sentimentality and decadent staticity—in a late-nineteenth-century Italian cultural context still dominated by Romantic overtones, Mantegazza's contribution to early science fiction, albeit not unique, is certainly of a higher standing than most Italian output of the time. Beyond the notoriety of its author, by far the most prominent of the few writers who contributed to the genre, *The Year 3000* is also more cogent and sophisticated than the era's other works, which are often marked by mechanical or unsubstantial plots, stylistic unevenness, and a gratuitous use of stereotypical situations. It is hence all the more surprising that, despite its relevance to the expanding futurist utopian panorama and the international popularity of its author, *The Year 3000* is still often neglected in scholarly discussions in the field.[18]

The Fourth Millennium at the Touch of a Button

L'anno 3000. Sogno tells the story of two young people, the scientist Paolo Fortunati and his companion Maria, who, in the year 3000, leave Rome, the capital of the former United States of Europe, heading to Andropolis, the capital of the United Planetary States, located in Asia, at the feet of the Himalayas. There, after a five-year engagement, they plan to celebrate their "mating union." Aboard the ultramodern electric spaceship that will allow the two protagonists to visit several curious places before landing at their futuristic destination, Paolo reads to his beloved a work entitled *L'anno 3000* (*The Year 3000*), a novel penned by a physician who, ten centuries earlier, had attempted to guess what the world would look like in the fourth millennium. In addition to functioning as a literary solution that highlights Mantegazza's proverbial self-centeredness, this interplay of narrative levels sets up a more visible contrast between the real conditions of the author's times and the dynamics of this futuristic world. The fact that Paolo has to *translate* the book from the dead Italian idiom into the newly established Cosmic language as he reads to Maria is indeed the first in a rich series of situations that illustrate the dramatic changes that have occurred between fin-de-siècle Italy and Europe and the two protagonists' civilization. Further, this gap enhances the credibility of the future scenario. Mantegazza's realistic logic works to authenticate the truthfulness of narrated events, events that the characters do not dream of, but actually live. Therefore, the reference to dreams in the novel's title here acquires the value of prophecy more than pure, inconsistent fantasy. The *sogno* of the year 3000 is Mantegazza's own wishful anticipation of a future that, the author hopes, sooner or later will become present. The value of this future is emphasized in the novel's first pages, in the contrast that the stop in LaSpezia creates between the alluring scenario of the fourth millennium and the past buried for good in the Necropolis—over "twenty thousand years of human history" (59) sleeping forever in silence, collected as in a museum.

By the year 3000, after a catastrophic war that lacerated the European countries and subsequently led to their political unification, conflicts have been abolished. The entire world is now in the hands of an oligarchy of wise and honest individuals, under whose auspices all residues of territorial rivalries, economic barriers, and cultural differences have disappeared, and the quality of life has remarkably improved, thanks to the suppression of physical pain. Paolo and Maria's journey from Rome to Andropolis hence enacts a displacement in both space and time, in line with Bakhtin's concept of a "chronotope," each of its legs offering insights into a particular phase in the social, institutional, and scientific evolution of this utopian universe.[19]

For instance, on the Isle of Experiments, which corresponds to Ceylon, the couple stops in the Republic of Turatia, named after the late-nineteenth-century Italian socialist Filippo Turati and modeled upon his egalitarian vision. Elaborating on what had already emerged during the previous stop in the Land of Equality, and reflecting Mantegazza's own political ideology, here Paolo criticizes the pervasive interference of the State in the citizens' lives and the apathy generated by its leveling effect. Denouncing the failure of the egalitarian ideal of the 1789 French Revolution, he ultimately declares to Maria that the political project of egalitarianism will be soon overcome by new institutional experiments aimed at fostering individual initiative and competition. Paolo and Maria are no less cautious with the opposite ideological extreme—namely the political and religious despotism of the small state of Tyrannopolis—yet they also express deep skepticism toward what may at first seem the golden mean between socialism and tyranny, represented by the parliamentary model of Logopolis. Indeed, despite some worthwhile reforms the City of Words also appears to Paolo as a corrupt, inefficient, and whimsical regime that uses rhetorical verbosity to cover up its absence of substance and coherence.

The fact that these and several other political and social organizations are all located in Ceylon seems to reassert the stereotype of the island as the primary locus of the utopian imagination. In fact, however, Mantegazza here resorts to the condition of its insularity to question, rather than reinforce, the normative utopian ideology it embodies. Indeed, as he groups together on the island the ideals he dismisses as surpassed or nonviable, Mantegazza also explicitly criticizes the persistence of their naively impractical ambitions across time: "Human nature is so elastic, so proteiform, that it allows us, over long intervals, . . . to hold on to the same strange utopias. . . . It is enough for a hundred people to think up a new social utopia or rethink an ancient one that has been buried for centuries, and they know that on the island of Ceylon they can always find a small or large virgin territory for founding their new republic or theocracy" (79). This polemical and self-conscious approach to the stylistic marks and narrative conventions of the utopian genre compensates for other structural elements that, if taken in isolation, would fix *The Year 3000* within the category of the traditional utopia—for instance, the common choice of toponyms often ending with the suffix *-polis* (Centropolis in Bodin, Cosmopolis in Verne, Andropolis in Mantegazza), or the predominance of descriptive, static elements that advance the plot by accumulation instead of enriching it with deep characterization and unexpected plot twists.

Just as it tests various political and institutional systems, Paolo and Maria's journey also delineates different technological phases, culminating with the accomplishments of Mantegazza's imagined fourth millennium. On the Isle of Dynamo, for instance, Paolo and Maria familiarize themselves with the changes that, across ten centuries, led from the technology of steam and electricity to what in the year 3000 has become the production of a general form of clean and silent energy, called *pandynamo*. Generated by living beings, it is distributed to the whole planet through little tubes and converted on demand into light, heat, movement, or electricity. Mantegazza hence transcends the widespread fixation with electricity as the ultimate source of energy—a fixation shared by most of his contemporaries and immediate predecessors, including Verne and Salgari, among many others—and also suggests the principles of other machines and inventions he will display in subsequent chapters. The technology that fostered the unquestionably major leap in nineteenth-century mechanics is by now material for the Historical Museum, which the protagonists visit. After Watt and Volta, the locomotive and the battery, a new era has come, that of "the artificial production and application of nerve force to mechanics" (83). The fourth millennium owes this technology to Macstrong, a much-venerated English scientist who died in 2654. Mantegazza's conception of energy is not only innovative but also ecological, his vision as significant to the health issues of his time as it is pertinent to our own environmental concerns. Unlike the notoriously appalling conditions of workers in post–Industrial Revolution Europe, no shrill noise, dangerous fumes, or excessive workloads plague the Dynamo energy plants: the "cleanly dressed" and "vigorous-looking" (82) employees are almost indistinguishable from their bosses. This encouraging portrait of savvy factory production reinforces the narrator's earlier remarks in praise of the nonpolluting and waste-free technology powering the English electric mail boat *Cosmos*, which brings Paolo and Maria to Ceylon. An "economical, very simple battery" breaks down saltwater "to provide hydrogen, the new fuel, and distill it into drinking water" (67)—an interesting anticipation of current awareness-raising efforts in favor of sustainable and renewable energy systems, prominent among them clean hydrogen.

Not surprisingly, once the two protagonists land in the capital of the United Planetary States, many more pioneering finds await them. Despite the exotic, archaic, and mystic resonances of its Indian setting, Andropolis is in fact not so much a memorial to glorious past stages of civilization as the locus of groundbreaking advances in all sectors of everyday life. Without questioning the foundational value of ancient wisdom—and for Mantegazza Indian culture is the quintessence of this wisdom, as he makes plain in his travelogue *India*—it is possible to aspire to physical, intellectual, and emotional well-being only by trusting in the new horizons of the postindustrial reality. In the United Planetary States this translates in part into displays of futuristic instruments for their own sake—electric engines with sophisticated flight and navigation instruments, instant telecommunication, synthetic foods and drugs, flexible materials to construct prefabricated homes that can guarantee fast accommodation to everybody. Yet Mantegazza seems once again particularly concerned with the human and social benefits of scientific and technological progress. Considerable improvements in medicine and hygiene now allow people to live longer and healthier lives. Thanks to sports and hydrotherapy, nervous illnesses and boredom have disappeared. Safer factory conditions and more tolerable working schedules free up more time for education and entertainment. Cosmic citizens also enjoy a bureaucracy-free existence and are not subject to any state religion. Women have the right to vote, and divorce is a well-established practice. The prevailing social harmony and universal dialogue that ultimately erased crime have even made possible the abolition of the Ministry of Justice and the police force.

With his proverbial eclecticism, however, Mantegazza does not succumb to the ideology of order and symmetry that character-izes many imaginary cities. Mantegazza here avoids uniformity and monotony—which he abhorred in his writings as much as in his personal life—not only by conceptualizing an urban space featur-ing a plurality of styles—from homes made with various materials to the vast array of fountains, each with a unique form—but also by allowing room for individual activities and tastes. The wealth of opportunities for the entertainment of both mind and heart is well demonstrated by the "over fifty large theaters" (155) and by the abundance of performances at the largest and wealthiest of them, the Panopticon. Here, furthermore, the blend of "the cleverest discover-ies of science and art" (156) that Mantegazza extols applies not only to the production of entertainment but also to its fruition: thanks to the "aesthesiometer," an instrument installed in each theater seat, spectators can experience different degrees of visual, auditory, and olfactory sensations while watching a show.

Unquestionably, the fictional world of *L'anno 3000* synthesizes many issues that Mantegazza developed more systematically in his cultural and scientific studies, tropes that also expose the author's response to the conditions of the newly created Italian nation. Unified in 1861 after decades of struggle, Italy at the turn of the twentieth century was still coping with fundamental political, institutional, and social questions affecting the "making" of the Italian people. These questions are transposed and sublimated in the pages of Mantegazza's novel, from the role of the State in the management of the new terri-tory, to the importance of improvements in public health, preventive medicine, and factory conditions (in the year 3000 child labor has been abolished—an urgent concern not only in nineteenth-century Italy

but also in much post–Industrial Revolution Europe), the standard-
ization and radical reform of the educational system, and the need
for higher moral and aesthetic norms in Italian life.[20] Mantegazza,
however, transcends the status quo by endorsing such controversial
practices as easily available divorce, abortion, and euthanasia—issues
that would polarize public opinion for the entire twentieth century
and that still have a strong resonance in our own world. For instance,
although Italy legalized divorce only in 1970, Mantegazza, over one
century earlier, in The *Physiology of Love*, stated that "divorce should
be written into our laws as soon as possible; happy couples demand
it in order to ensure their dignity, offended by a tyrannical bond;
unhappy creatures implore it on bended knee, whom misfortune or
guilt condemned to the greatest of human tortures, that of a slavery
without redemption, a yoke without repose, a scourge without balm,
a sorrow without hope" (296).

Furthermore, while aware of the broad nature of the utopian and
futuristic genre to which his novel belongs, Mantegazza also gave a
personal touch to *The Year 3000*, enriching it with autobiographical
references. The love story between Paolo and Maria, for example,
echoes Paolo Mantegazza's own recent union with Countess Maria
Fantoni, thirty years his junior, whom he met in 1891 soon after the
death of his first wife and to whom he dedicated the novel.[21] Likewise,
the novel is dotted with references to places linked to Mantegazza's
own whereabouts (from LaSpezia to India), members of his intellectual
entourage (Regalia, De Amicis, Turati), authors he loved (Porta)
or hated (D'Annunzio), and his personal views on the crucial social
issues that scroll throughout the various chapters.

However, it would be reductive to treat *The Year 3000* as a mere
roman à clef, slavishly reproducing Mantegazza's experiences. Indeed,
the protagonists' journey to the United Planetary States reveals the
author's awareness of and participation in a specific European historical and cultural conjuncture, of which *The Year 3000* offers many
hints. Turn-of-the-century Europe perceived its present and future in
contradictory ways. On the one hand, it saluted the approaching year
1900 with a strong belief in scientific and technological progress; the

certainty that society was heading toward greater prosperity, happiness, and refinement; and confidence in the prospect of higher moral standards. This view was mainly upheld by the optimistic doctrine of positivism, with its ideology of rational and social advancement, but also by the self-confidence of several European nations, like Great Britain and France, whose imperialistic operations strengthened their economic and political power. At the same time, however, popular superstitions and a general sense of precariousness contributed to fear of an imminent apocalypse as the climax of a process of degeneration, despite the apparent security that technology seemed to offer. This more problematic approach to the new era and the anxiety it fostered emerged, for instance, in a growing interest in the study of human behavior, of the psyche, and of the occult. Works like Émile Durkheim's *Suicide* (1897) and Sigmund Freud and Joseph Breuer's *Studies on Hysteria* (1895) shattered the individual's integrity and self-control, raising doubts about the conviction that the rational and material aspects of life alone can account for reality as a whole.

On the one hand, what underlies Paolo and Maria's adventures is Mantegazza's proverbial quest for human well-being and happiness. In *The Year 3000* these goals seem attainable through progress as a guarantor of unlimited improvement, in line with the Darwinian theory of evolution, which, by invalidating the notion of the fixity of species, had reconceptualized the life of organisms as subject to continuous and progressive modifications with the passage of time. A follower of Darwin, Mantegazza was also intrigued by the wider sociological and moral implications of the endless variability of species, which had inspired Herbert Spencer's concept of the perfectibility of human nature. In *The Year 3000* the scientist on the Isle of Dynamo replies as follows to Maria's inquiry about the relationship between mechanical and moral civilization: "Dearest lady, I as an engineer cannot concern myself with mechanical progress alone; please believe that it almost always moves in parallel with moral progress" (89). The narrator's comments about the management of fertile marriage at the end of the novel further consolidate the author's own asserted belief in the intellectual but also redemptive power of science, seen at once as a rational, moral, and hence civilizing resource. If "in barbaric times" (191) "the right to transmit life to future generations . . . had been granted to all" (191), in the allegedly culturally more advanced fourth millennium it is above all necessary to have "the consent of science" (191), with the assumption that only scientific authorization can prevent painful consequences.

An implicit response to the negative portrayal in the novel's first pages of science and technology as instruments of past terrible bloodshed, this edifying image of science (according to Mantegazza's personal hierarchy of values) seems like the final word on the problem that haunts Mantegazza—namely, as we can understand from Paolo and Maria's conversation, the problem of suffering and pain, of the "lament rising up from the entire planet, which weeps and asks heaven why there is life and why there is suffering" (64). Just as the performative nature of Mantegazza's scientific imagination in *The Year 3000* aims to overcome many physical ailments, the novel purports to extend the moral and social benefits of science even to the less tangible and more complex manifestations of human life—that is, to the psychological and spiritual ones, which, as Mantegazza repeatedly claims in many of his writings, were the major challenge confronting the nineteenth century. Paolo's invention of the "psychoscope," which wins him the cosmic prize from the Academy of Science of Andropolis, corroborates confidence in a future finally able to promote "a new era of morality and sincerity among humans" (190) precisely because of its unprecedented ability "to read into our brain" (190). If, as the secretary of the Academy states, "the dream of all the ages" and the main hope for happiness is the synergy of moral and intellectual progress (191), the psychoscope will guarantee each individual's physical and mental well-being by helping them overcome contradictions between thoughts and actions. From the perspective of fourth-millennium scientists (and of their nineteenth-century predecessor) the avowed social usefulness of the psychoscope in the diagnosis of mental illness for educational and psychological purposes seems to overcome the risk of an Orwellian totalitarian degeneration in the applications of this technology, a danger that we can presume possible as we learn, for instance, that with the intervention of this "terrible optic device" "lying will be banished or become rare" (191).[22]

Just as the psychoscope raises concerns about the ambivalent uses of science—even though the novel mitigates and often suppresses the possible negative ramifications of this radical confidence in the science of tomorrow—various other disquieting elements cast a shadow upon the apparent hopefulness of these futuristic scenarios. Scientific, technological, and social growth may as well be a panacea, but sometimes the means and costs of attaining an allegedly better life leave room for perplexity or even horror. For instance, the United Planetary States unveils its dystopian side when the narrator discloses the methods adopted to get rid of physical defects and moral deviance. In the name of eugenics all fertile couples are obliged to comply with a rigorous health policy implemented by a tribunal that grants the right to procreation only after a satisfactory medical checkup has ruled out hereditary diseases and consanguinity between the partners. An even more appalling measure affects newborns, whose brains are scanned and magnified with special equipment aimed at detecting physical, mental, or moral pathologies. In the case of any anomaly—for instance, a documented predisposition to delinquency—the baby is eliminated (with the mother's consent). While not as extreme as his contemporary and rival Cesare Lombroso in his interpretation and normalization of criminal behavior, Mantegazza nonetheless, in studies such as *Physiognomy and Expression*, supported connections between physical traits and intellectual and moral features. Beyond his expressed position, however, he also offers at least as much evidence of his interest in—if not attraction to—those very manifestations of deviance, especially of a sexual nature. Nevertheless, from the reading of human perfectibility (or lack thereof) through physiognomy, to the need to block the transmission of hereditary diseases, Mantegazza's search for happiness was often supported by a Malthusian perspective that is ready to sacrifice (selectively, with scientific authority and adequate technical support) weak, imperfect, or inadequate members of the present society for the sake of the physical and mental improvement of future generations. He hence became one of the first to introduce the prospect of eugenics in Italy when the theories of Francis Galton, who first coined the term in 1883, had just begun to spread. Already in 1878, in *Igiene dell'amore* (The Hygiene of Love), Mantegazza had highlighted his own pioneering investigation into heredity, claiming priority over Galton's own studies.[23]

On the one hand, if, as the subtitle of *L'anno 3000* claims, this fantastic journey into the world of the fourth millennium is "a dream," the era's developing Freudian psychoanalysis would suggest that through this dream Mantegazza was trying to fulfill his wish for an ideal future, tailored precisely to his most personal aspirations. Yet on the other hand, although carried away by his fertile imagination, Mantegazza did not gag his critical spirit and hence seems to interrogate his own yearning for progress and perfection, ultimately revealing that a dream, without the restraint of ethics and common sense, may shade off into a veritable nightmare. This awareness of limits and of the risks entailed by excess causes his future to oscillate between utopia and antiutopia, negotiating between materialistic and idealistic impulses and involving characters and readers in the struggle between fear and hope. However, just as the ending of *The Year 3000* is a happy one, despite the many darker aspects that we glimpse in its projections, Mantegazza himself remained an optimist until the end of his novelesque life. Just one year before his death his 1909 volume *La Bibbia della speranza* (The Bible of Hope) would celebrate hope with the same enthusiasm that animates the narrator's explanation of Paolo and Maria's eastbound journey: flying eastward means reaching "the light of day [that] has always brought man hope, the hope that never dies" (64). This hope—significantly the imperative carved on the statue at the gate of Andropolis's city of the dead, later even emerging as the value worshipped in the largest and most beautiful temple of Andropolis—goes beyond blind faith in the power of science tout court. More broadly this hope centers on the belief that humankind is ultimately heading toward better times, no matter what principles and instruments its members choose to adopt to imagine and build the future.

With this aspiration Mantegazza exemplifies the position that Robert Scholes has assumed, in favor of the free speculation allowed by what Scholes defines as "structural fabulation," that is, "a fictional exploration of human situations made perceptible by the implications of recent science" and hence "modified by an awareness of the nature of the universe as a system of systems, as a structure of structures. . . . The insights of the past century of science are accepted as fictional points of departure" (41–42). Structural fabulation, for Scholes, grants us unprecedented freedom to speculate, because "where anything may be true—sometime, someplace—there can be no heresy. And where the patterns of the cosmos itself guide our thoughts so powerfully, so beautifully, we have nothing to fear but our own lack of courage. There are fields of force around us that even our finest instruments of thought and perception are only beginning to detect. The job of fiction is to play in these fields. And in the past few decades fiction has begun to do just this, to dream new dreams, confident that there is no gate of ivory, only a gate of horn, and that all dreams are true. It is fiction—verbal narrative—that must take the lead in such dreaming, because even the new representations media that have been spawned in this age cannot begin to match the speculative agility and imaginative freedom of words" (38).

To be sure, regardless of Mantegazza's ultimate standpoint vis-à-vis the imaginative and speculative leap he took in this ultramodern planetary civilization, the novel's most surprising elements are its author's intriguing political, economic, and social forecasts, most of which have turned out to be accurate or, in some more extreme instances, may hit their targets in the future. Mantegazza's amazing perceptiveness largely compensates for the often unexciting prose of *L'anno 3000*. Unquestionably the book deserves attention above all for its documentary value and its originality, more than for purely aesthetic reasons. On the technological front the novel bestows upon readers visions of surprising discoveries and inventions based upon scientific principles—inventions that would actually change daily life in the next two centuries or even surpass current conditions. If, as we have seen, this technological futuristic imagination was anything but rare in nineteenth-century Europe, Mantegazza nonetheless left his personal mark by presenting ideas and devices that evolved from issues and interests he explored throughout his scholarly career.

For example, well beyond William Röntgen's discovery of X-rays only two years before the novel's publication, Mantegazza imagined medical examinations with machines that, like CAT scans, are able to provide a full, three-dimensional model of the whole body. If by the end of the nineteenth century Justus von Liebig had already devised beef extract as an alternative to real meat, we should not be surprised to learn that in the United Planetary States people can feed upon synthetic foods, resorting to pills to satisfy the needs of not only their stomachs but their souls. Artificial intelligence imitates the thinking of real brains, and even research in bioengineering is cutting-edge in Mantegazza's futuristic universe: wounds can be healed and physical deformities corrected through the creation of artificial tissues that attach to live skin cells and grow to replace damaged muscles. Bodies enjoy thorough massages with the aid of a sophisticated machine—electrically operated, needless to say. The homage to electricity goes so far as the conception of an alloy—the "electro" (126)—as radiant as electric lighting.

From a historical point of view *The Year 3000* accurately predicts the outburst of World War I. Above all, however, in line with what would become the actual international agenda from the early decades of the twentieth century onward, Mantegazza also highlighted the institutional and ideological role of Europe in the peaceful reconstruction of a shattered Old Continent. Indeed, Mantegazza's references to the "United States of Europe" can be considered a landmark in the larger historical and cultural discourse on Europeanness, more pertinent than ever in the present context. Furthermore, by extending the European federal dimension to a universal scale, *The Year 3000* opens up crucial issues of globalization and cosmopolitanism, touching upon their political, linguistic, and economic implications. The global currency circulating in the Planetary States, for instance, envisages, on a larger scale, the ongoing process of euro-area enlargement in Western Europe and in the so-called new accession countries.

Although, surprisingly, these issues have so far been neglected in Mantegazza scholarship, *The Year 3000* stands out not only in the context of futuristic proto–science fiction but also in the framework of Italian and European political and cultural history at large. Mantegazza's novel is one of the earliest and only literary examples of a sustained engagement with Europeanism and federalism as models of thinking and acting beyond the nation, paradoxically coming at a moment of Italian history—the Risorgimento—that coincided with Italy's longed-for nation-building process. While, as observed earlier, Mantegazza's treatment of a *specifically European* political, economic, and institutional structure as a template for a planetary political system probably owes credit to Della Sala Spada and Ghislanzoni, *The Year 3000* conveys a more substantial political message than the peripheral and somewhat gratuitous references to the "confederation of all the states of the world" in *Nel 2073!* and builds a more cogent scenario than the hallucinatory, convoluted spatial and temporal framework of *Abrakadabra*.

Coming from a patriotic family himself (his mother, Laura Solera, an activist for the cause of Italian independence, made him participate in the Five Days of Milan revolt against Austria when he was sixteen), Mantegazza could not be insensitive to the powerful ideals of political and intellectual figures like Giuseppe Mazzini and Carlo Cattaneo, who advocated the creation of the United States of Europe even before Victor Hugo's famous address to the leading European powers at the 1849 Peace Congress in Paris. Hugo envisioned a peaceful future moment when—just as different provinces had been combined into France—all "nations of the Continent" would be "blended into a superior unity, and constitute the European fraternity" without losing their individuality (Hugo 5). In his pioneering 1829 essay "D'una letteratura europea" Mazzini, even before laying out his political project of a Young Europe, had extolled literature as the paramount institution able to demonstrate that the particular history of nations was about to end and that European history was about to begin—a history that, by putting an end to the prejudices and aberrations of patriotic sentiment, would succeed in turning the inequalities caused by dissension among peoples into simple differences. (Mazzini 70, 42). Carlo Cattaneo, inspired by the American and Swiss democratic models founded upon a reduction of the absolute sovereignty of the nation-state, claimed that true peace would only be possible through the creation of the United States of Europe, presenting federalism as the only political solution that might build a Europe free from the international conflicts triggered by borders (244).

The symbolic realm of Mantegazza's fourth millennium appropri-ates such pronouncements, also transposing into reality Ghislanzoni's visionary scenarios. Significantly, in the projections of *Abrakadabra* a European parliament would already exist in 1930, with representatives of the "European peoples" elected by universal suffrage and—with a far more optimistic outlook than the actual vicissitudes of the 2009 ratification of the Treaty of Lisbon—already implementing by 1977 a European constitution aimed at reconciling the greatest individual freedom with guarantees of security and public order (58). Faithful to the federalist principle of administrative decentering, Ghislanzoni's European Union functions according to a synergy of local and global organisms: it is composed of twenty-four departments, divided into smaller communes, whose leaders represent a cohesive *"European people"* in the general congresses that are scheduled—in an uncanny anticipation of the dynamics of the real European Council—twice per year, but in this case in Berlin. In the name of tolerance and fraternity the Union accepts all sorts of terms to designate politi-cal and administrative leaders—"mayors, principals, kings, emper-ors, heads of households, fathers, czars, sultans" (58–59). However, complying with its transnational mission against discrimination, it has normalized their tasks. It is precisely the sacred principle of egalitarianism that has abolished capital punishment and incarcera-tion and instituted the right to existence, according to which every European citizen receives lifetime lodging, sustenance, and clothing from his or her commune. Yet this same principle is also responsible for the abolition of cultural differences through the homogenization of local and national languages into the "Cosmic language," which, although apparently confined to the European territory, reveals its potential for unlimited extension, since, in Ghislanzoni's vision, it will ultimately render other languages useless not only in Europe but also in other continents.

Curiously, Ghislanzoni's hypothetical scenario becomes reality in Mantegazza's fourth millennium, where the Cosmic language has indeed already attained global status, just as the "United States of Europe" has now expanded into the "United Planetary States," whose universal governance has superseded not only state sovereignty but also the political and cultural differences inside and outside the European federation's territorial lines. In *The Year 3000*, furthermore, if twentieth-century Europeanism offered the Old Continent a peaceful and permanent antidote to collective fratricidal violence, Mantegazza's internationalism on a universal scale ultimately also materializes what the renowned British journalist and reformer William Stead would soon urge, only two years after the publication of *The Year 3000*. Stead, in his 1899 volume *The United States of Europe on the Eve of the Parliament of Peace*, promoted the prospect of a brotherly "Federal Union, without hostile frontiers and without standing armies, and with a greater expenditure upon education than upon armaments," that would eventually become the blueprint for the "United States of the world" (12, 20). This development would come thanks to the abatement of all commercial and institutional barriers—above all "the pestilent nuisance of the *douane*" (12), a residue as barbarous as the passport, which obliges "the wayfaring man to admit the existence of independent, rival, or hostile States" (12) even in the face of consciousness and evidence of established forms of "international freedom and union" (14) (e.g., the postal system and the financial system of circular notes). For his part, Mantegazza had already abolished protectionist measures and introduced a universal paper currency, in addition, of course, to extensive means of transportation and communication, from the more plausible railways and telegraphs to futuristic electric spaceships that, by bringing people closer, help them avoid hate and warfare.

Linking 1897 to our own current debates, we could argue that with these global networks of national political governments and international nongovernmental formations that evolve from the European federative model, Mantegazza, even more than Ghislanzoni, sketches what political scientists have recently proposed as "cosmopolitical democracy." Such groupings are able to "involve the world's citizens in decision making" without either reproducing "the state model on a world scale" (Archibugi 9, 8) or dissolving the state structure altogether. They are founded upon a representative organism for transnational political life, such as a unifying parliamentary body for general and special interests.[24] If, for contemporary proponents of global governance, democracy has to be realized "on three different interconnected levels: within states, between states and at a world level" (Archibugi 8), cohesion in the planetary administration of Mantegazza's year 3000 is guaranteed precisely by the relationships among, and autonomy of, all components of the global federation, from the "supreme Council" and "partial assemblies within each department" (all elected by universal suffrage for only a one-year term) down to the commune, which is "the state's organic molecule" (106). The recipe for a successful political globalization, according to Mantegazza, hence features decentralization with a vengeance and emphasizes individual responsibility. This for him demonstrates "how easy and straightforward it is to govern the whole of humanity from the center of the globe when men, families, and communes are self-governing" (106).

However, while alleged accountability and tolerance at all levels seems to promise a plurality of identities thanks to a synergy of particular and universal, local and global forces, Mantegazza in fact does not neglect its more problematic side either—namely, what in a contemporary context would be the risk of globalization as homogenization rather than the harmonization of differences. Connected and merged through the intensification and expansion of cultural flows made possible by means of communication and environmental changes, peoples and races of the fourth millennium lose their individual traits and create "a new type, indefinitely cosmopolitan, the fruit of the deep and intimate cross-breeding" (170).

Interestingly, Félix Bodin had already presented this inevitable loss of ethnic distinctions as a mark of the future: "The interbreeding of races and the mixing of nations have been effected more and more profoundly: the original types of the different varieties of the species have been gradually erased; languages have grown more similar and few have almost disappeared. . . . The word 'nationality' is beginning to lose any but a vague significance" (*Novel* 93–94). As Émile Souvestre reiterates about his own fourth millennium, this "blending of racial characteristics was the natural result of social progress. The blood of all the different races had been mixed" (*World* 51). But behind the rosy promise of a harmoniously diverse humankind as just one happy family of equals, this ethnic and social creolization also sweeps away cultural niches and local feelings of belonging, raising the dystopian specter of institutional leveling and normalization.[25]

The caveat against the dangers of imposing global democracy against peoples' will (Archibugi 8) applies very well to these futuristic fictions. Indeed, the cosmopolitical creation of the "fraternal Continent," whether Ghislanzoni's European Union or Mantegazza's planetary extension of it, is not exempt from a democratic fundamentalism that, targeting global equality, ends up reintroducing differences through restrictions, exclusions, and marginalizations. As we have seen, instead of translating into an extension of egalitarian and libertarian principles, the worldwide federative expansion in Mantegazza's *L'anno 3000* ultimately reinstates the need for a Nietzschean moral and intellectual aristocracy: after it has buried the "stupid majorities" of the socialist European phase, the United Planetary States decides to be governed by the elite—"wise and honest minorities" who in fact implement inflexible Malthusian rules regarding the right to procreation. Likewise, Mantegazza's idea of a Cosmic language certainly arises from that same desire for universal brotherhood, which at the end of the nineteenth century fostered the creation of artificial international languages like Volapük (1879) and Esperanto (1887). The price to pay for this supposed equality without borders, however, is the death of national and regional languages—an outcome that suggests the tensions inherent in the linguistic policies of our own increasingly globalized world, negotiating between the erasure of cultural barriers (as in the current widespread tendency to adopt English as a lingua franca) and the preservation of local heritages and identities.

Seven years after *The Year 3000* was published, H. G. Wells, in *A Modern Utopia*, revisited the notion of a future world state that deliberately conceives itself as utopian, but with a substantial difference with respect to its antecedents: unlike the "all perfect and static States," where "a balance of happiness won for ever against the forces of unrest and disorder" (5), Wells's modern utopia "must be not static but kinetic, must shape not as a permanent state but as a hopeful stage" (5). Instead of resisting and overcoming "the great stream of things" (5), it should "rather float upon it" by building "not citadels, but ships of state" (5). Although not so lucidly as Wells and probably not even totally intentionally, Mantegazza likewise allows us to catch a glimpse of the weaknesses and obstacles inherent to his apparently "healthy and simple generation enjoying the fruits of the earth in an atmosphere of virtue and happiness" (Wells 5). By tracing a Wellsian "flexible common compromise" (Wells 6) between different visions and measures, *The Year 3000* builds a dynamic future, characterized by a dialectic between the apparently boundless human possibilities granted by the "other" logic of utopia and the limitations and flaws of "the world of Here and Now" (8).

Introducing his ideal model of futuristic fiction, Félix Bodin envisioned a narrative "fantastic, romantic, philosophical, and somewhat critical at the same time; a book in which a brilliant, rich and vagabond imagination can be deployed at its ease; and, finally, a book that is amusing without being futile" (*Novel* 41), able to eschew both the excesses of fantasy and the aridly critical and illusion-breaking philosophical perspective. *The Year 3000*, we could argue, would probably make Bodin happy. Famous for the claim "in science the true, in art the beautiful," which seems to decree an unflinching belief in the need to separate rational, objective truth from the subjective pleasures of the aesthetic realm, Mantegazza in fact offers us an intriguing combination of the two domains. The narrative itself confirms this: "The men of the thirty-first century no longer separate the beautiful from the true, and science and politics also enjoy dressing festively; . . . joy and beauty are no longer divorced from civilization, as in the times of great intellectual decadence and great hypocrisy" (109). Thematically and conceptually blended in the construction of this futuristic fantasy, science and art encourage the nineteenth-century imagination to transcend its temporal and spatial boundaries and travel in an ideal, apparently liberating elsewhere. At the same time, however, the novel suggests the need for a critical approach to dreams.

At a moment when Italy did not yet enjoy an established utopian, science fiction tradition, Mantegazza did not simply reproduce the stylemes and conventions of the genre, but rather offered a personal reelaboration of them, with interesting deviations from established models. Thus, *The Year 3000* should not be dismissed as blindly celebratory, satiric, or simply anachronistic, as has been too hastily affirmed.[26] Rather, it deserves to be reevaluated for its many "predictive" and "investigative" (Alkon 126) sparks, which invite us to use reason and emotions together, to test the technical possibilities but also the ethical limits of intellectual and material progress and of the quest for human happiness. Euphoric about the new, but also conscious of the inevitable shifts between triumph and downfall that the future holds in store, Mantegazza problematizes both extreme visions while gearing his and our imaginations to the challenges of an increasingly complex, more or less imminent, tomorrow.

A Note on the Text

First published in 1897 by Treves, *L'anno 3000. Sogno* was translated into German that same year by Willy Alexander Kastner as *Das Jahr 3000 ein Zukunftstraum*, published by Jena Costenoble.

Interestingly, the original subtitle "Sogno" (Dream) is less ambiguously rendered in German as "utopia." The effect is a more rigorous literary categorization of Mantegazza's novel—and hence the loss of the connections the title draws with the topoi of dreaming and sleeping as vehicles to the future, which Mantegazza's novel revises. Even before being translated into German, *L'anno 3000* was reviewed by the *Frankfurter Zeitung und Handelsblatt* (May 4, 1897).

The year 1897 also saw the publication of a Dutch edition in Leiden by Adriani (more faithful to the original Italian title: *Het jaar 3000: Een droom*) and a Portuguese edition by A. Varela (*O Ano 3000*). In 1898 there followed a Polish translation by M. Lag, *Rok 3000-ny: Marzenie przyszlosci* (Lódz: nakl. Ksiegarni L. Zonera)—"Year 3000: The Dream of Things to Come"—and a Russian translation, Будущее человечество (3000-й год), or *Budushee chelovechestvo (3000-i god)*—"The Humankind of the Future (Year 3000)"—an even more highly interpretive rendition that dissolves any allusion to imaginary (oneiric, utopian) worlds and brings to the foreground the factual value of the novel's representation. By relegating the reference to the year 3000 to a subtitle, the Russian translation also diminishes the importance of the specific temporal target, instead emphasizing more generally future generations themselves.

No French edition was available before 2003, when L'Harmattan published *L'an 3000*, translated, edited, and introduced by Raymond Trousson. No English translation of *L'anno 3000* exists prior to this one, apart from the incipit of the novel, which was anthologized in *The Physiology of Love and Other Writings* (University of Toronto Press, 2007): 513–14.

The Italian press did not devote to *L'anno 3000* the same close attention it paid, for instance, to Mantegazza's first novel, *One Day in Madeira*, which was an enormous editorial success. According to Mantegazza's bibliographer, Erasmo Ehrenfreund, only a few reviews of *L'anno 3000* seem to have been written in Italy between 1897 and Mantegazza's death in 1910, in such journals as *Gazzetta dell'Emilia* (May 14, 1897), *Illustrazione italiana* (August 21, 1898), and *Corriere di Catania* (July 24, 1899) (Ehrenfreund 137). Interestingly the article in *Illustrazione italiana*—which refers to the novel as "a curious book" that reaped success—is in its entirety a report on the content of a French review of Mantegazza that appeared on May 9, 1898, in *Journal des Débats*.[27] This review presented the utopian political scenario of *L'anno 3000* in positive terms but used Mantegazza's work as a sort of illusion-breaking tool to moderate the French electorate's hopes of immediate happiness. Just as France apparently would have to wait until the fourth millennium to get a glimpse of the perfect government, the French reviewer suggests, so the Italian people would almost certainly not elect Mantegazza to Parliament on the basis of the political ideas he expresses in his novel. These views, the reviewer implicitly suggests, were quite different from those of the actual Italian government of his time, although he ironically concludes that the Italian Parliament would probably not miss Mantegazza too much, as it already had another "Deputy of Beauty" in its ranks—Gabriele D'Annunzio. This is an intriguing textual rapprochement of two prominent intellectual figures who were surely linked with each other by the anxiety of influence.

On the whole the rather subdued Italian reception of *L'anno 3000*, despite the circulation of several foreign translations, is puzzling. Mantegazza's fame as a novelist might have still been linked to *One Day in Madeira*, and the century was probably also already experiencing the avant-garde surge that would soon sweep away the old academies and ultimately pave the way for Fascism, no less hostile to the modalities of nineteenth-century science. Paradoxically the total eclipse of Mantegazza also condemned his futuristic novel to oblivion in precisely the decades that lay the groundwork for the official birth, in the late 1940s, of what is considered the consistent and cogent production of the science fiction genre.

Readers would have to wait until the late 1980s to find *L'anno 3000* back on the Italian bookshelves, in the 1988 edition by Lubrina, with a preface by Alberto Capatti. A more recent Italian edition by Lupetti appeared in 2007, with a postface by Davide Bigalli. The present English translation is based upon the original 1897 edition by Treves and on the 1988 Lubrina edition. In the English rendition I have regularized the most obtrusive of Mantegazza's frequent present-past tense shifts but have left the others unchanged so as to give readers a taste of the author's narrative style.

As part of a wider rediscovery of Mantegazza's pioneering

contributions to various scientific and humanistic areas of culture, critics in various countries are also devoting new attention to Mantegazza as a science fiction writer, as the following selection of scholarly articles shows.

Bigalli, Davide. "Paolo Mantegazza: Il sogno della quiete perpetua." *L'anno 3000. Sogno.* By Paolo Mantegazza. Milan: Lupetti, 2007. 147–59.

Boni, Monica. *L'erotico senatore. Vita e studi di Paolo Mantegazza.* Genova: Name Edizioni, 2002. (The first chapter, "I sogni di Paolo Mantegazza," pp. 13–43, mainly discusses *The Year 3000.*)

Capatti, Alberto. "Prefazione." *L'anno 3000. Sogno.* By Paolo Mantegazza. Bergamo: Lubrina, 1988. 9–19.

Hudde, Hinrich. "Zwischen Utopie und Antiutopie: Mantegazzas *L'anno 3000.*" *Archiv für das Studium der Neueren Sprachen und Literaturen* 212 (1975): 77–94.

Marchioni, Massimo. "Scienza e invenzione narrativa: I romanzi di Paolo Mantegazza." *Ipotesi* 14, no. 2 (1985): 3–53.

Pireddu, Nicoletta. "Memorie del futuro. Archeologie letterarie d'Europa." *Balleriniana.* Ed. G. Cavatorta and E. Coda. Ravenna: Danilo Montanari, 2010. 212–36.

Roda, Vittorio. *"L'anno 3000. Sogno." Dictionary of Literary Utopias.* Ed. Vita Fortunati and Raymond Trousson. Paris: Champion, 2000. 54–55.

———. "Tra scienza e fantascienza: Il cervello umano in alcuni scrittori postunitari." *I fantasmi della ragione.* By Vittorio Roda. Naples: Liguori, 1996. 125–60.

Trousson, Raymond. "Introduction." *L'an 3000.* By Paolo Mantegazza. Paris: L'Harmattan, 2003. 7–35.

Notes

1. Anonymous and unnumbered introduction to Mantegazza, *Anthropological Studies.*

2. For more comprehensive discussions of Mantegazza's life and cross-disciplinary scholarly achievements in late-nineteenth-century Italian and European culture, see Pireddu, "Paolo Mantegazza"; Pireddu, "Primitive Marks."

3. Mercier's title literally translates as "The Year 2440: A Dream if Ever There Was One," but it was rendered in English as *Memoirs of the Year Two Thousand Five Hundred.* See, e.g., the translation by W. Hooper (Dublin: W. Wilson, 1772). This choice eliminates the reference to the dream that

in fact, together with sleep, would become a leitmotif shared by numerous European futuristic novels.

4. In his introduction Bodin explicitly ridicules the "honest and sometimes amusing declaimer Mercier, who aspired, 50 years ago, to dream of the year 2440" yet "did not even push so far as representative government, underwear and close-cropped hair" (53). To Bodin's eyes, therefore, Mercier provides an inadequate political perspective, insofar as his "philanthropic monarchy" appears as a mere "modification of absolute power" (53) and is hence insufficiently progressive for Bodin's standards. For its part *The Novel of the Future* foresees not only the abolition of slavery and the end of wars but also a decline of monarchies that will go hand in hand with an increase in democracy. Interestingly we find the main elements of Bodin's vision in Mantegazza.

5. Literally, then, the protagonists' experience is not exactly a dream, but Souvestre still resorts to a sleeplike state to account for their spatiotemporal leap.

6. At least fourteen translations of Souvestre's works were circulating in the United States by the second half of the nineteenth century, sixteen or more in the United Kingdom. See Clarke xi.

7. One eloquent passage can be found in chapter 22 of *The Physiology of Love*: "Today matrimony is one of the most fruitful sources of misfortune; it is a slow poison that kills domestic happiness, the morality of a nation, the economical development of the forces of a country. Matrimony is often a patent which gives free irresponsibility to woman and an easy and unpunished polygamy to man; it is a false mask of virtue, with which they cover the vice of modern society; it is a safeguard which justifies all smuggling of infidelity, all treachery; it is a flag that hides a domestic slave-market, an exchange of easy lechery, or a bigamy tolerated with enviable longanimity by offenders and offended.

"Matrimony in modern society is the most cruel, the most inhuman parody of faith, of the oath, of eternity. . . .

"Matrimony should be a free, a very free election, as much for the woman as for the man; it should be the election of elections, the typical election. In our country, on the contrary, it is only the man who selects; woman generally accepts or yields to the choice. . . .

"The common consciousness in two creatures of choosing each other freely and loving each other without any bond of interest, any pressure of authority, prejudice or ambition, is the sacred stone on which the most splendid temples of conjugal felicity are erected" (290, 291, 292–93).

8. See Durr; Esposito; Gooday.

9. See Orizio and Radice; Mori; AA.VV.

10. *Paris in the Twentieth Century* was written and rejected for publication in 1863, discovered in 1989 by Verne's great-grandson, and published posthumously in 1994. *In the Year 2889* is believed to have been cowritten with Verne's son Michel under the influence of Robida's *Le vingtième siècle*. It was first published in English in 1889 and one year later in French as *Au XXIXème siècle: La journée d'un journaliste Américain en 2889*. For a discussion of the controversies surrounding Jules Verne's futuristic production see Evans 65.

11. In *Paris in the Twentieth Century* we already find "two hundred pianos wired together by means of an electric current" that "could be played by the hands of a single artist" (209).

12. See, e.g., Bellamy chapter 21.

13. A shorter version of Grifoni's novel, entitled *Da Firenze alle stelle*, was published in 1885. As for F. Bianchi's novel, its full title is *Da terra a Marte: Romanzo umoristico, scientifico-filosofico. Combatte la teoria della reciproca attrazione dei pianeti, contiene la scoperta della vera teoria del volare* (From Earth to Mars: A Humorous Scientific-Philosophical Novel. It Fights the Theory of the Reciprocal Attraction of Planets. It Contains the Discovery of the True Theory of Flying). This novel tells the story of Eugenio Barmann, who, after financial and family misfortunes, undertakes a journey to Mars, interacts with its inhabitants (including the local scientist), and perfects the project of a flying machine and a system to communicate with Earth. Despite extensive research I have been unable to identify Bianchi's full name, which is not even listed in the catalog of the Italian National Library in Florence. This gives an idea of the very limited diffusion and knowledge of such works and of the persistent difficulties in pursuing scholarly research on them, unlike their French equivalents.

14. "Interessantisimo romanzo fantastico-scientifico" (Grifoni iii). Significantly, when the first portion of the novel was initially published, a review in *Nuova Antologia* welcomed Grifoni as a new "Giulio Verne italiano" (Italian Jules Verne) but criticized precisely the long scientific digressions that are the hallmark of Grifoni's Vernian technique, claiming that they allegedly harm the "immaginazione sbrigliata" (unbridled imagination) that should characterize the novel, although it belongs to "il genere della fantasia scientifica" (the genre of scientific fantasy). See "Il Mondo dell'avvenire" 579. This demonstrates Italian public opinion's difficulties in coming to terms with unconventional literary styles and new genres.

15. Turin and Milan remain the main locations, even though the characters in both Della Sala Spada's and Ghislanzoni's works also leave their respective headquarters and travel to other parts of the world (even trying to contact creatures from other planets in *Nel 2073!*).

16. *Il pianeta Marte* (The Planet Mars, 1893), *La vita sul pianeta Marte* (Life on the Planet Mars, 1895), and *Il pianeta Marte* (The Planet Mars, 1909). Schiaparelli's writings on this topic have been recently republished as *La vita sul pianeta Marte*. The hypothesis that there was life on Mars was also supported in part by the misleading English translation of *canali* as "canals" rather than "channels," hence suggesting man-made structures.

17. See Marinetti. Curiously the remarks in *The Year 3000* that seem to come closest to a thematization of Marinetti's formal perspective on expressive speed appear in chapter 7, which presents writing in the elementary schools of the United Planetary States—"ten times faster than the ancient sort" because, unlike the "old-fashioned writing that lasted up until the twenty-first century, in which vowels and consonants all had to be represented by a letter," schools now teach a kind of "stenography in which the vowels are all omitted or indicated with the simplest marks" (127). Marinetti would go well beyond the school curriculum of Mantegazza's fourth millennium, not only by urging the destruction of syntax, the abolition of punctuation, adjectives, and adverbs, and the use of infinitive verbs for the sake of mechanical simultaneity but also by provocatively practicing all he preached in his own aesthetics.

18. Mantegazza, e.g., does not appear in Inisiero Cremaschi's overview of Italian science fiction precursors (*Universo e dintorni*) or in Gianfranco de Turris's "Quando la bandiera sventolò su Venere." But even more surprisingly he is not even mentioned in the article "Science-Fiction," included in the recently published *Encyclopedia of Italian Literary Studies*.

19. This is the literary expression of an intrinsic connection of "temporal and spatial relationships" that "[define] genre and generic distinctions." See Bakhtin 84–85.

20. Mantegazza's negotiations between a historical perspective on major social plights and its seemingly incompatible counterpart offered by a Utopian projection toward an imaginary future exemplify what Fredric Jameson calls "Utopian circularity"; that is, the ability of the representation of the future not only to act as "a political vision and program" but also to "return upon our present to play a diagnostic and a critical-substantive role." See Jameson 147–48.

21. "Alla mia Maria raggio divino di sole che illumina e riscalda l'ultimo

crepuscolo della mia sera" (To my Maria, divine ray of sunshine that brightens and warms up the last crepuscule of my evening) (Mantegazza, *L'anno*).

22. Although the novel subordinates the disturbing potential of Paolo's invention to humanitarian causes, the topos of mind-reading technoloogy and the question of its more or less acceptable applications provide further evidence of Mantegazza's cutting-edge imagination. Indeed, more recently both reality and fiction have offered poignant investigations into precognition abilities, elaborating premises found in *The Year 3000*. In 2007 a team of German and British neuroscientists adopted high-resolution brain scans to probe human mental activity and identify patterns associated with the development of specific thoughts and intentions (Sample). This milestone in brain-reading technology immediately raised scientific and ethical debates that conjured up the specter of a *Minority Report* society, where—as in the 2002 movie directed by Steven Spielberg, based upon Philip K. Dick's 1956 short story—precognition abilities, coupled with advanced equipment, promote preemptive disciplinary measures that allow the ability to punish the guilty before a crime has been committed and ultimately to eliminate crime altogether, just like the foreknowledge granted by the psychoscope in *The Year 3000*.

23. Francis Galton—interestingly Darwin's cousin—illustrated the purposes of "the science of improving stock" in his 1883 volume *Inquiries into Human Faculty and its Development* (25), but he had already divulged his ideas on the physical and mental improvement of future generations, with special attention to racial qualities, in his 1865 article "Hereditary Talent and Character." For an overview of eugenics in late nineteenth-century British culture see Richardson. For more recent bioethical issues entailed by the nineteenth-century dream of human perfection see Rotschild. For Mantegazza's references to Galton and his own groundbreaking research in the field see Mantegazza, *Igiene* 211.

24. See Falk and Strauss 216.

25. Souvestre, though, with his usual parodic intent, ultimately connotes "universal brotherhood" as "universal ugliness," since, in an interesting inversion of the myth of progress as unlimited improvement, racial interbreeding had in fact led to the predominance of "the least well-favored races" (51).

26. See, e.g., Roda 54–55; Trousson. The intellectual and cultural context of Mantegazza's novel is in fact more complex. Far from ignoring the alleged crisis of positivism, Mantegazza himself expresses the tensions inherent to the movement. Debates regarding the role of science within this framework were far from over in those years. Yet Mantegazza projected himself even beyond

positivism itself, seeming to think of a more extended and general path toward the future. With precisely this farsightedness he transcended the more provincial sensibility and imagination of his contemporaries, certainly pushing characterization beyond the figure of the scientist-alchemist-sorcerer (whether positive or negative) that seems to prevail in proto–science fiction.

27. "Giudizii della stampa."

Works Cited

AA.VV. *Milano illuminata*. Milan: AEM, 1993.

Alkon, Paul. *Origins of Futuristic Fiction*. Athens: U of Georgia P, 1987.

Archibugi, Daniele. "Cosmopolitan Democracy." *Debating Cosmopolitanism*. Archibugi, *Debating* 1–15.

———, ed. *Debating Cosmopolitanism*. London: Verso, 2003.

Bakhtin, Mikhail. *The Dialogic Imagination*. Trans. Caryl Emerson and Michael Holquist. Ed. Michael Holquist. Austin: U of Texas P, 1981.

Bellamy, Edward. *Looking Backward. 2000–1887*. Ed. Alex MacDonald. Peterborough CA: Broadview Literary Texts, 2003.

Bianchi, F. *Da terra a Marte: Romanzo umoristico, scientifico-filosofico. Combatte la teoria della reciproca attrazione dei pianeti, contiene la scoperta della vera teoria del volare*. 3rd illus. ed. Milan: Tip. Del Commercio, 1895.

Bodin, Félix. *The Novel of the Future*. Trans. and intro. Brian Stableford. Afterword by Brian Stableford. Encino CA: Black Coat P, 2008.

Cattaneo, Carlo. *Dell'insurrezione di Milano nel 1848 e della successiva guerra. Memorie*. Milan: Feltrinelli, 1973.

Clarke, I. F. Introduction. Souvestre xi–xxv.

Cremaschi, Inisiero. *Universo e dintorni*. Milan: Garzanti, 1978.

Durr, Michel. "Jules Verne et l'électricité." *La France des électriciens: 1880–1980*. Ed. Fabien Cardot. Paris: PUF, 1986. 335–58.

Ehrenfreund, Erasmo. *Bibliografia degli scritti di Paolo Mantegazza*. Florence: Stabilimento Grafico Commerciale, 1926.

Esposito, Bernard. "Les voyages extraordinaires de Jules Verne au pays de l'électricité." *Bulletin d'histoire de l'électricité* 35, no. 35 (2000): 143–76.

Evans, Arthur B. "The 'New' Jules Verne." *Science Fiction Studies* 22 (March 1995). Available at http://www.depauw.edu/sfs/backissues/65/evans65art.htm. Accessed November 28, 2009.

Falk, Richard, and Andrew Strauss. "The Deeper Challenges of Global Terrorism: A Democratizing Response." Archibugi, *Debating* 203–31.

Galton, Francis. "Hereditary Talent and Character." *Macmillan Magazine* 12 (1865): 157–66, 318–27.

————. *Inquiries into Human Faculty and Its Development.* London: Mac-Millan, 1883.

"Giudizii della stampa. Il governo dell'Anno 3000. Maurice Muret." *Illustrazione italiana* 25, no. 34 (August 21, 1898): 146–50.

Gooday, Graeme J. N. "Electrical Futures Past." *Endeavour* 29, no. 4 (2005): 150–55.

Grifoni, Ulisse. "Al lettore." *Dalla terra alle stelle. Viaggio meraviglioso di due italiani ed un francese.* Illus. E. Mazzanti and L. Edel. 5th ed. Rome: Edoardo Perino Editore, 1890. v–vi.

Hugo, Victor. "The United States of Europe. Presidential Address at the International Peace Congress, Paris, August 22, 1849." *Five Views on European Peace.* Ed. Sandi E. Cooper. New York: Garland, 1972. 3–9.

Jameson, Fredric. *Archaeologies of the Future.* London: Verso, 2005.

Mantegazza, Paolo. *L'anno 3000. Sogno.* Milan: Treves, 1897.

————. *Anthropological Studies in the Sexual Relations of Mankind.* Trans. and intro. James Bruce. New York: Falstaff, 1932.

————. *Igiene dell'amore.* Milan: Brigola, [1878]. 15th ed., Bemporad, 1896.

————. *The Physiology of Love and Other Writings.* Ed. and intro. Nicoletta Pireddu. Notes by Nicoletta Pireddu. Trans. David Jacobson. Toronto: U of Toronto P, 2007.

Marinetti, Filippo Tommaso. "Technical Manifesto of Futurist Literature." *Modernism: An Anthology.* Ed. Lawrence S. Rainey. Oxford: Blackwell, 2005. 15–19.

Mazzini, Giuseppe. "D'una letteratura europea." *D'una letteratura europea e altri saggi.* Ed. and intro Paolo Mario Sipala. Fasano: Schena, 1991. 27–75.

Mercier, Louis Sébastien. *Memoirs of the Year Two Thousand Five Hundred.* Trans. W. Hooper. (Dublin W. Wilson, 1772). Trans. of *Rêve s'il en fut jamais.*

"Il Mondo dell'avvenire: Da Firenze alle stelle." "Romanzi." *Nuova Antologia* 20, second series, vol. 51 (1885): 579–80.

Mori, G., ed. *L'industrializzazione in Italia (1861–1900).* Bologna: Il Mulino, 1977.

Orizio, L., and F. Radice. *Storia dell'industria elettrica in Italia, 1882–1962.* Milan: La Culturale, 1964.

Pireddu, Nicoletta. "Paolo Mantegazza: A Scientist and His Ecstasies." Mantegazza, *Physiology of Love* 3–53.

————. "Primitive Marks of Modernity: Cultural Reconfigurations in the Franco-Italian *Fin de siècle*." *Romanic Review* 96, nos. 1–2 (2006): 371–400.

Richardson, Angelique. *Love and Eugenics in the Late Nineteenth Century.* Oxford: Oxford UP, 2003.

Robida, Albert. *Voyage de Fiançailles au XXème siècle.* Paris: Conquet, 1892.

Robinson, Victor. Introduction. *The Sexual Relations of Mankind.* By Paolo Mantegazza. Trans. and intro. Samuel Putnam. New York: Eugenics, 1935. ix–xiv.

Roda, Vittorio. "*L'anno 3000. Sogno.*" *Dictionary of Literary Utopias.* Ed. Vita Fortunati and Raymond Trousson. Paris: Champion, 2000. 54–55.

Rotschild, Joan. *The Dream of the Perfect Child.* Bloomington: Indiana UP, 2005.

Salgari, Emilio. *Le meraviglie del Duemila. Avventure.* Pref. Felice Pozzo. Postfaces Pier Luigi Bassignana and Piero Gondolo Della Riva. Turin: Viglongo, 1995.

Sample, Ian. "The Brain Scan That Can Read People's Intentions." *Guardian,* February 9, 2007. Available at http://www.guardian.co.uk/science/2007/feb/09/neuroscience.ethicsofscience. Accessed November 28, 2009.

Schiaparelli, Giovanni. *La vita sul pianeta Marte: tre scritti di Schiaparelli su Marte e i "marziani."* Ed. A. Mandrino, A. Testa, and P. Tucci. Milan: Mimesis, 1998.

Scholes, Robert. *Structural Fabulation: An Essay on Fiction of the Future.* Notre Dame: U of Notre Dame P, 1975.

"Science-Fiction." *Encyclopedia of Italian Literary Studies.* Ed. Gaetana Marrone Puglia and Paolo Puppa. New York: Routledge, 2006. 2:1717–21.

Souvestre, Émile. *The World as It Shall Be.* Ed. and intro. I. F. Clarke. Trans. Margaret Clarke. Middletown CT: Wesleyan UP, 2004.

Spada, Agostino Della Sala. *Nel 2073! Sogno di uno stravagante.* Ed. and intro. Simonetta Satragni Petruzzi. Alessandria: Edizioni dell'Orso, 1998.

Stableford, Brian. Introduction. Bodin, *Novel* 5–25.

Stead, William T. *The United States of Europe on the Eve of the Parliament of Peace.* London: Clowes and Sons, 1899.

Suvin, Darko. *The Metamorphoses of Science Fiction.* New Haven: Yale UP, 1979.

Trousson, Raymond. Introduction. *L'an 3000.* By Paolo Mantegazza. Paris: L'Harmattan, 2003. 7–35.

Turris, Gianfranco de. "Quando la bandiera sventolò su Venere." *Le Aeronavi dei Savoia.* Ed. Gianfranco de Turris, with Claudio Gallo. Milan: Casa Editrice Nord, 2001. i–xxiii.

Valla, Riccardo. "Storia della fantascienza italiana." *Delos Science Fiction* 54 (March 2000). Available at http://www.fantascienza.com/magazine/speciali/6813/storia-della-fantascienza-italiana/. Accessed July 22, 2009.

Verne, Jules. *The Complete Twenty Thousand Leagues under the Sea*. Trans. and intro. Emanuel J. Mickel. Notes by Emanuel J. Mickel. Bloomington: Indiana UP, 1991.

————. *Journey to the Centre of the Earth*. Intro. David Brin. New York: Random House, 2003.

————. *Paris in the Twentieth Century*. Trans. Richard Howard. Intro. Eugene Weber. New York: Random House, 1996.

————. *Une ville idéale*. Ed Daniel Compère. Amiens: Editions CDJV—La Maison de Jules Verne, 1999.

Wells, H. G. *A Modern Utopia*. Intro. Mark R. Hillegas. Lincoln: U of Nebraska P, 1967.

THE YEAR
3000
A DREAM

1

PAOLO AND MARIA SET OUT FOR
Andropolis. One evening in the
Gulf of La Spezia.

PAOLO AND MARIA LEFT ROME, CAPITAL
of the United States of Europe, in the largest of their *aerotachs*, the
one intended for long trips.

This is an electrically run airship. By releasing a spring, they
convert the two comfortable armchairs in the middle of the ship into
quite comfortable beds. Opposite the chair-beds are a compass, a small
table, and a quadrant bearing the three words *motion, heat, light*.

With the touch of a button the aerotach sets off, reaching speeds
of up to 150 kilometers an hour.[1] With the touch of another button
the room can be heated to the temperature of your choice, and the
touch of a third button lights up the ship. A simple switch turns the
electricity into heat, light, movement, whatever your pleasure.

The walls of the aerotach are stocked with enough provisions to last ten days: condensed juices of albuminoids and carbon hydrides, representing kilograms of meat and vegetables; very cohobated aethers replicating the scents of the most pungent flowers and all the most exquisite fruits; a small canteen with a plentiful supply of three elixirs that stimulate the brain centers that regulate the major forces of life: thought, movement, and love.[2]

There is no need in the aerotach for mechanics or servants, since everyone from early school days has learned to drive it wherever they want to go. One of the quadrants tells you the kilometers covered, the room temperature, and wind direction.

Paolo and Maria brought just a few books with them, among them *The Year 3000*, written ten centuries earlier by a physician with a bizarre imagination who tried to guess what human life would be like a millennium on.

Paolo said to Maria:

"It's a long trip, so I'm going to help while away the boredom by translating the strange fantasies of this ancient writer from his native Italian. I'm really curious how well this prophet guessed the future. I'm sure there'll be some beauties to laugh about."

Bear in mind that by the year 3000 Cosmic has been the only language spoken for over five centuries. All the languages of Europe are dead, not to mention the languages of Italy: in chronological order, Oscan, Celtic, Latin, and, finally, Italian.[3]

The trip Paolo and Maria are setting out on is very long indeed. From Rome they plan to reach Andropolis, the capital of the United Planetary States, where they hope to celebrate their mating match, having already been together for the past five years in a love match. Now they must appear before the biological Senate of Andropolis, whose Supreme Assembly of Sciences has to judge their suitability to transmit life to other humans.

But before they cross Europe and Asia for the world capital at the foot of the Himalayas, formerly known as Darjeeling, Paolo thought his fiancée should see the great Necropolis at La Spezia, where the Italians of the year 3000 have, as in a "museum," collected all the memories of the past.[4]

Maria has traveled very little up until now. She is familiar only with Rome and Naples, and the thought of the unknown is intoxicating to her. She is only twenty, having thus given her hand in love to Paolo at fifteen.

The flight from Rome to La Spezia took only a few hours and went without a hitch. They arrived near evening, and after a brief stay in one of the city's best hotels, they brought out of the aerotach a sort of rubber blanket called a *hydrotach*, which, when blown up by a piston, in just a few moments turns into a comfortable, safe little boat. Here again there is no need of boatman and servants. A small electrical machine, no bigger than a mantelpiece clock, guides the hydrotach over the waves, at whatever speed you desire.

The Bay of La Spezia was heavenly that evening. The moon, from on high, in the tranquil peace of its light, shed a sort of gentle breath of melancholy over everything. Hills, monuments, islands seemed cast in bronze; motionless like some figure dead for centuries. The scene would have been too sad had the murmuring waves, which seemed to gossip and laugh among the endless silver net that enmeshed them like thousands of small fish caught in a fisherman's net, not given the bay the pulse of life.

The couple held hands and looked into each other's eyes. They too saw one another as though veiled in that dusky light that robs objects of solidity and makes the souls of things gigantic.

"Look, Maria," said Paolo, once he could find his voice: "here all about us are sleeping in the silence more than twenty thousand years of human history. How much blood has been spilled, how many tears have been shed before the peace and justice we enjoy today could be attained, far though they are still from our ideals. And how lucky for us if all that remains from the first centuries of human infancy are a few stone weapons and some confused memories. I say lucky because the further back we go in history, the fiercer and wickeder human beings were."

As he spoke they were nearing Palmaria, now turned into a large museum of prehistory.

"You see, Maria, here, in a cave ten or twenty centuries ago, lived men who knew nothing of metal and dressed in the pelts of wild animals. At the end of the nineteenth century an anthropologist from Parma, a man named Regalia, first showed the world this cave, called the Cave of the Turtle-Doves, describing the human and animal remains he had discovered in it.[5] At that time, though, the end of the nineteenth century, the whole island was covered with cannons, and a big battery of artillery, a true miracle in the art of murder, was defending the bay from enemy assault.

"And the whole bay itself was one giant trap for killing people. On the hills, cannons; on the shores, cannons; on the ships, cannons and rifles: all an inferno of horror and destruction.

"Yet even centuries before this bay bore memories of bloodshed. There, in the east, over Lerici, you see that ancient castle? It was prison to a king of France, François I, after he lost the battle of Pavia.

"We no longer see the hecatombs of bones that must be down on the bottom of the sea, because at the start of the twentieth century a terrible naval battle occurred, in which all the fleets of Europe took part, while, by a fateful coincidence, another great battle was being waged in France.[6]

"They fought for peace and for war, and Europe was divided into two camps—those who wanted war and those who wanted peace. But to want peace they had to fight, and a great bloodbath darkened the waves of the Mediterranean and soaked the earth. In just one day during the battles of La Spezia and Paris a million people died. Here, right at this spot we are now, enjoying the delights of this beautiful evening, in one hour twenty battleships were blown up, killing thousands of strong, handsome lads; almost all had mothers waiting for them, all a woman who adored them.

"The slaughter was so vast and cruel that Europe finally recoiled in horror, frightened by itself. The war killed war, and from that day on the first stone was laid for the United States of Europe.

"Those black giants you see floating in the bay are the ancient battleships that emerged unscathed on that awful day. Every nation from that time is represented: there are Italian ones, French ones, English, German. They're visited today like museum curiosities;

we'll see some tomorrow. You'll see how, in that time of barbarism, ingenuity and science were united in supreme efforts to kill men and destroy cities. And just imagine that large-scale killing was then considered the greatest glory, and the victorious generals and admirals were carried in triumph. What sorry times, what sorry humanity!

"Yet even after war was abolished the family of man still had no peace. There were too many hungry and unhappy people; and the pity of suffering, not reason, led Europe to socialism.

"It was not until the last pope (I think his name was Leon XX) that a king of Italy spontaneously stepped down from the throne, saying he wanted to be first to try the great experiment of socialism. He died among the benedictions of a whole people and triumphs of glory. His colleagues fell cursing and protesting.

"A great war ensued, only now it was one of words and ink, between republicans, conservatives, and socialists; and the last of these won the day.

"The generous but rash experiment lasted four generations, which is to say a century; but people realized they had taken the wrong path. They had suppressed the individual, and liberty died at the hand of the very people who sought to sanctify it. The tyranny of king and parliament was replaced by a more vexing, crushing tyranny, that of an artificial mechanism that, to protect and defend an anonymous collective, stifled and extinguished the seeds of individual initiative and the sacred struggle for supremacy. By suppressing inheritance the family became a mechanical factory of child-breeding and sad, sterile tedium.

"A large assembly of sociologists and biologists buried socialism and founded the United Planetary States, governed by the best and most honest through a two-phase election.[7] The government of dull-witted majorities was replaced by a government of knowledgeable, honest minorities. Nature's aristocracy was copied by humankind, who made it the basis of human society. But unfortunately we are still only halfway there. The art of choosing *the best* has not yet come; and men and women thinkers, the priests of thought and priestesses of feeling, still toil to find the best way, so that every man born to woman should have the rightful place nature accorded him at birth.

"Soldiers were suppressed, as were duties on consumption, customhouses, all the instruments of the old barbarism. Physical suffering was suppressed, and average life grew longer, extending to sixty years.[8] Yet disease still exists, and hunchbacks, the mad, and delinquents are still born, and the dream of seeing all people die at an advanced age, free of suffering, is still far off."

Maria was listening in silence, and Paolo too fell silent, as though overcome by a great melancholy. Twenty thousand years of history seemed to him too long a time to cover such a small distance on the road of progress.

Maria wanted to break that silence and lift that melancholy, and, with that clever, mobile agility all women have, wanted to get her companion's thought to take a large leap.

"Tell me, Paolo, why, among so many dead languages, did you study Italian with such special fondness? I've been curious about that for quite a while, and you've never satisfied my curiosity. Would it by any chance be to read *The Year 3000* in the original?"

"No, my dear, it's because Italian literature has left us *The Divine Comedy* and *Giovanin Bongé*, Dante and Carlo Porta, the two greatest poets of the divine and the comic.[9] You and I should read those two great poets, and you'll see that I've a hundred reasons to want to study Italian ahead of every other dead language.

"No one has known how to touch all the strings of the human heart like Alighieri, and no one has made us laugh more humanly than Porta.

"But to understand Porta it's not enough to know Italian, one has to study Milanese, a heavily Celtic dialect that was spoken ten centuries ago in much of Lombardy, when Italy had more than twenty different dialects.

"And then, even without Dante and without Porta I would have studied Italian ahead of every other dead language, because it was the first and favorite daughter of Greek and Latin, and concentrated in itself the juices of the two greatest civilizations in the world, and added a third to them, no less glorious than they. Speaking Italian, one thinks back to Socrates and Phidias, Aristotle and Apelles; to

Caesar and Tacitus, Augustus and Horace, Michelangelo and Galileo, Leonardo and Raphael. Never did another language have a nobler, greater genealogy. That is also why, when they founded the United States of Europe, Rome, by unanimous consent, was chosen as its capital."

"Paolo, dear, you're swelling my head for being Roman!"

And again the couple fell silent, while their hydrotach skimmed over the waves of the bay, at every movement breaking the meshes in the silver net cast over the water's surface.

Meanwhile they were approaching La Spezia's old Arsenal, and its mournful, monotonous sound was reaching their ears—at times confused and barely perceptible, at times clear and distinct, depending on the vagaries of the night breeze.

Paolo's and Maria's eyes turned to where the sound was coming from and where it seemed to rise out of the waves, where a round body was floating over the water like a huge sea turtle.

They steered their little boat toward that point as the sound grew louder and sadder. They stopped the hydrotach a few paces from that floating body.

"What is this?"

"It's an ancient buoy; the barbarians of the nineteenth century would tie their biggest battleships to it. It's stayed here for centuries and centuries, rusting and forgotten, the memento of a time in human history that luckily won't return."

Meanwhile the sad, monotonous sound coming from the buoy grew crystal clear.

It was a double, piercing sound, made up of two notes: a lament and a thud. First there was a shrill, protracted *ihhh* and then, after a brief pause, a deep, lugubrious *boom* and another pause, with incessant repeats of lament and thud.

The human heart too measures the brief turn of life's quadrant with two alternating sounds, a *tick* and a *tock*; but those are glad, almost joyful sounds.

This *ihhh* and *boom*, on the other hand, seemed the beatings of a giant, broken heart counting out the time of our planet.

"Good God, tell me, Paolo, why is that buoy lamenting so? It sounds like it's crying in pain."

"Why, you silly," he replied, with a forced smile. "That 'lament' is the buoy groaning from the rust around its ring, that thud you hear is the wave slapping against the empty hulk."

Paolo, however, providing the physical explanation for that alternating sound, was taken up with other thoughts, his mind adrift in a higher, more distant world.

And the two of them again fell silent for a long time.

"Let's move on, let's head back to land, this buoy frightens me, it makes me want to cry."

"You're right, let's move on. This dirge is making me sad too. It calls to mind the painful image of all of human history. A lament rising from the bowels of newborn children, from lovelorn youth, from the aged stricken with the fear of death; from all those who are discontented, hungry for bread or glory, wealth or love. A lament rising up from the entire planet, which weeps and asks heaven why there is life and why there is suffering.

"And Fate, Fate in its deep, dark thud, replies to that planetary lament:

"So it is, so it must be, so it shall be forever."

"No, Paolo, that's not how it is and not how it must be forever! Think of those murderous battleships that no longer exist; think of progress, which never stops. Even this buoy, whose beats seem to be repeating to us the eternal lament of humanity and the cruel answer of Fate, will be silent someday, dissolved by the waters of the sea . . ."

"I hope so," said Paolo, speeding up the little boat's motion to escape the nightmare of that harrowing, plaintive sound . . .

The next morning the sun shone brightly in the sky over La Spezia, brighter than the moon before it. The bracing life of labor put the night's melancholy behind it, and the couple, after visiting some carcasses of old battleships and climbing back into their aerotach, flew eastward, where the light of day has always brought man hope, the hope that never dies.

2

FROM LA SPEZIA TO THE ANCIENT
pyramids of Egypt. From the
pyramids to the Isle of Experiments.
The Land of Equality. Tyrannopolis.
Turatia or the Socialist Republic.
Logopolis. Other governments and
other social organizations.

CONTINUING THEIR FLIGHT FROM LA
Spezia, Paolo and Maria soon found themselves heading over Sicily,
where from their lofty height they saluted Mount Aetna, completely
extinguished now for several centuries.

The next day they were in Egypt and with a decent telescope
could see the pyramids, still firmly in place after such a long course
of history. They had remained indestructible in their granite impas-
sivity, but at their feet were lapping the waves of a new sea, which,
through the giant operations of men, had come to replace all the
deserts of Africa. Water had replaced sand, thus cooling the climate
of Europe by many degrees, yet without the return of a glacier age.[1]
In the year 3000 people so deftly controlled the forces of nature that

it was enough to direct a strong current of warm air toward the poles to melt the immense ice formations that once occupied much of the polar zone.

Maria showed a desire to visit the pyramids, and Paolo immediately obeyed her, lowering the aerotach in just a few minutes to the foot of those stone giants.

They stepped out to the pyramids, and Paolo explained the phrases and names carved into the stone in long-dead languages by a people that had vanished centuries ago.

They ate on the beach and, asking a local fisherman for a small net, decided to go fishing.

In less than an hour their little boat was full of fish, since fishing now was very easy. The net, extremely fine yet firm enough to withstand all resistance, was lowered in a semicircle, and in the middle of the arch it formed was hidden a little electric lamp that, in the sea's depth, shed a very bright light, summoning to it from far away the water's great and small inhabitants alike. After a half hour the net closed, clasping in it, as in a bag, all those creatures intrigued by the light, and the easy prey were gathered into the boat.

Paolo, choosing from the great mass of fish only the most exquisite, put the others back into the sea.

On the beach they lunched on their catch and the provisions they had brought with them from the aerotach, and they spent the night stretched out upon the soft sand, contemplating the moon and remembering the ancient Egyptians and the Turks and the Italians, who had followed one another in dominion of this land once desert and now so fertile.

Maria enjoyed this sea outing so much that she said to Paolo, with a sigh:

"Tomorrow, why don't we just keep on boating?"

"Yes, why not?" answered Paolo. "This very night the *Cosmos*, a mail boat bound from London for India, stops at Ceylon. Air travel doesn't keep people from traveling by land and water, so let's go to Ceylon on the English mail boat. Even by aerotach I'd have put down on that strange island, where all the forms of past governments have been preserved, as though it were a museum. That is why it is also called the Isle of Experiments."

That evening the *Cosmos* cast anchor at the feet of the pyramids, letting out the many passengers who wanted to visit them.[2]

The *Cosmos* differs considerably from ancient steamers. It is tiny compared to the older vessels, since its engine runs not on steam but on electricity, and the saltwater is broken down by an economical, very simple battery to provide hydrogen, the new fuel, and distill it into drinking water. There is no longer need for a huge storage space to carry coal, which is what the ancient steamers once burned.[3]

The boat is built with a special bronze made of aluminum and iridium, a metal at once very light yet stronger than iron. No fumes, no foul smell, and great speed of movement—so that, landing somewhere new every day, the passengers always have the freshest food.

With seasickness completely eliminated, since the waves barely create any turbulence, the prow sprays out an oily substance that stretches over the water and, as though casting a spell over it, calms the storm's tumult.

Furthermore the *Cosmos* has all the comforts and amusements of a large, wealthy city.

No more narrow, stifling cabins with all the most disgusting smells from the kitchen, the steam engine, and imperfect ventilation.

The rooms are spacious and well-furnished, since they accommodate only a few passengers. Music and flowers are everywhere, the kitchen available to all, providing for their every desire, at all hours. A fine library, games of all sorts. The service invisible, since everywhere, by merely pushing some buttons, you can communicate your wants and needs. The captain, more a friend to all than a commander, is host to long hours of amusement and conversation.

Every evening a small theater alternates dramatic with musical presentations, and the passengers, in their amateur roles, are both entertained and entertaining.

The ship's almost total motionlessness also allows for dancing and even billiard playing, which has been set up so skillfully that the ship's slight oscillations do not in the least disturb the movement of the balls, which are also different from ours.

It took our travelers only two days to go from the pyramids to Ceylon, and just a few hours before their arrival the delightful island already announced its nearness with an intense perfume of roses, a balm to the air and an enchantment to souls.

They disembarked at the port of Equality, one of Ceylon's cities, and its most modern.

The Egalitarians had founded it, a people convinced they had resolved the question of human happiness by giving equal rights and obligations to all people—equalizing them in their wealth, their dress, in everything.

No sooner had they landed than Paolo and Maria found a crowd of people eagerly awaiting the arrival of the English mail boat. They were all dressed identically, in the whitest silk, and all were beardless, so that you couldn't even tell their sex. The women too wore their hair short and cut just like the men's. It was only when they spoke that their voices gave away their sex. It was also hard to discern their age, since the older ones dyed their hair black—all always done in tribute to universal equality.

The harbor opened onto a large square, completely lined with houses of the same height and color, fanning out into twelve large streets. These streets in turn had houses of the same height and color.

Paolo and Maria picked one of these streets at random, looking to left and right to discover something different to distract them from the cold, boring monotony.

The inhabitants were all walking with the same gait, neither slow nor hurried, and all seemed to express the same thing—that is, a vast boredom, an indifference to everything and everyone. They even seemed all to have the same physiognomy.

Hoping that these egalitarians understood the Cosmic language, Paolo asked one passerby:

"Where can we find lodging for a day, and who is head of this city?"

"You can knock on any door, and whoever answers will give you the same hospitality. As for the head, you'll find him at Sixth Street, number 1000, since our houses differ only in their numbers: just as we, when we're born, aren't given names but numbers, which tell us apart from others and accompany us even to the tomb.[4] But when one of us dies, the first person to be born after takes that person's number, so the series is not broken. The highest number is that of the last-born and also represents the exact number of the population, which today is ten thousand.

"As for your other question, the head of the city is called the Different One Today, because every day each of us over the age of twenty, whether man or woman, takes a turn being head of the city for just a day; the number 1000 settles any problems of order that might otherwise arise. That person metes out justice and, all in all, does whatever hundreds of employees do in Andropolis.

"Furthermore, governance of Equality is extremely easy, since in the house of the Different One Today the code is posted for all to see, and that determines and regulates everyone's life.

"We live in horror of difference, since it offends justice, our goddess; each of us immediately reports to the Different One Today anyone who behaves differently from others, whether in dress, eating, or anything else."

Maria could not keep from laughing at this speech of the egalitarian, though the latter had no time to notice: bidding the travelers goodbye, he or she had already set off on his or her rhythmic, monotonous way.

"Why, Paolo, we've entered a cage of mad people! Let's get out of here, and fast."

"No, my darling Mariuccia! I find this realm of Equality quite curious and would like to study it more closely. Over eleven hundred years ago the French had a terrible, bloody revolution to achieve, among other things, *equality*. They severed thousands of innocent heads with guillotines, yet people continued to be born different from one another, and social hierarchies were set down in the society in which we live today, where justice no longer grants the same thing to all people but rather what each deserves. Yet here on the Isle of Experiments we find, renewed after eleven centuries, the old dream of 1789."

"Luckily I don't see the guillotine here, and these lunatics of egalitarianism have come together freely to achieve their dream."

"Well I, my sweet companion, am feeling quite hungry and would like to knock at the first door we find to ask for hospitality."

And so our travelers did.

At number 365 of Sixth Street in Equality they entered a house whose door, like all the doors there, had been left wide open.

In the hallway they found a white-clad creature. Man or woman?

It was quite hard to tell, but once the person began to speak by way of greeting, they realized it was a woman and one who, like everyone else, did indeed speak Cosmic.

"Pardon, madam, they told us there are no hotels in this city and that every house offers travelers hospitality. If that is true, we would like to ask you to give us a meal."

"Come in and sit down. I'm so sorry to have to tell you, though, that breakfast time is over, and you'll have to wait for the lunch hour, which is at 17:00."

"Forgive us, madam, but we're very hungry and would be satisfied with the smallest snack: two eggs and a bit of bread."

"I couldn't disobey the law of Equality. Like the good travelers that you must be, surely you have some small provisions with you that will allow you to wait until lunchtime, which is a communal event. Meanwhile, you'll find the guest room open to you and unoccupied."

Paolo and Maria always had in their small travel bag some condensed albuminoids and nervine foods, and for that reason, begging a thousand pardons of the egalitarian, they repaired to the guest room, laughing like two mad people at the peculiarity of this country's customs.

When lunchtime arrived they heard an electric bell ring to announce it, and with it all the other bells of the city.

Led into the dining room, they saw seated at the table five people, the father, mother, and their three small children. No manservant, no maid. By turns first the father, then the mother, then each of the three children rose and from a counter window in the wall took their food, prepared by them in the kitchen with scant personal effort and highly ingenious mechanical and chemical devices.

The master of the house, scarcely distinguishable in his features from the mistress of the house, and completely identical to her in dress, was cheerful and extremely gracious to the guests. He had them tell of their travels, gave useful information about the city of Equality and the island's other states, but above all fervently praised to the skies the social perfection of the government under which he lived.

"Look how admirable this system is, sheer order and symmetry! At this very hour in our city everyone is dining, and everyone eating the same thing, and at many tables the same number of people are sitting, since celibacy is forbidden—as it is forbidden to have more than three children. Only if something bad happens to one of them can we replace that child with a fourth.

"On the first of every month all the heads of families send a proposal for food to the house of the Different One Today, the food to be eaten for breakfast, lunch, and dinner, and the majority of those proposals becomes law for all. In that way the food and the mealtimes depend on the seasons and on public health. Don't you think that's ideal for a society? No one first and no one second; but all equal. No ambition, no power struggles, since we each get to have power for a day—no envy. What do you think?"

Paolo did not want to humiliate a man so kind nor disabuse him of the blessed sureness of his convictions. He contented himself with saying:

"No doubt your social organization is very curious, very original . . ."

"Oh, my dear sir, it is not only curious and original; it is perfection, the ideal of all human governments."

"But how do you manage to make everyone enjoy the same things? People are born so different from one another . . ."

"That may be, but accustoming them to the same things makes them more and more equal, and we hope with time to make them be born all equal, all with the same strength, the same intelligence, the same tastes. A law passed in this very year requires all men to fecundate their wife only on the first of May. As for love, we all make it at the same hour, every hour, when the special bell of the Government House tolls. Don't you find it beautiful and poetic to think that you eat, sleep, stroll at the same hour as all your fellow citizens?"

Here Paolo, barely managing to hold back a smile, could not help saying:

"My dear sir, as early as 1600 the Jesuits of Paraguay thought the same thing, and a certain bell tolling in the morning enjoined citizens to pay their tribute to the fertile Venus . . ."

"I don't know who these Jesuits were that you speak of, but I find that an idea that endures after so many centuries must have a serious foundation in the needs of human nature . . ."

"I think, on the contrary," put in Paolo, "that human nature is so elastic, so proteiform, that it allows us, over long intervals, to repeat the same experiments and to hold on to the same strange utopias, which is what I consider this egalitarian republic of yours to be."

—•—

The next day our travelers left Equality and headed for Tyrannopolis, a small state where the people lived under the despotic regime of a petty tyrant, Nicholas III, who bore the title of *czar*, in memory of the emperors of Russia who, many centuries earlier, had governed much of eastern Europe and western Asia.

They stayed but a day, indignant at the moral cowardice of the populace, who obeyed one man who had no other merit but having been born to Nicholas II, who in turn had inherited the throne from Nicholas I, founder of the dynasty.

Tyrannopolis was teeming with soldiers who did not have to defend the country, since it had no enemies; instead they served as gendarmes and guards of public safety, reporting every day to the Chief of Police what they had seen and heard in their constant spying.

A single irreverent word uttered against the czar was punished with prison, and every effort at rebellion earned the death penalty, which was carried out by strangling.

Nicholas was not just an absolute king; he was also the religious leader. This was an extremely simple affair: adoration of a single God and his saints, all of them tyrants famous throughout history. Augustus, Tiberius, Nero, Ezzelino da Romano, Louis XI, Louis XIV, Henry VIII of England, Napoleon I, King Bomba of Naples, Peter the Great, and numerous others were saints, with their temples and their cults to prove it.[5]

Around the throne was a double aristocracy, civil and religious, drawn together by ties of kinship and a common solidarity. Its members bore various titles according to the hierarchy to which they belonged and, in exchange for the services they rendered the throne, were handsomely paid, having nothing to do but defend throne and altar.

Tyrannopolis was surrounded by liberal states, and some citizens had managed to flee the tyranny of Nicholas III by reaching Equality, the metropolis of socialism, the parliamentary state. But emigration was rare and difficult, being punishable by death, should the culprit be captured. In other cases it was the culprit's nearest relatives who were punished.

Emigration, moreover, was quite rare for another reason. The inhabitants of Tyrannopolis, born of two generations of slaves, came into the world already resigned; patient in their enslavement, they obeyed the most absurd and tyrannical laws.

The smartest and proudest among them hoped for a Messiah who had yet to come, who would kill the tyrant and destroy the dominant aristocracy, bringing the light of freedom to all.

Just as Paolo and Maria, horrified by the sorry spectacle of that society of slaves, were about to leave through the country's border, they met a young gentleman whom Paolo had known in Rome when the former was studying there and who had since gone, for the sport of it, to Andropolis. Ever since he was a boy he had tyrannical instincts, and once he became a man, in public lectures and in newspaper journals, he preached the need to strengthen the Government of the United States of Europe with restrictive laws. The supreme court of Andropolis had now ordered him to spend a month on the island of Ceylon to see with his own eyes what a fine thing a state was when governed by ancient tyranny.

He himself told the couple the purpose of his voyage, and Paolo, laughing, told him:

"Go, go to Tyrannopolis, and a month will be too much time there. It will cure you of your authoritarian ideas."

—•—

Continuing on their voyage of exploration Paolo and Maria reached Turatia, capital of a small state governed by collective socialism.[6]

Matters were fairly similar to what they had seen in the city of Equality and were no less odd and ridiculous.

Finding a young boy walking down the street, they asked him the address of a hotel, and as he accompanied them they entered into conversation with him, asking him whose child he was:

"I don't know, no more than any of the other inhabitants of this country knows. I only know who my mother is, but since she had many lovers, several claim to have brought me into the world. Here we use our mother's last name, because love is free and marriage does not exist. The children are all children of the State, the great father of all."

Maria further asked the young socialist boy why their city was called Turatia.

"It's in honor of a certain Turati, who lived in Italy around the end of the nineteenth century and who was one of the most honest and reasonable socialists of his day, one who with his pen and his word prepared the coming of the great socialist republic that later governed Europe."

Maria was keen to study Turatia, and Paolo gave her a succinct history of the great and generous utopia of socialism, which he defined as arcadian soft-heartedness coupled with the deepest ignorance of human nature.

"You see, Maria, from 1895 Europe had in it socialists of various stripes. A certain Bianchini, a sharp, profound writer of that time, came to identify three distinct categories.[7]

"In the front ranks were the *scientific socialists*, their science not always entirely pure in substance, although on the outside it jealously sought to appear grave, systematic, and dignified.

"These socialists would point to the day, hour, and minute of the imminent social transformation and the related demise of the bourgeoisie. Their inventions could not be faulted for excessive variety. Whether one worked too much or not at all, whether there was an actual obstacle or gross incompetence, whether it was drizzling or storming, all they could see in the world was infamous capital at the root of everything and on high the God Marx, a great forerunner of Turati.

"Then there were the *literary socialists*, some of them men of talent, others mediocrities, and trailing after them the infinite herd of authors betrayed by fate, to whom the advent of socialism smiled as a vindication of their own misunderstood genius, in that sacred work in which capitalist tyranny would no longer clip the wings of their boundless flights of thought.

"They dreamed of the happy day in which publishers' sordid greed would no longer clash with the ineffably sweet groan of the printing press, and that dream exalted them, roused the most ardent and sensitive parts of their heart.

"The socialist man of letters was an enthusiastic, expansive animal, convinced to the point of absurdity of his own ideas but personally quite harmless.

"Lastly, Bianchini identified the *professorial socialists*, whom he found in his day to be few but singularly stubborn.

"They were frightfully erudite men who, with the most heroic courage, had dived into the *mare magnum* of judicial laws and institutions to come up with the infallible recipe that would delete from the dictionary of humanity the sad word *suffering*. Their speculative work unconsciously separated them from the world of the living to carry them into a milieu in which they acknowledged but one divinity, *the law*—which was all, and was obliged to all, and was capable of all. There was no physiological or natural requirement they deigned to consider in man, but that they perfected it with the greatest insouciance, turned and overturned it entirely as dictated by the needs of their preestablished system. And beside these *maestri*, these simple, temperate laborers, deluded in good faith, there arose the lightweight, superficial disciples who went strutting about in their pretentious garb of easy superiority.

"But studying the history of socialism, my dear Maria, I think that, to the three kinds of socialists so masterfully delineated by Bianchini at the end of the nineteenth century, one must add a fourth, which might even have been the most numerous, namely the *socialists out of pity*. Among them was Edmondo De Amicis, a famous Italian writer of the nineteenth century.[8]

"These are precisely the kind we find here, after eleven centuries, wanting once more to make the ancient attempt, founding the State of Turatia here on the island of Ceylon.

"Physical suffering no longer exists, but there still do exist ever so many forms of moral suffering, despite efforts to suppress from birth the innate delinquents and all the monsters and all the organisms destined to die either prematurely or of hereditary diseases. Sometimes the expert biologists make mistakes and let live people who are condemned by their constitution to suffer or make others suffer, if not physically, morally—for altruistic pity is acutely painful.

"Add to this the struggle of individuals perhaps too free in their movements and who often create conflicts, contradictions, inequities.

"From the little I have seen in Turatia it seems to me that the experiment, which has lasted only five years, won't have a long life. The great mass of the socialist populace is made up of the ignorant and people of extremely weak character, who have come here hoping to find a panacea for their ills. At the head of them I have seen clever men, but with more heart than head, straining to achieve a sort of squaring of the circle—namely giving to all their due, measuring with one and the same scale the value of labor, which differs so widely in different human organisms.

"The State has become a sort of gigantic tumor that absorbs all with the sacred intention of distributing to all an equal quantity of blood and life. But this distribution is made by men, who for all their intelligence and goodness are after all just men, with their sympathies and their passions—which explains the many causes of error and dissatisfaction.

"Note, then, that the impossibility of gathering the fruit of one's labor to leave to one's children takes all the nerve out of individual energy, and a great apathy reigns in the atmosphere of this State, where, even if there are neither oppressors nor oppressed, there is an absence of saints and powerful struggles for primacy, and the most beautiful and noblest energies abort, since their labor is denied.

"Yesterday, while you were sleeping, I had a long conversation with one of the principal leaders of Turatia, but I found in him a great poet rather than a wise statesman.

"He was enthusiastic about the new experiment and told me that the socialist republic has a great future before it and is destined gradually to absorb all the societies on the planet. To my objection that they have done away with God and the family, which is to say the temple in which we believe and hope and the nest in which we love, he, shaking his head with an air of compassion and in the warm, inspired voice of an apostle and a prophet, replied:

"'Yes, it is true, we have done away with God, because He is a lie. We have done away with the selfish, animallike family; or rather, we have greatly extended its boundaries. Here we are all brothers and sisters, and the young are the children of the old. Our kinship is not merely of the blood but of the brain, of the heart, of all the nerves that set human nature vibrating to the tremors of joy and pain. The joy of one is the joy of all; the pain of one is the pain of all.

"'The individual, whom you others on the planet have made a God, here among us is only a molecule, the social atom, a member of the great organism, which is the State. We feel no need for greater freedom nor for greater affluence, because the State thinks for us and metes out their due to all. We have copied what nature does when it shapes the organisms of the vegetable and animal worlds.

"'Does an arm or toe or one of our many internal organs complain of the work it has been assigned in life's great travail? Certainly not: each of our organs works for itself and for others and lives at once its own life and the collective life. You others, fanatical individualists, can rise as high as you like; you can feel powerful and extremely rich; and yet you remain a unit. Whereas I, as you can see, have quivering in me the life of all the thirty thousand brothers and sisters who now make up the Social Republic of Turatia, as though the conscience of my "I" were as large as that of all my fellow citizens.'

"And the socialist said many other beautiful things, and to him too I hadn't the courage to hurl in his face even a single one of the many objections that were on my lips.

"I contented myself with giving him a strong handshake and saying:

"'I admire and envy you, although of opposite opinion on the form of social governance you have chosen for yourselves. All enthusiasm, all ardent faith, is always a matter for thought, which surprises and also brings happiness to anyone capable of it.'"

—•—

From Turatia our pilgrims, traveling into the interior of the island, reached Logopolis, or the City of the Word, a new reconstruction of an ancient parliamentary state.

There they found little new and interesting. Logopolis is a perfect copy of Old England when it was an independent state ruled by a parliamentary government. The only difference is this: that the king is not a hereditary but rather an elective head.

Every five years the Chamber and Senate hold a joint assembly to cast their vote in the election of the king.

This king, however, is a largely symbolic head of state, who merely signs decrees and has not even been granted the right of dispensing favor or mercy. He receives a rich annuity and carries about him the majesty and the trappings of his high office.

Beyond that there are ministers, representatives, and senators, as in the ancient states with parliamentary regimes. The same intrigues, the same corruption to be elected members of one or another chamber, since senators too are elected in Logopolis. Both are handsomely paid, although barred from performing any real function—as are all the lawyers and those who have common interests with State concerns.

The representation of the people, however, has become a little more earnest and serious, for with every important vote, with every political act of any real gravity, whether that of a minister, a representative, or a senator, the voters of the College have the right to assemble in an extraordinary committee and cast a vote of disapproval of their representative. From that moment on he ceases to be a member of Parliament or the Cabinet and must be replaced through a new election.

This and other minor reforms in Logopolis have improved the ancient parliamentary form, but it continues to have these two organic diseases:

One of creating laws through a commission of too many individuals, making them mutable according to every accident or incident of persons or things;

And the other, of always changing with the vagrant whims of the voters, those who must frame laws and steer the rudder of State.

—•—

Our companions did not visit all the states of the Isle of Experiments, but only the main ones.

Beyond the egalitarians, beyond Tyrannopolis, Turatia, and Logopolis, there are other peoples and other countries under different governance. It is enough for a hundred people to think up a new social utopia or rethink an ancient one that has been buried for centuries, and they know that on the island of Ceylon they can always find a small or large virgin territory for founding their new republic or theocracy.

And thus the experiments are made and remade: thus rise and fall cities and phalansteries and strange new organizations, which then serve as sport yet also as schooling for the politically minded people of the United Planetary States.

Paolo and Maria knew in fact that, in addition to the states they visited, Ceylon comprises:

Poligama, a little state with a semidespotic government, in which every man has many wives;

Polyandra, another state, in which, on the other hand, every woman has many husbands;

Cenobia, a vast hieratic city from which women have been barred and where the men live in continuous asceticism;

Monachia, a small city made up entirely of nuns devoted to the cult of Sappho;

Peruvia, a communist state that imitates the ancient socialist regime of the Incan Empire and where property, belonging entirely to the State, is lent out to all according to their needs, broadening its boundaries according to the number of children. Thus work is also distributed on the various days of the week for oneself, for the poor and the sick, for the king and the princes, and for the expenses of worship.

3

VOYAGE TO THE ISLE OF DYNAMO,
one of the four great laboratories
of planetary force. The Historical
Museum of our planet's mechanical
evolution. The three great historical
epochs. Macstrong's discovery
and the pandynamo. The central
distribution office of cosmic forces.

OUR TRAVELERS, AFTER RESTING A FEW
days in one of the Isle of Experiments' delightful hotels, and after
strolling in the shade of those woods and rose-wreathed palm trees,
after inebriating themselves with all the perfumes of that divine,
endless flora, waited for an Italian steamer to take them to the Isle
of Dynamo and from there to India.

The Italian vessel took them in just a few hours from Equality
to Dynamo.

In ancient days this island went by the name of Andaman, inhabited
first by a savage race of pygmies that disappeared like so many others upon murderous contact with the European races. It became an
English colony and then, after the founding of the United Planetary

States, one of the four largest accumulators of cosmic energy, called Dynamos, of which one was placed on Malta, another on Fernando de Noronha, a third on one of the Kurile Islands, and the fourth, as mentioned, on what had been Andaman.

Paolo wanted Maria to see one of these great laboratories, where the planet's energy was gathered and then distributed through wires to all regions of the globe.

The Indian Dynamo, where our travelers now put ashore, had become a city and a school. The city was inhabited by the engineers who directed the giant workshop and school to which students came running from every part of the world, eager to earn degrees as *dynamologists*, or doctors in the science of physical forces.

Landing at Dynamo you heard no shrill noises, smelled no foul fumes to announce an energy workshop, as had been the case with earlier plants. Nor did you find anyone on the streets dirty with coal or grimy with pork fat, or with a face made haggard by unhealthy or excessive labor. The workers were cleanly dressed, vigorous looking, and differed in almost no way from their bosses, the dynamological engineers.

Perpetually green trees clustered together in small woods, and fragrant flower beds separated the various divisions of the giant workshop.

Our two travelers asked if it might be possible to see the general director of the island, and they were immediately led to his room, in which he was studying.

Just a few moments later a very pleasant young man introduced himself and put himself at their service.

"Well, my guess is you're not specialists and would like to take a quick tour through our workshop to get a general idea of how we produce the forces here and distribute them to the farthest countries in the world. Since our planet has three other main centers as large as ours, we have divided the earth into four departments; ours corresponds with all of Asia and Micronesia."

From the Director's small residential building they stepped down into a large garden. The small building was in the middle, and from it, by several diverging streets like spokes in a wheel, one reached various laboratories.

"If you would like," said the engineer, "we can go first to the Historical Museum and there, as shown through various models, see the rapid evolution of mechanics over the centuries."

Maria, who knew nothing of the existence of the great planetary force distributors but their names, was all eyes and ears, darting from one curiosity to another, one marvel to another.

"Look here," said the engineer, entering the first room of the museum. "The first prehistoric specimens of mechanics—the first animal strength used to benefit humankind."

They saw the first ox-driven ploughs, the first carriages, wheelless first, then with full wheels, then spoked wheels, drawn by horses, donkeys, mules. Represented there were all the animals that in very ancient times had lent their muscles to man, from the elephant to the homing pigeon, from the dromedary to the ostrich, from the dog to the reindeer.

In the next room they saw the first applications of the elements of nature: the windmill and the watermill, the small boat and larger ship guided by sails, all the applications of fire as a great modifier of raw material.

Paolo too, quite unlearned in the history of mechanics, could not understand how those big wheels moved with windmill sails or how ships once moved only by wind.

"Look here," said the engineer, stepping into a new part of the museum. "Here is the great leap mechanics made in the nineteenth century, finding new forces in steam and electricity, which men had hitherto overlooked. One could say that the locomotive and the battery mark a new era that now has had eleven centuries of life. And then we come, further on, to a third era, the last (for now), marked by the artificial production and application of nerve force to mechanics—perhaps the greatest of human discoveries, which we owe to the great Englishman Macstrong, who died in the year 2654 and whose statue you can see in the park here, beside those of Volta and Watt.

"Here where we're standing you see represented in various models all the applications of steam and electricity, ancient locomotives, very ancient batteries, then more modern ones; the ancient telegraphs, the telephones, the phonographs, and all the ingenious devices that opened new horizons to the family of man at the end of the nineteenth century and throughout the twentieth century.

"I think that rapidity of communication," continued the engineer, "achieved with steam and with the telegraph, contributed more than all books, all newspapers, more than all parliaments, all legal codes, and all religions, to destroy the ancient, wicked era of wars between peoples and to create a new morality, one that was wholesome and honest.

"Toward the end of the nineteenth century the Christian faith, which was that of the most civilized people of the era, had almost lost all moral influence. While the ancient temples where for so many centuries men had prayed and hoped crumbled away, eaten away by time and science, while priests and soldiers and kings on every side kept propping up the decrepit edifices, honest people—that is, the poets of the future and the gentlemen of the present—were totally dismayed by human morals, which seemed to decline day by day, falling into a base speculation of easy, mercenary pleasures. Without an administering God how could the ship of morality be saved?

"Meanwhile everyone bemoaned the present, feared for the future; but no one knew how to save the family of man from shipwreck, who could preach the new Word that would save humankind from decay. They were repeating what had been seen in the ancient world roughly eighteen centuries before, namely awaiting a Messiah, a man would regenerate humanity and proclaim a new era in history.

"Amid so many agonizing fears and so much decline of churches and gods, it was science that inadvertently prepared, quite despite the philosophers and theologians, the new era. It was mechanics, it was physics, it was chemistry, that without bombastic theories or scholastic sophisms—but with railroads, with the telegraph and all the other ingenious devices invented in that era—brought men closer to one another, making hatred more difficult and war impossible. To make acquaintance, to see one another each day, to be able to speak even poles apart, is to love, clasp hands, double one's joy, and give comfort in shared sufferings.

"The new morality came precisely out of those laboratories that the priests had cursed as workshops of iniquity; and poetry, which the shortsighted of their day assumed to be buried forever, rose up lovelier than ever, refreshed with new leafage, finding new inspirations in the indefinite freedom of human energies and the informed contemplation of the forces of nature.[1]

"The Gospel of Christ was in its day a sacred work, a great battle won by universal justice, but in the twentieth century Edison's school wrote another book on the applications of electricity that exerted a much more powerful influence on the morality of the future."

The engineer serving as guide to Paolo and Maria was young and in love with his science, and the warmth of his words exhilarated the two travelers, who hung on his lips. All they beheld there was new to them, and all they were hearing seemed to have, as it were, a vivid light about it, which leaving behind the darkness of the distant past, illumined the darkness of the future . . .

"And now," said the engineer, "let's leave the era of Watt and Volta and move on to that of Macstrong, the last and most fertile of them all.

"I think it's no exaggeration to say that Macstrong's discovery is the greatest of all those that honor humanity, both in its originality and for the results it has brought and the giant step it has meant to civilization.

"And though you may not believe it, this discovery owes itself to a firefly.

"This small insect was for that great man what the lamp in Pisa Cathedral was for Galileo and the falling apple was for Newton.[2] And yet how many centuries had men seen fireflies circling about at night, lighting and extinguishing their little love-flame!

"One summer evening the great Englishman was walking along the Ticino at Pavia, admiring, as millions had before him, the thousands of fireflies glinting in the air.

"Seated on the riverbank, his head resting in his hand, he was deep in meditation when all at once he rose in an impetus of joy and creative enthusiasm and, as Archimedes had so many centuries before him, shouted: *Eureka!*

"The great discovery had been made!

"And in his memoirs he left written record of the evolution of thought that led him to his immortal and fruitful discovery.

"Here, he thought, is a tiny insect, which without batteries or any large devices turns on a light at will, then puts it out at will. But mightn't the other animals also be able, without complicated apparatuses, to produce heat, electricity—all the forces, then, that man generates through intricate mechanisms, with machines involving metals, wheels, highly powerful acids?

"Don't the electric ray fish and the *gymnotus*, with their tissue, produce an extraordinary quantity of electricity?[3]

"And don't all warm-blooded animals, constantly perhaps, produce heat, heat that in some of them can exceed forty degrees?

"And don't pigeons move through space faster than locomotives, and don't insects produce a muscular force that in relation to their volume is higher than that of our best machines?

"Thus the animals can, without metals, boilers, batteries, or acids, produce motion, light, electricity. Let us study how they produce this force, and let us imitate them. All our inventions, which we with excessive pride call our creations, are but imitations of nature, merely applications of forces that have existed before us and without us.

"From that day hence Macstrong shut himself up in his laboratory, studying, with the microscope and with chemical analysis, the intimate characters of the protoplasm of living bodies. And after some years of research he found a way to produce it artificially, without organic synthesis, and he gave it the name *pandynamo*—since out of that omnipotent substance, with easy handling, one can release light, heat, electricity, movement, magnetism.

"With the pandynamo locomotives, batteries, and all the intricate contraptions of ancient mechanisms take on secondary importance, reduced to very small volume and easy application. Here in the museum you see the whole set of phases through which Macstrong's great discovery passed, to be perfected later by his disciples and successors over centuries of research and study.

"In the central laboratory of this island you will see how we have obtained the pandynamo, which distributes the various forces it releases to the farthest regions of our planet.

"With light compressions and special reagents a simple worker sends a current that will provide as much light, heat, electricity, or mechanical force as one pleases, depending on the demand from the distant, indeed extremely distant, workshops. And the wires that carry and guide these currents are no longer metal, as in the ancient telegraphs and telephones, but little tubes of an elastic and extremely tough albuminoid substance, closed inside one another and separated by a special liquid. A single tube can in this way, and contemporaneously, carry various sorts of currents that will emit light, heat, or movement.

"The current Director, who is one of the most profound and famous of our scientists, is now studying the way to transmit force without need of conductor tubes (which are, after all, nothing but a copy of our nerves) through the earth's cortex and hopes to succeed at this. For when it is a single force that is to be transmitted one can, from this island, for instance, suddenly light the whole chain of the Himalayas, as last month's experiment did."

Maria was astonished, moved, ecstatic at the words of the splendid engineer guiding them and could not help but say to him:

"But do you think that one day we will be able to artificially produce thought too in protoplasms we have created?"

"And why not?" responded the young enthusiast. "Thought too is a force released by cells made out of protoplasm, and when we can perfect Macstrong's pandynamo in such a way as to render it similar to that which makes up the gray matter of our brain, we will be able to make it capable of thought, just as today it is capable of giving us light, heat, and electricity. The limits of the possible, to our great fortune, have been marked out by no law, and we can hope to advance it always further with every new human generation, with each discovery we make, with each invention. But let's go to visit the office of the distribution of forces, which is, in a sense, our post office."

And a post office it truly was, since an infinite number of wires converged in it.

It was a great octagonal room, in which the clerks sat at their posts receiving dispatches and transmitting the forces requested from different points on the globe. As happens with our nerves, the same wires that were everywhere conducting light, heat, and electricity were allowing correspondents to express their needs.

The engineer approached one of the transmitter offices and said:

"Come here and look. Here is a dispatch from Peking:

"Big festival tomorrow to honor Confucius. We need intense blue light, alternating with red light, all night long.

"And tomorrow we will send what they're asking for from China."

He then went into another office, the one that distributed mechanical force.

"Come here. Here is a dispatch coming in this very moment from Dhavalagiri in the Himalayas:

"In the tunnel being dug across the Himalayas a very hard quartz rock found. We need a triple force of perforation.

"And we will immediately supply their demand for the force they require."

After stopping at various distribution offices the engineer led our two travelers to the middle of the room, where above a round table was a giant map on which were marked in red all the regions with which the Isle of Dynamo corresponded.

"You see," said the engineer, "on this map every evening we mark the requests for forces that are made from the various points of our region, their intensity, and the necessary suspensions of delivery.

"Every day the map is updated, and at the start of the year all the maps are gathered into a volume, which thus gives us the way to create our balance sheet. The other three planetary centers do the same work, and thus, when we put the four volumes together every year in Andropolis, we have marked with mathematical precision the overall budget for planetary civilization."

Maria ventured to say:

"For mechanical civilization, but . . . not moral civilization."[4]

"Dearest lady, I as an engineer cannot concern myself with mechanical progress alone. Please believe that it almost always moves in parallel with moral progress. And in Andropolis, if you go there, you will see how every year they also gather the figures that mark the moral progress of humanity."

—•—

Our travelers, going from one marvel to the next, visited, one after another, all the laboratories of Dynamo and, after thanking the gracious engineer who had accompanied them, left the island, prouder than before to be human.

4

DEPARTURE FROM DYNAMO AND
arrival in Andropolis. The overall
look of the city. Its houses, their
construction and architecture. The
plazas of Andropolis. The dynamics
plant. The market. Arrest of a young
thief, and justice meted out.

OUR TRAVELERS, HAVING LEFT THE ISLAND
of Dynamo, climbed into their aerotach, eager to reach the world's
great capital, and headed toward India. In just a few hours they
glimpsed the Ganges, the ancient river of the Hindus. From their
current altitude they could faintly make out below them a large
city in the site once dominated by Calcutta, which sloped along the
banks to the sea.

From there they steered their small ship northward to where, broad
and majestic, the boundless chain of the Himalayas stretched.

They were gradually nearing that mountain chain, whose summits seemed to be silvered by their cover of eternal snow, and other
aerotachs filled the air. They seemed like great black birds: they

were of all sizes and shapes, and all across the horizon they were converging upon the same point—like blood vessels coursing from the whole periphery of a body to its heart.

And Andropolis truly was the heart of our globe, the center of planetary civilization.

Andropolis was founded in the year 2500 by Cosmete, an English citizen and the greatest of the world's legislators, who in a plenary gathering held in London in 2490 laid the foundations for the United States of the Earth.

Envoys from all countries took part in that meeting, and after more than a month of discussions it was resolved that the planet's capital should be founded at Darjeeling, judged to be the world's most beautiful and healthy region.

The discussion was long, heated, and at times even furious, since many Europeans wanted the City of Man to be founded in Rome, which many centuries earlier had been the world's capital and the cradle of three civilizations.

The Americans, on the other hand, wanted the planetary capital to go up in Quito, where the volcanoes had been extinguished and there were no more earthquakes, and which enjoyed an eternal springtime.

The Asians of the Far East wanted the capital to be in Japan, the Australians would have liked it to be in New Zealand; the Africans insisted on the central plateau of their continent. But in the end those who wanted Andropolis to be at the foot of the Himalayas triumphed.[1]

At the time of Paolo and Maria's visit the city was only five centuries old yet already counted ten million inhabitants.

More than a city, however, it could be called an immense agglomeration of a hundred cities, which from the mountains and hills descended into the valleys, which were then all joined together by land and air routes.

Our travelers descended to Andropolis and took lodging in an excellent hotel suggested to them by the guide they had with them—a hotel in the very center of the city.

This was the one part of Andropolis built in perfect symmetry.

From a large circular plaza seven streets radiated out like the beams of a star, and in the plazas there proudly stood the Government Building, the Academy of Sciences and Fine Arts, and the Temple of Hope. In the streets leading into the plaza were the hotels, the main department stores, the Archives, the Libraries—all the public buildings essential to the life of a great people.[2]

This part of Andropolis could be called the public City; all the other vast extent of houses contained the inhabitants who, having come from every country in the world, had gathered together there through that irresistible instinct man shares with the ants, the bees, and all the other sociable animals.

The public City had no symmetry to it, but followed the vagaries of the terrain, now clambering up the hills, now descending into the valleys and spreading over the plateaus.

The building law imposed no other restriction than that of leaving open the road between the mass of houses, assuring free movement to pedestrians, velocipedes, carriages, and all the other varied means of transportation that were used in the year 3000, depending on each person's taste and wealth.

Not all the roads were straight, nor did they bisect at right angles as in the monotonous checkerboards of America; at times they were winding, at other times oblique, and at still other times straight, depending on the accidents of the land and the whim of the builders. The only thing mandatory was their width, which for all roads was at least twenty meters.

The houses were all one-story, or more often two-story, including the ground floor. Those with only a ground floor were for the poor or for bachelors, the taller ones for the wealthy and men with wives. Every bachelor and every family had a house to themselves, and every house had its own little garden. Light, heat, motor force, and water were distributed to every house from the city's large dynamics center.

As for the architecture that had guided the construction of the houses, it was bizarre and highly varied. All ancient styles were represented, along with new and very new ones, in fantasies owners and architects hatched every day. Everyone could apply his talent to his own house, with the result that you would find alongside a Gothic edifice a Pompeian house, a chalet near a small Greek palace, and minarets near Baroque-, Lombard-, or Renaissance-style houses.

For a man of our time visiting this city, however, the most original feature was not the extraordinary variety of architectural styles, but rather the novelty and diversity of material with which the houses were built.

In the nineteenth century all houses were made of wood, brick, or stone, in rare instances of iron. They all required substantial time and considerable cost, so that the bulk of the population could never enjoy the great, healthy joy of living in a house of their own. In the year 3000 the poorest man in the world always has his own small house, built either by himself or by others in a single day, at modest cost.

To build a house you do roughly what you usually do to cast a statue in plaster or bronze. There are prototypes of houses at various prices, made of a ductile, rust-resistant metal alloy. You put the model where you are going to put up the house and then, through a hole, pour the liquid substance into the mold, which, solidifying after a while, forms the partitions and main walls of the structure.

The liquid material used can be of the most varied nature, its cost ranging anywhere from a few *lire* to thousands of *scudi*.[3]

Housing for the poor is made with a blend of plaster and aluminous soil, which hardens like stone and may come in various shades, depending on the owner's taste.

There are liquid compounds that, when they solidify, simulate genuine marble that acquires all its splendor with polishing; there are others that imitate jasper, agate, lapis lazuli, jade—all the most beautiful and most precious stones.

Other compounds imitate shinier and more precious metals, without having their dangerous conductivity, and houses can be seen in Andropolis that seem to be made entirely of gold and silver, aventurine or bronze, but that have instead been built with a material that conducts heat poorly—thus combining the beauty of a building with its healthiness.

To the men of the thirty-first century it seems strange that for so many centuries their fathers should have toiled so hard to solder together bricks and stones with lime, when they can make houses through this simple pouring technique, as you do with any small plaster statue.

All the streets have a name and the houses a number, and the city is divided into so many regions, distinguished by their astronomic position.

In the center of Andropolis, undeniably, the noise is somewhat annoying, although considerably less than in the streets of ancient Paris or ancient London.

With the elimination of locomotives and carriages drawn by horses or other animals, they have already removed the larger problem of deafening sounds and smoke; but electrical vehicles of earth and air are not silent, and the comings and goings of thousands of people crowding into the middle of the city create a very loud steady din. Literary men and calmer folk know as much and thus always live far from the center, in the more solitary streets, where, furthermore, as in the rest of the city, the sidewalk, being made of a material similar to cork and rubber, to a great extent mutes the noise of wheels and the tread of passersby.

All this our travelers saw on their long strolls in the streets and plazas of Andropolis.

They were waiting to visit all the city's great public buildings, the real place to study the life of this, the world's great metropolis. Meanwhile they wanted to visit the big dynamics plant and the market, the great centers of energy and food.

In this, their voyage of discovery, they were not satisfied with admiring the multitude of large open plazas into which so many streets flowed.

These plazas were square, rectangular, octagonal, hexagonal; but mostly they were round, all very spacious and adorned with trees, flower beds in bloom, and picturesque fountains, of which they could not find two that were identical. Beneath the trees they saw comfortable seats, where anyone could sit to relax or admire the statues, flowers, fountains.

The fountains could be neither more beautiful nor more fanciful. In one of the main plazas was erected an artificial hillock, made of large rocks picturesquely piled on top of one another. Amid the stones were planted shrubs and alpine plants that hung shaggily from crags and landslips; lichens and ferns and soft moss gave the stones a fresh, cheerful life imitating that of a mountain. The water spurted out from high above, now noisily hurtling down into small precipices, now gathering into a silvery streamlet, now scattering over a rock black as anthracite and glistening with fine mica crystals, like the rich tresses of a nymph who had loosened her hair for the air to caress. And all these waters reunited at the base, in the calm bosom of a little lake in which big and little fish of every color darted, and swans calmly, majestically glided close to ducks and aquatic birds from the most far-flung regions of the globe.

Other fountains were in the style of classical antiquity, others baroque, with dragons and dolphins spewing water from their faces.

An Icelandic geyser too was represented in another fountain in which, beside rounded masses of blond agate, there rose heavenward a hundred jets of water that in the night, illumined by the electricity's polychrome light, gave the eye a feast of colors you could never tire of admiring.

Nor were the statues erected haphazardly; every plaza was meant to illustrate the glories of some historical epoch or some country. The historical element, however, outweighed the geographical, the civil men of the thirty-first century being readily convinced that the geniuses of an epoch were more alike than the great men of a single country. Time is a complex of infinitely accruing elements, whereas the geographic element is just one factor, often uniting in a single family, and by chance, men who are very different and often contradictory.

In one plaza, for instance, you could see statues of the great men of ancient Greece, in another those of imperial Rome; in a third were gathered the geniuses of the Tuscan Renaissance, who were numerous enough to people one of the major plazas of Andropolis. Elsewhere you could admire the statues of English politicians, or those of German philosophers, and so on ad infinitum. At the feet of the statues were only a name and the dates of birth and death.

Paolo and Maria had to rent an electric tandem for a couple of hours to visit the dynamics plant, which was very far from their hotel.

That plant stood out from the other houses, all of them low, like a colossus among pygmies. It was a true palazzo, a true public edifice, simple and severe in its architecture: here the beautiful had been sacrificed to the useful and indispensable.

The Director, to whom they had been referred, served as their guide, but after having seen the Isle of Dynamo they had little new to admire and little to discover.

The plant received from that island all the motor energy necessary for the huge metropolis and had only to distribute it.

What was most admirable was a quadrant placed in the middle of the building, where all the various forces were marked out that had to be distributed every day to private individuals and public buildings. A single workman supervised this regular, daily distribution, while in a nearby room several workers were handling the requests for extraordinary forces—which at this moment were for more light, more heat, and a larger supply of water.

They stopped for a half hour in that division to marvel at the orderliness with which requests came in and the promptness with which they were met.

One employee took care of water, another light, a third heat, a fourth mechanical force, another electricity, whether the old kind or the new.

The requests came in not via the ancient telephone, which had been greatly perfected, but via telegraphic dispatches that were automatically written in luminous characters in a small black box kept in darkness.

The Director showed Paolo and Maria some of these requests.

In the distribution bench for mechanical force, after a little bell went off that put the worker on alert, they read:

Farm machine factory. Edition Company. Region South-West. Volta Street, no. 37. Tomorrow there will be a third more workers. A third more mechanical force is needed.

Shortly thereafter another ring alerted the worker at the light bench that he had a request coming in.

And indeed in the dark square they could read these words:

North-east region. Homer Street, No. 59. Family dance tonight. Triple light needed all night.

In a special section was written: *Accidents.*

And the small bell was calling the worker to attention.

In fact, the camera obscura said:

Central region. Palace of the Academy of Fine Arts. Small fire has broken out in Print Room.

Here the Director himself rushed with some concern to the station and took the worker's place, answering by telegraph:

Open the small faucet of carbonic acid at once and point the gas conductor tube to where the fire has broken out. If the fire is not immediately put out, please advise.

Moments later the camera obscura read:

Fire put out. Many thanks.

The Director sat down again and turning to his visitors said:

"You know, along with my advice I would gladly have telegraphed those members of the Academy of Fine Arts a slap in the face.

"You should know that every public building has a reserve of liquid carbonic acid to which elastic tubes can be fitted in just a few minutes, tubes you can turn wherever you want; they direct a strong gas current onto the flames or burning objects, and the fire is extinguished in a matter of moments.

"But these blessed artists disdain science, which they often heartily make fun of. Almost invariably they know nothing of the elements of physics and chemistry, which doesn't keep them, when there's some little mishap, from tearing their hair and calling on the science of which they've been so dismissive. You have witnessed one of these scenes. But let us forgive these willfully ignorant people their whims, since their admirable works are a blessing to our life."

On another day our two pilgrims wanted to visit the market, or I should say the markets, since they take up an entire small hillside in Andropolis. Since the ascent is rather steep, you go up and down it with funicular lines. Some of these are for transporting the food, others for people.

All that movement of trains continually going up and down, all those cars of flowers, fruits, game, fish, meat, form a curious, strange, highly interesting spectacle. None of the food cars is open, but since they are sealed with highly transparent glass, what you can see inside looked excellent.

Atop the hill stretches out a broad plateau where in the different buildings they see here fish, there meat, further on greens, vegetables, fruit, flowers. And everywhere a coming and going of people who load the wagons with goods for a specific address. No one carries goods on his own; rather, a company has its clerks deliver the purchases to individual houses.

The cook, the house servant, the master of the house, only choose what they wish to acquire and consign it then to distribution agents.

Paolo and Maria made fairly long stops in the flower and fruit markets.

In the former was a most dizzying feast for the eyes and fragrance enough to remind one of love's delights.

In the nineteenth century gardens were already wonders, because in small spaces they joined together flowers that had come from all parts of the globe, and both hothouses and coldhouses allowed for the cultivation of tropical plants, even in temperate countries and cold zones. Imagine that even then certain wealthy gentlemen in Russia harvested grapes in their vast hothouses and made wine from them, and in Norway they cultivated Central American orchids.

By now, however, the art of cultivating flowers has made giant strides. Not only can the gardener combine flowers of the six parts of the world in one bouquet, but he can produce new flowers with highly complicated devices of artificial fecundation and chemical fertilizers. They have even managed to make plants grow and fruits ripen in all seasons of the year.

Once the sun's light could not be replaced by any other light, and fruits obtained beyond their natural season were tasteless—like flowers without their perfume and beauty. Today a fruit or flower harvested in the winter in hothouses cannot be distinguished from one that nature provided in summer under the sun's powerful force.

The number of flowers cultivated today is almost a thousand times greater than it was in the nineteenth and twentieth centuries, not only because there is no longer the smallest corner of our planet, nor the farthest forest, that has not paid the tribute of its plants and its flowers; but also because art has managed to create new species that at first sight don't seem to have any kinship with the species that grow spontaneously in fields and woods.

In the flower market they were also selling living plants and embalmed flowers that fooled everyone's eye.

From the flower market Paolo and Maria entered the fruit market.

Here too was delight for the eyes, perfume for the nose. The beauty of the flowers equaled that of the fruit, their perfume equal too.

With flowers beauty is the first charm, which makes them the earth's dearest creatures. It can be said that in flowers the greatest colorist of the Venetian School has allied himself with the prince of design of the Greek School, the profusion, the variety, and the intricacy of colors outdone only by elegance, purity, or strangeness of design. There where the enamored colorist, in the exaltation of his love for color, tosses his invention out with his hands full, in excess, risking a fall into the baroque, the painter of design takes over, in originality of elegance of line creating a frame for the orgy of colors, so that all can say:

"Oh, what sacred, dear allies! Oh, how well they are partnered in the fertile creation of the beautiful!"

And when design would be too severe, too simple or rigid, the colorist immediately comes with his inexhaustible palette to give life and youth to the too miserly chalice, the too classical cup. The flower seems to respond to its two parents:

"Thank you, thank you!"

If the flowers are beautiful enough on their own to dictate an aesthetic treatise to anyone (provided he's not a philosopher), their scents too are a poetry of perfume that has in them perhaps more notes than music has.

And don't they also have about them the delicacy and transience of a dream that, among half-shut eyelids, appears and disappears and is guessed more than sensed?

And don't they also perhaps have a note of the warmest and most ardent aroma, the deep voluptuousness that seems like the contact of love-struck flesh, piquant, sparkling, ethereal, and vaporous, tickling and delighting in countless other ways, to which our so imperfect language denies the impress of any word?

And so in the fruits forms, colors, and aromas stand among themselves in like relation, as the beauty of forms and the mildness of scents do in their parents and siblings, the flowers.

The perfume of fruits has not the poetry of that of flowers, and if, in admiring the latter, the soul's first cry is: "Oh, how beautiful!" in admiring fruit the cry is: "Oh, how good!"[4]

Thus the forms of fruits are much simpler and fewer, just as their fragrances have fewer notes. They can be pleasant but rarely intoxicating, strong but rarely or never voluptuous. They have aromas that are almost flavors and are related to those of flowers as friendship is to love.

And aren't flowers perhaps plants' loves?

And aren't fruits perhaps the friendships generated by love?

All this our travelers were pondering and sensing as they roamed from the flower market to the fruit market.

Here too they saw and admired, gathered into a single shop, strawberries, raspberries, mangos, mangosteens, a hundred varieties of bananas, coconuts, pineapples, cherimoyas, pears and apples, and so many, so many other fruits that the nineteenth century still did not know. Among them was the *pata*, which an Argentinian knew enough to take from the virgin forests of his country and cultivate in Europe, making a fruit that in its fragrance and flavor rivals the peach. And yet a certain Mantegazza made mention of it as early as the nineteenth century, citing it as a forest fruit entirely unknown to Europeans.[5]

Paolo and Maria, passing by a stall in which were displayed mountains of oranges and mandarins, saw an urchin snatch one of the finest and biggest and sneak off—though not fast enough to escape being seen by the woman vendor, who shouted:

"Thief, thief!"

Scarcely was this cry heard than all around the market one heard the loud exclamation of men, women, children:

"Justice, justice, justice!"

In the year 3000 there are no longer gendarmes, nor policemen, nor public security guards; every honest citizen is a gendarme, a policeman, and moreover also a judge.

In just a few minutes six citizens had gathered around the little scamp; together with the gentleman who had grabbed him they were just enough to improvise the tribunal called the Justice of the Seven.

The public, after recognizing that the tribunal had been formed, stood back, making a circle around those eight people: seven judges and one guilty person.

"Why did you steal this orange?" asked the person who had first arrested the little delinquent.

"Because I was thirsty."

"But that orange wasn't yours."

"No, but the fruit seller has a hundred, a thousand of them."

"That doesn't matter. Those oranges weren't yours. You should have asked or bought it. You've stolen, and now you're going to the House of Justice."

Then one of the seven said:

"I'm going down into the city, and I live close by. I'll take him there myself. Give me the sentence."

One of the seven tore off a small page from a portfolio he had in his pocket and wrote:

Boy, thief of an orange.

All seven signed the paper, and the man accompanying him took it and went off with the urchin, who, putting up no resistance except for whimpering, followed him.

And all was restored to its former order.

"Look at that, Maria," said Paolo. "You've witnessed a trial and sentence as it is carried out for all crimes, even the greatest.

"In this case it was a matter of only the simple theft of an orange, but if that ragamuffin had stolen a diamond or a wallet filled with money or knifed a companion of his, they would likewise have shouted:

"'Justice, justice!'

"And in the same way seven gentlemen would have joined forces and made a summary judgment and led the culprit to the House of Justice.

"And this House is by no means a jail, as they were in earlier times, but a sort of school, where they correct the guilty, where they lovingly study the causes that can have led someone to commit a crime."

Maria interrupted Paolo:

"But you've said that certain specialists examine children's brains when they're just born, and when they discover in them an irresistible tendency to crime, they eliminate them."

"That is true," answered Paolo, "but they destroy only the born delinquents—that is, those who by a peculiar, fatal organization of their brain cells are necessarily destined for crime. They would kill and rob even if they were born rich, even if fortune put them in the most felicitous conditions. But these are the rarest exceptions.[6] All other people are born honest but are the children of very distant fathers, who have lived the savage life that has made violence necessary and have preserved in their brain a hidden seed of crime, which in favorable circumstances can be developed and lead them to kill or steal. There is not a man on this earth who in a sudden fit of passion cannot, through hatred or revenge, make himself guilty of a homicide or a theft.

"Our civilization has for centuries tried to educate man in such a way as to eliminate, stifle those ancestral seeds, while on the other hand it has tried to organize social life in such a way that the crime is useless and harmless to the person who commits it. Once human justice was concerned only with punishment; today, however, we are trying to prevent misdeeds, making them difficult or impossible. And that this work of civilization is not for naught can be documented by the statistics on crime, which is becoming increasingly rare. This is not to deny that we still have thieves and murderers among us. Moral progress is rather a slower matter than intellectual progress, but we should not despair that one day the one will reach the same level as the other."

"Then crimes are no longer punished today?"

"That's correct, but the sentence is reduced to temporary loss of liberty. Doesn't it seem to you to be punishment enough to be isolated from human society?

"In the House of Justice the thief, the assassin, are shut away, while people try to demonstrate to them the enormity of the crime they committed, persuading them that the crime is not only a wrong, but an error and a bad speculation.

"The confinement lasts only a few days or a few weeks, and it is a very rare case that extends to several months. But the punishment does not end there, because when the guilty person has his freedom restored he wears for some time on the lapel of his jacket a badge of infamy, so that all view him with distrust and suspicion. Thieves wear the color yellow; murderers or all those who have committed acts of great violence wear red. And that sign is not removed until the culprit has shown by his conduct that he has reentered the fold of upright people."

"And if the delinquent relapses?"

"Oh, then the prison sentence is doubled or tripled, depending on the case, and the culprit, on leaving the House of Justice, wears two ribbons instead of one. But that happens only in the rarest of cases and, moreover, with born delinquents who were spared elimination by errors in their brain exams."

—•—

Soon after Paolo and Maria made their way down from the market, having bought many flowers and many fruits, and returned to their hotel.

5

TRIP TO THE GOVERNMENT PALACE.
Forms of government and political
organization around the world in
the year 3000. The four wings of
the Palace. Land, Health. School.
Industry and Commerce. The
Office of Finance.

PAOLO AND MARIA, AFTER SEEING THE
dynamics plant and the market, went to visit the Government Palace,
located at the center of Andropolis.

Maria had wanted to save that trip and kept putting it off from one
day to the next, telling her companion that she understood nothing of
politics and that to think the world could be governed from a single
building made her head spin.

"Paolo, dear, I'm an ignorant little woman who finds it hard enough
to govern a house and is bewildered at the notion that just a few
humans can govern the entire world from the Government Palace
of Andropolis."

Paolo smiled, giving her a little love pat.

"No, you are not an ignorant little woman, and the central government of Andropolis is not a cabal nor such a dark, intricate mechanism that you can't understand or admire it. The art of governance once seemed to revolve entirely around complicating administrative and political gadgetry, creating newer and newer staffs, new wheels and castors; it all came to seem like some acrobatic or juggling act. And with each new use of this machinery, with each new mechanism of transmission, registries, protocols, with each new administrative department one encountered, affairs moved in more complicated ways; so that the machines were breaking down almost daily, and the huge forces expended to put it all in motion were almost worn away already from the friction.

"And to think that in the nineteenth century, after civilization had made giant steps, when the French Revolution, from the heights of 1789, had proclaimed the rights of man; when almost the whole of Europe was already being governed in republics or in parliamentary states, an Italian minister could discover that a lira paid by a taxpayer in Sicily or Sardinia, by the time it arrived in Rome, had become a soldo.[1] The other nineteen soldi had gotten lost on the way, gone to pay government employees, to move and oil the wheels of the intricate financial machinery. And that happened not just with taxes, but with everything else: with war and with all the institutions of public life.

"Power was parceled out among hundreds and thousands of people who wielded only a part of it, and the conflict among the various authorities, all jostling each other, was so absurd, so complicated, that it created obstacles and contradictions each step of the way.

"With the exception of the king all those who exercised any authority were children of free election, but the responsibility was subdivided so finely into impalpable molecules that when you wanted to take hold of it, it slipped from your grasp, as if you were trying to grasp fog.

"The mayors represented the communal councilmen, who in turn represented the administrative electors; but the communal Councils were subject to the oversight of provincial Councils, which were led by prefects nominated by the central government.

"And there were two Chambers, which contradicted one another though one couldn't decide anything without the consent of the other; and over the Chambers and the Senate was the king, who could dissolve those Chambers and apply the veto to the laws voted on by the Chamber and the Senate. The ministers, it is true, represented the majority of deputies; but they in turn couldn't govern without flattering the vanity or greed of the deputies or reaching agreements with the parties, of which there were three, four, and even eight in a single Chamber.

"And the ministers, who just to orientate themselves would have needed to give months and months of study to the ministry they'd been entrusted to, were overwhelmed by the capricious or self-interested votes of the Chamber. Laws followed laws in a giddy succession, robbing the social order of any stability and the laws themselves of any authority.

"A giant step was made with the elimination of kings and standing armies, but the inauspicious experiment of collective socialism set civilization back by at least a century. Then after endless decentralization responsibility would fall to the individual, returning to him and his family what had been taken away and forming the commune, or city-state, as the state's organic molecule.

"When you visit the Government Palace today you will also see how easy and straightforward it is to govern the whole of humanity from the center of the globe when men, families, and communes are self-governing.

"Here in Andropolis one can't help but affirm the great unity of the United Planetary States. Only the cosmic questions of potentially universal interest are taken up.

"The delegates (as they are called) of all the planetary regions meet here just once a year, and then only for a month, and only a few staff stay here permanently, preparing the work for the following year or by mandate dealing with unforeseen accidents—earthquakes, floods, or other cataclysms.

"The delegates are elected by every single region of the globe by majority vote and by universal suffrage (including women) and are paid for their work. As soon as they arrive here they elect a leader among themselves, known as the *Pancrat*, who holds office as long as the cosmic delegates, which is to say just a year. But during this brief period he can at least boast of holding in his hands all the world's reins of government. No matter how many times he is sent back to Andropolis as delegate, though, he can never be reelected.

"Here at this site in Andropolis every year the Supreme Council holds permanent session for a month, presided over by the Pancrat.[2]

"It is made up of the directors of the central offices, which are few, as we'll see when we visit the building; they preside over the affairs of Land, Health, Education, Commerce, and Industry. These correspond to the ministers of the old governments.

"While the Supreme Council is in session heads of the regions and the communes may come to Andropolis to have their special issues resolved, or they can send their demands here.

"People have understood a little late that we, in science as in politics, in the arts as in the pettiest affairs, must copy nature, whose children we are. Whenever passion or faulty thinking takes us too far from nature, we commit mistakes if not crimes, whereas we reach truth, beauty, and goodness whenever we stay loyal to her.

"Our overweening pride would have us believe that our discoveries, our inventions, are our own creations, whereas in fact they are imitations of nature. We can do nothing new that does not already exist in the world in which we live and out of which we have been born; the supreme effort of our brain can do no more than apply the forces of nature and variously combine the elements that exist prior to us and without us. Just as the bird can only weave its nest from the blades of straw, the bits of bark, and the tufts of wool it finds, so we can make a house, a painting, or the cleverest machine only by putting together the material we find about us.

"Once people realized this great truth in the political ordering of society, as simple as everything that is truly great, they had no choice but to copy our organism, which is shaped in the unconscious mystery of the mother's womb with the aid of our thought and our will.

"And just as with our body every organ, every cell, has its own independent life and only maintains itself in a linkage with the great federation and the great unity of the organism by means of the nervous and blood systems, so on our planet every commune lives by itself, but through the telegraphic wires that represent the nerves it communicates with Andropolis, which is at once the brain and the heart of the giant planetary organism. Between the communes and the center, then, dwell many minor centers, which are the *regions*, representing the ganglia.[3]

"And right away you can see how simply, how neatly life circulates in this great political organism.

"Every commune is self-administrated, with a mayor and the small body of a Council.

"Every region has a head, called the *Podestà*, who also has his own Council, which creates the regional laws after hearing the opinion of all the mayors.

"And while here in Andropolis they address only questions of a universal order, they never meddle in changing communal or provincial laws, which can be laid down only by those born and raised in the country they have to govern."

Maria listened carefully to her faithful companion's words, amazed that she could grasp the great issues behind world politics so easily.

After this speech that Paolo thought he should make to Maria, to prepare her for their visit to the Government Palace, they walked up a magnificent staircase that took them into a huge entrance hall at which four large buildings begin, like the branches of a cross.

Around the entrance hall spacious rooms have been assigned to the Pancrat and his staff; the Supreme Council also holds its annual assemblies there.

The four wings of the palace represent the four great concerns of cosmic civilization: agriculture, health, education, and industry fused with commerce.

For three centuries there has been no more war on our planet, and all the gigantic forces that our forefathers devoted to killing are now used to improve the climate, make the earth fertile, and increase humankind's treasury of joy.

Our travelers entered the building dedicated to agriculture, on which is carved the word *Land*.

Here too statues and very beautiful pictures adorn the entryway to the agricultural department, all symbolic of agricultural questions—since the men of the thirty-first century no longer separate the beautiful from the true, and science and politics also enjoy dressing festively; since joy and beauty are no longer divorced from civilization, as in the times of great intellectual decadence and great hypocrisy.

A pleasant government worker led Paolo and Maria into the various areas of the Land Department, speaking to them of the great issues that many of the scientists who work for that department were then studying.

They had to admire a huge relief map representing in a planisphere the whole surface of our planet, marking out the uncultivated, lightly cultivated, and intensively cultivated parts.

At a glance you can see in the white parts the still-uncultivated terrain, in the green-painted parts the lightly cultivated parts, and colored in red the intensively cultivated terrain.

"You see," said the clerk, "how much of the earth still remains to be cultivated after so many centuries of civilization and three centuries after the planetwide abolition of war. You can devote to agriculture all the boundless forces that arms and battleships used to require.

"The issue being studied today is this:

"What should we do with the immense forests that border all the Amazon or those found in the middle of Africa?

"Should we destroy them to plant coffee, cocoa, bananas, and all the other tropical fruits, or should we simply make them healthy by draining and clearing them, pulling up the useless and even unattractive plants in them? The botanists, farmers, and economists have very different views on this question, and the inhabitants of these locales have been asked to give new information and urged to express their opinion.

"Meanwhile, however, the central government of Andropolis has sent some scientists to Africa and America to study this great question on site, since destroying or conserving thousands of square kilometers of forest is bound to modify the climate of vast regions of the planet.

"And on the other hand, broadening or restricting the cultivated zones can, in a different way, resolve the great Malthusian question that after so many centuries still plagues the family of man.

"By limiting marital fertility we have already in large part settled the question, yet we still have against us the anti-Malthusians, who would gladly remove all obstacles to human fertility and who argue that much of our planet still remains to be cultivated and that agricultural production could, in little more than a century, be tripled.

"Today another problem occupies our experts in this central government department, and that is the reclamation of the swamp regions we still have in Africa, America, and much of Malaysia.

"The experts in two sections are currently working together on this issue, those in Land and those in Health, since this is a complex issue that can only be resolved with the joint forces of physicians and farmers.

"In Europe not a single marsh is left, but we still have countless others in the countries to which civilization came later and in which we still find at our feet forests that are themselves the source of miasma; it is painful to destroy them but dangerous to conserve them.

"In this department dedicated to Land we have an entire section concerned with roads and all the means of communication among the different countries of our planet.

"In former times people traveled only by land and water; today we have added air. For this reason we have land, water, and air engineers who compete to shorten and make more comfortable the paths by which peoples join together, persuaded as we all are that this extends life and augments and enhances fraternity within the human family.

"Here, in another planisphere, you can see the whole layout of the world's highways. Since these are of interest to all sorts of people on earth, the highway issue can be termed one of the most universal, thus justifying its presence in Andropolis.

"On this issue too there is dissent among engineers and economists. The former, to hear them talk, would immediately turn the whole surface of the earth into so many highways, leaving not an inch of it for agriculture. They say that air navigation does not satisfy everyone's taste and that it is suitable always to leave open the electric routes for those who prefer land to air."

From the Ministry or Department of Land our pilgrims proceeded to that of Health, where the most world's most learned physicians study these two large issues in their laboratories:

Stamping out diseases.

Prolonging human life and removing all pain and terror from death.

Even in the year 3000 there continue to be people who are weak and destined to live short lives, and even though pathological newborns are destroyed, many imperfect organisms still remain who can neither find life at all pleasant nor make it useful to themselves and others. Furthermore they reach the age of fertility, at which point they can pass their ailments on to another generation.

Couples' visits to be authorized for fertile marriage have fairly well diminished hereditary diseases, but they still exist, through the errors of visiting physicians and through vices that ruin good constitutions as well.

In the nineteenth century medicine took a giant step with the discovery of disease-carrying microbes, yet epidemics continued their reign over the earth until the twenty-fifth century, when a well-known French physician discovered a powerful antiseptic substance like corrosive sublimate but able to be injected into the veins without impairing health.[4]

In this way whenever cholera, yellow fever, bubonic plague, or another epidemic sickness appeared, the whole population of an endangered country had to take the new vaccination, and the breeding-ground of infection was immediately quelled.

It is striking, however, that in the countries where they still would not adopt Malthusian limits on birth, and where the population consequently is rising, new epidemics still break out that current vaccination can no longer help. Thus they are now looking for the new microbes to find the agent that will kill them.

Indeed, it seems an inexorable law of cosmic life that when too much breeding occurs a new cause of death suddenly appears to restore balance.

"How much ink," said the physician who headed the Health Department, "has flowed to oppose Malthus and the inevitable consequences of his doctrine, when nature itself, ever since the appearance of life on the surface of our planet, has declared itself Malthusian and shouted to all living beings: 'If you must breed so much, be prepared for a great deal of death!'

"Human life too has been considerably prolonged, thanks to the rising prosperity of the poor classes and all the progress in hygiene. Whereas in the nineteenth century an average life span was between twenty-eight and thirty-six years, today the average planetary life span is seventy-two years and in some healthier regions up to eighty-five years. Before perhaps one out of a million inhabitants died without disease—that is, died a physiological death—whereas nowadays natural death accounts for some 30 percent of all deaths. We hope that one day it will be the only way that everyone dies.

"The hygienic issues studied here in this ministry often come up in the form of questions from sanitation authorities in the various parts of the world, since every region has a physician alongside the Podestà, concerned with all problems of public health."

From Health our travelers moved on to the School Department.

Their new tour guide explained to them what issues concerned the experts in this third section.

"Consider this: whereas in the department you've just come from they study how to improve people's health and extend their life, here we are dealing with educating and instructing, making lives better in feeling and more fruitful in thought. To nurture the heritage of intellectual joys and make them possible for all, this is the lofty and challenging aim of our studies. But don't think, however, that imperative laws are handed down from Andropolis, laws that impose special methods of instruction on different regions of the world.

"Every commune and every region provide themselves with the schools they want, and the central government exerts no authority over them. Here we advise, we suggest, nothing more, or we respond to problems they send us to solve. The city of Andropolis has a model school, which you can visit. As for the rest of the world, we are content to send inspectors out every year to the various regions, to examine the schools and study the methods that are adopted in them and then send their findings to the central government.

"In the latest report of last year, in which they surveyed the conditions of the schools on our entire planet, a fact was confirmed that had already been sensed but had not yet been confirmed, as it was this time. It filled with gladness the heart of all those who are persuaded that human happiness consists of these two great factors:

"*Good health.*

"*Harmonic balance of all the faculties of thinking and all the energies of feeling, so that all are active and none is worn out with excess fatigue.*

"Well now, whereas in the last century the methods of education and instruction were so varied in the different regions of the globe, today they have been reduced to a very few, and they are coming so close to one another that they will end up blending into one; this one, to our very great pleasure, is the one that has been adopted for perhaps fifty years in Andropolis, where the assembly of so many great men must have made much easier the task of achieving an ideal education.

"This concord of aims, this fusing of various pedagogical ideas into a few ideas and then into a single one, was predictable, since the shortest path that must conjoin two distant points is a single one. After many efforts, and much experimental groping about and trials, one must always fall into the single path that, because it is the shortest, must also be the easiest.

"The Director of the School Department is, after the Pancrat, the citizen placed highest in the social hierarchy, who might be said to be something like the pontiff of the ancient Catholic church.[5] The current Director, who is of Italian origin, has been in office for twenty years and today is considered the greatest genius in the world. He is also always consulted by the directors of the other ministries, and no Pancrat takes a step without asking his advice.

"It can be said that for twenty years he has collected in his brain the thought of the world, being at the head of all schools and conveying to all of them the current of his own ideas and of his own ardent feeling for the progress of humanity.

"Every year when he gathers about him his own counselors and the inspectors who present him their reports on the schools in all the regions of the planet, he will always say: *'And now let us feel the world's pulse.'*

"A phrase that in anyone else's mouth would seem too haughty, but that, uttered by him, expresses only a great and simple truth.

"Today the great man is taking up a major question, namely that of knowing how far woman can accompany man in higher studies. This is an issue old as the world, but one that has yet to be resolved.

"From the nineteenth to the twenty-second centuries we wanted to concede to our female companions a wider share in studies and the liberal professions, and there were woman doctors, lawyers, engineers.

"So far so good, but women's enthusiasm grew enough to create a serious professional competition between men and women, a source of domestic discord and endless quarrels. What is worse, our women companions, abusing the intellectual labor in which they have rather less endurance than we, lapsed into such states of nervous disorders as to alarm humanity. Nervous ailments, abortions, epilepsy, neurasthenia, and children growing up neurotic and terribly frail.

"As is only natural, this state of affairs set off a reaction, and from the excessive mental labor the women were forcing upon themselves they passed to an exaggerated inertia. And ever since it can be said that in various countries around the world the issue has always remained open: whether, that is, women should study and know as much as men or whether, on the contrary, either sex, having a different organism and a different mission to fulfill, should also have a different share in intellectual labor.[6]

"This is the eternal question that our illustrious Director is studying, and he hopes to settle it, because, he says, with that half-ironic, half-benevolent smile of his:

"'By virtue of my age I believe I can study this question without bias. Young men, in all questions concerning women, always feel too much that the female is "the other side." Just as women, even the most intelligent and honest of them, always think of a man as a male, expecting the height of sensual enjoyments from this, and the right to mother him.'

"Our Director is a great opponent of government intervention in school affairs, and he says that if the religions of State were an instrument of tyranny and obscurantism in the long-past barbaric ages, we must take care not to create an instruction or science of the State that would be just as fatal to human progress.

"Religion allied with government meant tyranny of conscience, slavery of thought, for whoever proclaims that he holds the keys to the life beyond can guide the souls of the common people, who always make up the great majority, and lead them where he pleases with the stick of fear and the carrot of paradise.

"Today faith is not imposed even if one governs from above, and everyone believes what he wishes and as much as he wishes. But if the government from a single center were to decree legislation of schools, it might guide thinking wherever it considered best and impose a new yoke, creating a second form of slavery.[7]

"And here we have only a few government schools, in which the great scientists and literati expert in this department attempt to apply the latest reforms, making them model institutes. Apart from these in Andropolis we also have schools founded privately or by associations, and they teach what they want, as they want.

"Every day in the newspapers of the capital you will read advertisements announcing a new school, a new teaching, a new teaching chair. There are free schools founded by wealthy gentlemen or by apostles of new ideas, who want to create disciples, and there are schools with tuition fees.

"The State intervenes only to authorize the exercise of a given profession, and in every region there is a council of the learned elected by the Podestà, which once a year examines those seeking a license to be a physician, engineer, or mechanic—in essence, any one of the hundred professions into which human labor is subdivided.

"To anyone who presents himself they never ask where he studied nor with whom. They do, however, put him through extremely rigorous theoretical and practical examinations, depending on circumstances, and then they grant or refuse the license he is seeking. There are no degrees of merit, so they are not offending anyone's self-esteem; further, as long experience has shown, as scrupulously impartial as the examining commissions are and as conscientiously and maturely as they conduct the exams, the judges do not always respond appropriately to the candidate's real merit.

"Naturally the schools of Andropolis are judged to be the best in the world, and thus the diplomas from the capital's university are highly prestigious. Every day aspiring students, even those who already have their degrees, come from the remotest countries, bent on earning the precious metropolitan diploma.

"Man, when he thinks and when he argues, is always a great decenterer, but when he acts he becomes a fierce centralizer. To this instinct of his, automatic if not almost animal, our modern scientists try to oppose themselves with all the weapons of criticism, persuasion, and indisputable authority that doctrine and experience afford them.

"Another problem that currently torments the thought of the high councilmen of our school is that of knowing individual attitudes, whereby private or public schoolteachers can guide the student in the choice of a profession, the selection of studies. Here, we think, lies the secret of all the effectiveness of instruction and education.

"There may perhaps be not a man on earth unfit to do something useful and good, but this attitude is not always conscious, nor does it always reveal itself even to the most acute observer of brains and intellects.

"The examining of central cells made with a penetrating light and with the sharp optical tools of our *psychohygeians* is still in the early phases of its possibilities. These learned experts are well able to tell us if a brain belongs to an individual whom it led to crime, if it belongs to an imbecile, to an ordinary man, or to a genius; but further than that they cannot yet go.

"Thus it still remains to the individual, to his parents and teachers, to discern the evolving course of thinking in the first ages of life, to discover which in his brain are the weak organs, which the strong, where to strengthen the former, and what best use to put the others to in the choice of profession and the direction of studies.

"We do not want displaced persons in our society, and whoever makes a mistake in the choice of career is a displaced person and thus an unhappy one."

—•—

Paolo and Maria, thanking the courteous clerk who had been their guide in the School Ministry, moved on to the last arm of the large government cross, which on its walls bore the inscription *Industry and Commerce*.

Here too they had a new guide.

At the entrance a giant statue of Liberty dominates, tall and sublime, as though to express the new direction taken by human labor in the year 3000, though started upon several centuries earlier.

"Look," said Paolo to Maria, "this statue represents a very handsome slave who has broken his chains, which lie shattered at his feet. He is supporting himself on a trophy of wheels, batteries, and other instruments; on the other side an aerotach and a boat stand for commerce.

"You see, Maria, these chains represent the fetters in which industry lived, or rather suffered, together with its brother commerce, in ancient times. The thought of those times horrifies me, and I feel a deep compassion for those distant ancestors of ours who patiently endured all the varied forms of commercial and industrial servitude.

"Just imagine that up until the twentieth century you could not enter many cities of Europe or all the cities of Italy without being put through a visit, often brutal and always tedious, from rough-mannered guards who rummaged in your bags and trunks, everywhere, to see if you had objects subject to the consumption tax, which loomed over all food provisions, over wine, over milk, and over a thousand other things.

"And when the city or village was by a seaside, whether you had come by a small boat from some distant country or from the one perhaps no more than three or four kilometers away, you had to pass through the red tape of two categories of guards—the financial ones, to see if you were carrying merchandise from abroad, and the municipal ones, to verify whether you were trying to get around the consumer tax.

"Quite a double burden to undergo in the course of an hour! Thank God, the consumption tax was abolished in all the cities of Europe by the twenty-first century. Then, gradually, as the United States of the world were forming, they also abolished customs offices throughout the world, and today economists no longer even remember the meaning of the words *protectionist* and *free-marketer!* Long live civilization! Love live progress![8]

"Today all countries around the world freely exchange their products, and customs duties have been relegated together with strongholds, in the museum of the ruins of the past."

And here the polite tour guide cut in to offer the necessary elucidations.

"In this department the economists, the industrialists, and the businessmen, who through their cleverness, their enterprise, and their studies have acquired a world reputation, examine the great questions facing cosmic commerce, responding with valuable advice, thanks to the statistical information gathered here from every part of the world, which all the industrialists and tradesmen on the planet consult.

"Here is an example of one of the functions exercised by this ministry.

"Three or four years ago in Canada a large factory was founded for a new construction material, which consists of reducing to pulp the maple trees of those immense forests, mixing it with various soluble silicates.

"The solidity and low price of this material, and its slight or nonexistent heat conductivity, quickly made it extremely popular, and its use spread to all countries around the world. The factory, encouraged by its success, doubled production of the paste and pushed it excessively, beyond demand.

"At the same time in Java another factory of the same sort opened, it too overproducing. The central government here, alerted to this fact and on the strength of the statistical data it had gathered on the production and consumption of the construction-paper paste, telegraphed both factories, urging them to confine their production to a necessary level. Without this warning, which went out just this week, one of the two manufacturers would soon have had to go under.

"And the same is done for all the other large industries, which also receive instructions and advice from this center.

"Another great mission of this ministry consists in having the appropriate laboratories study the products of the new industries, which often do not measure up in their value to the overly optimistic hopes of their inventors.

"Here many illusions are shed, but many catastrophes also averted.

"And commerce is handled the same way as industry. This ministry is not a fiscal organ, but a simple information office. Every great businessman from Peking or New York, Genoa or London, can, within the same day, know by telegraph the commercial movement of the whole world as represented by the boats entering and leaving the various ports and the nature and quantity of goods they carry in their bowels."

—•—

After thanking and bidding goodbye to their guide, our travelers left the Government Palace, admiring the order that reigns in it and proud to have been born in a era that has made such considerable strides toward civilization.

On leaving the building, however, Paolo and Maria saw alongside it a smaller single-story building out of which came an infinite number of wires, directed toward all points on the horizon. On the door is inscribed in large characters a single word: *Money.*

They wanted to learn what this office was. It was none other than the cosmic accounting office, or the financial organ for our planet, representing all the functions that once were exercised by an extremely complicated mechanism including the ministries of finance, the Court of Accounts, the Collector's Offices, and all the various torture instruments with which money was wrung from the purses of taxpayers to meet the government's expenses.

The four large sections of the State make up the central accounting of all that is needed for the universal expenses of reclamation, scientific exploration, and the safeguarding of public health. The chief accountant, after consulting with his few colleagues, once a year announces to the world the tax Andropolis must exact of it.

The Podestà of each region distributes the tax to every citizen according to his means. The tax rises geometrically with the earnings of every citizen. The poor pay nothing. This is the cosmic budget, but every commune also has its own budget, and here too the taxes are geometrically progressive and the poor exempt from all taxation.

Each region has a Council of Complaints to which are sent the protests of those who think they have been taxed excessively or unfairly. Andropolis has its own Council for complaints regarding the cosmic tax.

The judgments coming from this Council are without appeal.

Protests in the year 3000 are very rare, because taxes are paid only by the wealthy, because they are very modest, and above all because everyone knows he is paying to his own advantage—since the revenue is spent to the benefit of all and in the great universal interest.

6

THE GYMNASIUM OF ANDROPOLIS.

IN A PLAZA OF ANDROPOLIS COMPLETELY cultivated with green European plants stand two facing structures.

One is the Gymnasium, which indeed is devoted to gymnastics. The other is the School, devoted to instruction.

Over the entrance hall of the Gymnasium is inscribed in gilt lettering:

Be healthy and you will be halfway to happiness. Be strong and you will be free.

In front of the Gymnasium stands a beautiful colossal statue—a Hercules who is also an Apollo, representing calm in strength.

Our travelers visited this Gymnasium, which we shall describe through their words, but only in large excerpts, since, to enter into all the marvelous details of that School of Muscle, one would have to tell the athletic history of the year 3000, and that would be a volume in itself.[1]

The whole Gymnasium is divided into two large areas, one for men, the other for women; only on the occasion of great athletic festivals do the two sexes come together in a special circus for their competitions. In the women's section all the teachers belong to the fair sex. The Gymnasium's Director General, however, is a man.

In either of the areas the pupils' parents, relatives, and friends are welcome to attend the lessons, competitions, and shows that are periodically given.

Since in their general outlines the two areas, male and female, are perfectly equivalent, we shall describe only the men's area.

The first section, which you find on the right side as you enter the Gymnasium, bears a two-word inscription over its doorway in Cosmic, coinciding in this instance with the ancient Latin:

Alere flammam.[2]

Into this area, in fact, enter weak boys who want to grow sturdier, convalescents who want to quickly regain their strength, and all those who, without being weak, want to train themselves—who have to make long and arduous journeys or who wish, for whatever reason, to expend some extraordinary amount of force.

A good training, which turns a pale bookworm weakened by study into a stout traveler, lasts only a month.

The first activity to which the *trainee* must submit is the general cold bathing taken with thick sponges, along with a general massage, which is no longer performed by a masseur's hands, but with a most ingenious device known as the *pantomass*.

This is a small case inside of which the trainee's whole naked body is enclosed, meaning that its shape and size are expandable, since it must fit that body as perfectly as a well-tailored piece of clothing. Nor should any part of the body but the head remain out of contact with the pantomass.

The inner surface of this small case appears to be completely unified, but in fact it is formed like a Roman mosaic out of so many small square pieces, each a square centimeter in surface.

Each of these small squares is joined to a thread that transmits movement through an electric motor.

Once the trainee has stretched out in the pantomass, its current is sent through the feet, then the legs, the thighs, and so on upward, until all the small squares are transformed into so many little hammers that, like those of a piano, strike the body's surface, now gently, now more strongly, now fortissimo, according to the needs and requirements of each body.

The material the small case is made from is consequently that of each small hammer, ranging from a soft, smooth substance such as glove leather to metal and stone, so that the massage, varying with each individual, may be as sensual as a tickling caress along the entire body or as rough and violent as a slap.

The procedure lasts from just a few minutes to an hour. One leaves the pantomass red as a beet, and often in that state one is put under a cold shower.

The gentler procedures are given to the weak children and often too to the elderly, who want to extend their life and who in fact manage by these means to gain several years and, more important, to avoid suffering the infirmities of old age.

In the area devoted to strengthening the weak, treatment is not confined only to massage. Individuals also perform various exercises such as the swing, the mechanical mount, and others that are all applications of transmitted motion, so that, without useless and tedious expenditure of muscle strength, capillary circulation and vasomotor activity are kept vigorous and harmonic.

Some manipulations and exercises are quite tedious, but in these instances soft music relieves the boredom. Throughout the Gymnasium, incidentally, music accompanies and bolsters all forms of sport, even those reserved for the strongest and most agile. Hygienists in the year 3000 have long been convinced that any gymnastic exercise that seems boring or unpleasant loses at least half of its medicinal efficacy. In such cases it may even be injurious to one's health.

Beyond the general massage applied with the pantomass to the whole body, massages are administered to particular organs, always with mechanical apparatuses, again depending on individual conditions and specific therapeutic recommendations.

Often the massage is linked with electric, dynamic, or nerve current and with particular lowerings or raisings of temperature, so that it is possible, in the same individual, over the whole surface of the body or only over a square centimeter of a person's flesh, to convey a given quantity of motion, heat, and electricity, variously associated and different in intensity and tempo.

In individual sections of the Gymnasium pupils study riding, swimming, wrestling, jumping, racing, cycling—that is, all the exercises of sport.

One whole section is devoted to hygienic and curative hydrotherapy, and anyone who takes the trouble to compare the methods used in the year 3000 with the crude and primitive ones of the nineteenth century can be persuaded of the great progress this branch of hygiene has made.

The gymnasium is at once a school and a physical training center.

The school accepts youths and younger children who, on being visited by a physician, have been advised to follow a given gymnastic method, adapted to their age and constitution. After a certain time they may ask to undergo an examination and receive a certificate declaring them to be excellent or mediocre equestrians, swimmers, wrestlers, and so on.

In these times every person is likely to consider himself dishonored if he turns twenty without knowing how to swim, ride, run, jump, wrestle. Well-exercised muscle strength has almost totally eradicated from the earth the nervousness, the neurasthenia, and all the physical ailments that so tormented men and women from the end of the nineteenth to the twenty-first centuries.

Each year two or three large athletic festivals are held, the pupils and amateur participants of the Gymnasium displaying their skills. These are solemn festivals that draw the warm, lively curiosity of the entire populace, and the Pancrat also always attends them with his four main ministers.

7

THE PALACE OF SCHOOLS. THE
primary school. The middle school.
The school of advanced studies.
Lesson on the influence of passion
on the logic of thought.

FACING THE GYMNASIUM STANDS A STERN
and giant edifice made up of three buildings connected by a portico
and gardens.

In the Greek-style entrance hall appear these words:
Wishing is power if it also contains knowledge.

"Oh, what wisdom in those words! The whole science of life seems
to be contained in them. They can serve as a cornerstone to the art
of happiness and all pedagogy. Who'd have thought it?"

"Who'd have thought it? All people of good sense, I think, because
the seed of all the great truths lies in every well-organized brain.
But the first to utter those words was a citizen of Florence who lived
around the end of the nineteenth century. He was a representative,

the mayor of his city, and also a government minister. His name was Ubaldino Peruzzi, and he was sharp, active, full of Attic salt and good sense. And all you need to prove it are these sacred words carved here in gilt letters on the Palace of Schools."[1]

You enter the Palace by a broad staircase, at the top of which, in the middle, stands a colossal statue representing Science.

This statue has been cast in *electro*, a metal made from an alloy of silver, palladium, and aluminum; it is whiter than snow and in its splendor outshines the most dazzling metals known to antiquity. When the sun illuminates it, it glows with such light that you can scarcely look at it, and at night it is more radiant still, lit as it always is by electric lighting.

The statue has two large eyes made of diamonds that, in sunlight and electric light, seem like two stars. It looks smilingly toward the sky as though watching the distant horizon and with its raised right arm holds a torch that, with a contrivance of various rainbow-colored lights, spreads all around it like so many blazing beams.

The Palace of Schools is in a plaza set at a certain height, so that the statue, seen by night from every point of the city, seems like a beacon.

And the beacon of Andropolis it is indeed: it is the light of science, which from the capital of our planet seems to light the whole world.

And was it not science, perhaps, that guided men in the quest for the true and the good?

And was it not science, perhaps, that transformed the shaggy, fierce savage, prey of the beasts and hurricanes, into the beautiful, powerful man who harnesses lightning, drills through the continents, making him absolute master of his planet and giving him hope in the year 3000 that his voice will be heard by his planetary colleagues?

Paolo and Maria, entering the main hall of the palace, knew that the three buildings of which it consists are dedicated to the three branches of teaching:

Primary school.
Middle school.

School of advanced studies.

They wanted to visit the primary school accompanied by one of the teachers offered to them as a guide.

They quickly crossed through the spacious, ventilated rooms, flooded with light and pure air, in which the very young pupils sit—all sitting separately in comfortable seats with desktops.

The teachers walk among the benches, looking over the assigned work, giving advice and, if need be, correction.

In one of the schools the pupils were writing. It was not the old-fashioned writing that lasted up until the twenty-first century, in which vowels and consonants all had to be represented by a letter; it was a stenography in which the vowels were all omitted or indicated with the simplest marks—making this writing ten times faster than the ancient sort.

The teacher, who served as guide to our travelers, told them that the children arrive at these elementary schools after the age of six and that almost all have already learned to read and write in their families.

"Here we give practical instruction in morals, arithmetic, a bit of history, the art of expressing one's thought in Cosmic, the elements of physics, chemistry, and the natural sciences, subjects that can prove quite indispensable to the practice of life. No religious teaching, because every family has its own religion, and the parents, if it suits their thinking, instruct the children in the religion they have adopted.

"In this primary school boys and girls study together, and the teachers may be men or women, but parents have the right to choose a male or female teacher, as they prefer.

"Elementary instruction lasts only three years. The pupils almost all pay for their tuition. The State provides only for the poorest. The lessons last only three hours a day, with two days off a week."

From the primary school our travelers moved on to the Middle School, the equivalent of the ancient world's secondary school.

There they teach everything that aids in general cultivation, the teaching divided into two large branches.

Scientific studies.

Literary studies.

No ancient language: only the authors who have written in Cosmic are studied, and the critical analysis of their works is always geared to instilling a feeling for the beautiful.

History and geography are taught to all, forming the skeleton of teaching.

Philosophy has been banned for some time now, even in name, replaced by psychology and anthropology.

In scientific studies the emphasis has shifted to the teaching of the natural sciences, elementary mathematics, mechanisms, physics, and chemistry.

Laboratories and workshops are connected to all instruction, and the pupils, who must be at least twelve years old, complete their course of study over four years.

When the course is finished, a very strict exam leads to a certificate of general education. This is enough for all those who, not wanting to exercise any particular profession, have no further aspiration but to be cultivated people, to manage their own affairs and perfect themselves on their own, freely following lectures in higher-level courses.

The Middle School grants a literary certificate and a scientific certificate.

The first is necessary for anyone wishing to become a judge or writer, the second for anyone wishing to become an engineer (in any of the branches of engineering) or physician.

The School of Advanced Studies has different courses for professionals and for pure science, equivalent to the ancient university. The student needn't formally enroll, and the final exam is necessary only for those who want a professional diploma.

Here too men and women sit at the same benches, and some of the professors are women.

To be a teacher in the primary or middle school you must have a certificate, which is given out only after a very long and hard exam.

To give lessons in the Advanced School requires no exams, but you must present published works.

There are an infinite number of teaching chairs, because anyone who does specialized research can propose a course on a preferred subject, as long as the request is filed with the Higher Council of Schools, made up of three individuals representing the three branches of teaching.

Paolo and Maria wanted to look in on one of the many lessons being given that day, and entering by chance into a classroom, they saw announced the topic the professor would be discussing that day. The announcement read:

History of human errors. Influence of the passions on the logic of thought.

The class was to last only an hour and was a great delight for our travelers.

The speaker was very learned, eloquent, and prolix, with a sometimes barbed wit that made pleasant even the driest doctrine and the documented history of human errors.

—•—

The whole course for that year and the next was supposed to be devoted to the history of human errors, but on that day the professor turned his eloquence to the examination of ancient legal practice and the errors into which human reason had once been drawn by scientific experts whom the courts assigned to defend or prosecute delinquents.

"Back in the very distant barbaric age there was a time (said he) when, in attempting to elucidate questions of guilt, by casting too much light on judgments so that the truth would emerge neatly and clearly, they sometimes ended up blinding the eyes of judges, who then handed down the most absurd sentences.

"The judges, who should have been the only competent ones, had on the contrary a handful of men taken off the street, physicians or engineers or businessmen, who had never studied so much as the alphabet of judicial science yet who nonetheless were ultimately entrusted with sentencing, absolving, or condemning.

"And these poor jurors, innocent in their ignorance, fearful of their undeserved responsibility, turned to the technical experts, to the men of science who should have illuminated them, and the light shed upon them instead produced only an ever-thicker darkness.

"The experts for the defense would say:

"'There is no poison in the victim's entrails.'

"'There is poison.'

"And the poor jurors—faced with such shameless contradictions, dazed and confused by the clash of lawyerly eloquence, by the lyrical invectives of the judges, tossed amid science that was denying itself its own efficiency through flagrant contradictions, lost in the labyrinth of sophisms, paradoxes, and dialectic that fell upon their shoulders like so many missiles in a day of battle—ended up yielding to the promptings of feeling, the most unreliable of judges in the field of justice, and so passed sentence with their hearts instead of with reason.

"So that ultimately it was not judicial science, not the science of experts, that passed final judgment, but selfishness or compassion.

"The former told the jurors:

"'That man has stolen: if he is set free he will steal again, and stick his hand into your pockets.

"'So, off to prison with him.

"'That beautiful young woman has committed love crimes. How I would like to have sinned with her!

"'Poor thing! Set her free.'

"And when, on the other hand, compassion appeared or shook the sensitive fibers of the jurors, the culprit was absolved when compassion was stronger for him than for the victim. He was condemned, on the other hand, when the lawyers managed to convey greater compassion for the victim.

"As you can see," said the professor, "it was a question of elective affinity. It was a battle of sentiment against reason, and poor justice too often was overwhelmed in those very unequal contests.

"Such was justice ten centuries ago. But let us not be too proud, we other men of the thirty-first century, because we too do not always manage to neatly separate the heart from thought in our judgments."

The lecture, often interrupted by approving laughter, was thunderously applauded at its end, and our travelers left the Palace of Schools very glad to have made the visit.

8

TRIP TO HYGEIA. THE STATUE
erected to the preeminent physicians
of antiquity. The anteroom of the
sick. The divisions of Hygeia. A lung
doctor's visit to a tubercular patient.
Card money in the year 3000. The
Hygeians' department. Visit to
newborns. Elimination of a baby.
A mother both pitiful and cruel.

PAOLO AWAKENED MARIA, WHO WAS STILL
sleeping off her tiredness from a very long walk the day before, and
said to her:

"Please bear with me and get up at once, because the Director of
Hygeia has granted me an appointment for this morning to see the
great Institute of Health, where they treat the sick or injured who
need urgent care."

Maria did not have to be asked twice and in a half hour was dressed
and ready for the awaited trip.

With a short walk they climbed up a hill occupying the most
delightful and charming site in Andropolis; there the great building
of Hygeia stands, huge and majestic. All around it are evergreen

conifer trees from Japan and China, which cast a cool shade and spread about them a pleasant smell of resin. Beneath these plants you see many wooden benches where the convalescents sit.

On entering through the main door they found themselves in a spacious courtyard, entirely peopled with statues of marble and bronze set amid sweet-smelling flower beds.

At the center three statues stand out, those of the three great founders of ancient medicine.

"Look, Maria, this is Hippocrates, the Greek physician, who lived four centuries before Christ and was by many years the father of ancient medicine. He has left us the vastest encyclopedia of medical science ever written by a single man. His books contain truths that endure to this day.

"This other figure is Avicenna, an Arabic physician. This statue's been erected in his honor not for his jumbled, polypharmic compilation of a thousand prescriptions but because he wrote that medicine is the art of preserving health—thus prophesying what the art of medicine would be many centuries after him.

"This other figure is Galen, also a Greek physician, though one who practiced his art in Rome. He laid the cornerstone for human anatomy, which he derived from that of the monkey, since in his times it was not permissible to cut up a human corpse. Beyond that glory he made possible giant strides in medicine and surgery.

"All around you see more than fifty other statues, all of them erected to transmit to posterity the memory of illustrious physicians. Nor will I point them all out, because I should have to give you the history of the entire art of medicine, in all its multiple branches. My only request is that we stop a moment in front of the greatest of them.

"This is Jenner, who with the discovery of vaccinal pus and the smallpox vaccine paved the way for the discovery of Pasteur, who lived and died in France in the second half of the nineteenth century and who extended vaccination to anthrax and rabies, opening up a new era in curative art. And as you can see his statue has quite rightly been placed alongside Jenner's.

"Just after Pasteur's statue you see that of Lister, who, with his antiseptic cure, saved millions of victims, making the boldest surgical operations not only possible but almost entirely safe.[1]

"This other statue is erected to Doctor Micali, an Italian physician who, in the twenty-fifth century, by perfecting Röntgen light, managed to make the whole human body transparent, thereby allowing us to see with the naked eye the brain, the lungs, the heart, all the inner organs, and even the marrow of the bones.[2]

"This discovery made obsolete the pleximeter, the stethoscope, and all those other ingenious tools with which nineteenth- to twenty-fifth-century scientists sought to understand the profound alterations our inner organs undergo.

"This other statue, which in order of time is the last erected to the illustrious physicians, represents Doctor Yang-Feu, a Chinese physician who found a way to suppress physical suffering and even calm all moral suffering practically at the moment it arises—and this with a tiny device that everyone can keep in his pockets, called the *algophobus*.[3] It has two blunt tips, or, you might say, poles. One of these is applied to the crown of the head, the other to the center of the spine; through them a current passes that numbs all sensitive cells, immediately stopping any pain.

"Once dying a natural death was an extremely rare exception; you could count one lucky case out of perhaps a thousand, and everyone else died of illness. Today, though, the general rule is to die of old age, painlessly, because, as you will see, from birth on all badly made organisms are eliminated, and illness, which is detected at its first appearance, can almost always be cured and stifled at its inception. The only people who die of illness are those who did not manage early on to consult a physician or those who, through wounds or serious falls, present lesions too traumatic to allow them to stay alive."

As Paolo was attempting to inform his gentle companion of the infinite progress made by medicine over the course of centuries, the Director appeared before them. He had seen them from the windows of his study and hurried down to meet them.

Welcoming them, he accompanied them through the rooms in which the sick sit, or those who think they are sick, waiting for their consultation.

Maria immediately felt compelled to ask the Director of Hygeia: "But surely all these people must be only mildly ill if they've managed to come on their own two feet to consult your doctors."

"My dear lady, once one called a doctor only when the illness was already so advanced that the patient was forced into bed and so far gone that he was almost always difficult if not impossible to cure.

"Now, on the other hand, we know that almost no illness strikes us like lightning, but it is prepared by almost imperceptible ailments that simply escape the eye of poor observers.

"It is for this reason that, in all the schools, everyone is taught to observe carefully his own organism and its functioning. And the moment one notices the slightest pain or the smallest trouble, one rushes here or to another Hygeia to have his inner organs checked and thus nip in the bud the least ill that might threaten him.

"Just imagine, my dear lady, that at one time a single man would treat all diseases. In those days the physician was a surgeon, obstetrician, oculist; but in the nineteenth century our science had already progressed so that the doctors had to specialize, and then there were surgeons, oculists, ear doctors, chest doctors, stomach specialists, etc., etc.[4]

"This subdivision of medical work continued to expand until today, for every inner body part, we have a specialist, so many are the changes each organ can undergo and so many are the means to lead it back to normal functioning. Imagine, for the brain alone we have at least twenty specialists who treat the diseases of the motor and thought cells, who study the illnesses of thought, of the will, and so forth—just as we have *osteopathologists* for diseases of the bones, *hematopathologists* for blood diseases, *hepatopathologists* for liver ailments, *nephropathologists* for those of the kidneys, *gastropathologists* for those of the stomach, and so on.

"Likewise, we have the loftiest sort of hierarchy among the physicians, that of the *hygeians*, who study the healthy organisms to detect a person's predisposition to illness before that illness develops; it is they who visit the newborns to verify whether they are fit for life. And among them a subspecialty has formed, which is that of the *psychohygeians*, who, as we shall soon see, detect newborns' future attitudes to crime, in order to eliminate the delinquents before they can do damage to the society into which they have been born.

"But look, here is a doctor in attendance, reviewing the clients who have come this morning, to point them to the section in Hygeia they should go to be examined."

A young man was calling the clients by the number they had been given at the door, and after asking them what they were suffering from, told them whether they needed to consult the gastropathologist, the hepatopathologist, or the hematopathologist.

It was a very cursory visit, and the indication might also be wrong, but the specialist would later correct it when he visited the client with the perfected Röntgen light.

This distributive examination of the sick was conducted with the greatest orderliness, without quarrels or confusion, and in less than a half hour the room was empty, because everyone had received the indication needed to guide him to one or another department of Hygeia.

"And now that we have seen the waiting room," said the Director, "let us visit one of the many divisions in which the specialists observe the sick and prescribe a method of cure to them. If you have no objection let us go into the section of the *pneumopaths*, that is, those suffering in their respiratory organs."

Indeed, they stepped into this area, where many sick people of both sexes were waiting to be visited.

A delicate youth, pale and gaunt, was just then waiting to be called.

The pneumopathologist asked him to remove his clothes and, once he was entirely naked, asked him to go stand in a sort of niche where suddenly the light that was illuminating the room disappeared, and all was plunged into darkness. Immediately after, though, the doctor directed a beam of light onto the naked man, who became as transparent as if he were made of glass.

One could see the heart in its speeded-up, irregular beating, and see the lungs dilating and contracting rhythmically, and see all the viscera of the belly, as if that man had been opened by an anatomic knife; one could even make out the marrow in the depths of the bones.

The pneumopathologist looked at him for a long time with a double telescope, making the sick man pose in front of him, then to the side, then with his back to him, and then:

"Take comfort in this, your illness is just beginning and is quickly curable. You are threatened with tuberculosis, but it will be overcome with a good respiratory regimen and a good diet. Get dressed, and I'll write down what you need to do."

The doctor went to a desk and wrote out these prescriptions:

Go at once to Everest, to Darley station, which lies at an altitude of 2000 meters; take lodging there and stay for a full year. Then return for several years to this site, though only in the winter months. Meat and dairy diet. For the other details the patient should follow the advice of the physician who directs Darley Station.

The sick man, who came from a remote village and so lived far outside of the current of new civilization, asked the pneumological doctor:

"Won't I have to take any medicine?"

The doctor started to chuckle and then said:

"You mean to say that in your village you still have pharmacists? Here in Andropolis and in all the large cities of the planet pharmacies have ceased to exist for over a century. Pills, potions, bandages are relics of ancient medicine. Today they cure all disease with change of climate, diet, and the rational application of heat, light, and electricity.[5] Pharmacists for many centuries were the successors to the magicians who cured diseases with exorcisms, and with short verses from the Koran or prayers to God, the Blessed Virgin, and her saints. And the prescriptions were like letters sent off to people with 'address unknown.' Sometimes they accidentally reached the person who should receive them, but most of the time pills, powders, and decoctions, after a more or less rapid course through the gastrointestinal tube, ended up going down the drain, without having found the intestinal tracts they were intended for and that they should have treated and cured. Every physician had his prescription, and each school varied the method of treatment. It was in that era that a great French poet, who was also briefly president of the French republic, made the bitterest but truest criticism of the medicine of his day, calling it *une intention de guérir*, an intent to cure; but even for several centuries after Lamartine this definition was the faithful photograph of the art of curing the sick."

The pneumopathologist moved on to examine the other sick people, and our travelers with their guide left that area for the one in which the newborns were inspected.

Paolo and Maria had observed that the man with the chest ailment who had undergone his examination in their presence, on thanking the physician, had placed a small card in his hand.

It was his payment for the consultation.

In the year 3000 money stopped circulating quite a while ago, and the currency is made up of so many tiny cards, all the same size, that bear a stamp, that of the minister of finance, and have on them a line left blank, where everyone writes his own name and the amount he wants.[6]

The color of the card indicates the amounts that can be written on it, there being twenty series, each distinguished from the others by a different color:

From 1 to 100 lire—white card
100 to 500—gray card
500 to 1,000—light blue card
1,000 to 2,000—deep blue card
2,000 to 5,000—blue-green card
5,000 to 10,000—emerald green card
10,000 to 20,000—pale yellow card
20,000 to 50,000—orange card
50,000 to 100,000—light violet card
100,000 to 200,000—deep violet card
200,000 to 300,000—half-white, half-black card
300,000 to 500,000—pink card

500,000 to 600,000—deep pink card
600,000 to 700,000—half-yellow, half-green card
700,000 to 800,000—half–light blue, half-red card
800,000 to 900,000—half-green, half-red card
900,000 to 1 million—half-brown, half-red card
1 to 2 million—half-white, half-green card
2 to 3 million—silver card
3 to 10 million—gold card

The value of this currency is given, however, not by the signature of the person who spends it, but by that of the *optimate*, which can be read at the bottom right of the card.

The optimates are the most honest, wealthy, and esteemed citizens of the country, to whom the government's Superior Council, after lengthy deliberation and weighty examination, has given that honorific title. Just as there are cards of various values, so every optimate, according to the fortune he possesses, can sign a different category of card.

As is natural, the wealthiest optimates can also sign the silver and gold cards, and there are some so universally well-known that their signature is good over the entire planet. Those with more modest fortunes, known only in their village or their city, are authorized only to sign the cards in lower sums.

The optimates, to give these slips of paper a desired value, need no other signatures than their own and thus, so to speak, mint money in their own houses.

When you want to buy an object you give the seller a card that corresponds to its value, writing out the intermediate figures between those inscribed on it; when, with long use, this paper bill has become too dirty and too crumpled, you take it to a window at the state's central bank, where it is replaced. The only inconvenience with this money is its flammability, but in the event of a fire you can go to the central bank and, recommended by four optimates as honest, swear on your honor that you have lost a given sum, and you are fully, immediately reimbursed. If this misfortune befalls an optimate, his word is enough to credit his own declaration.

And this is how men are encouraged in the year 3000 to be honest, sincere, and perfect gentlemen, for honesty gives credit, and credit brings wealth.

It needn't be pointed out that twice a year in every city and every province the counselors of finance meet to establish the norms of circulation, which is always regulated by the wealth of the country and by the financial ability of the individual optimates who sign the cards.

This money, easy to use and guaranteed by the perfect honesty of its signer, has the same value in all countries in the world and has considerably simplified the flow of commerce and the functioning of all business.

The card with which the poor tubercular man paid the pneumologist was white, with the number 50 on it, a common fee these days for a simple medical checkup. The poor are given free checkups, or their consultations are paid for by the rich.

Our travelers quickly traversed the wards where the sick were treated, those who need prompt, urgent medication or who must undergo difficult or impossible surgical operations in private residences.

I call them wards, to use an old-fashioned word and because the rooms of the sick are placed one after the other, in two rows separated by a broad corridor, but every sick person has his own room, fairly spacious, in which well-placed ventilators freshen the air day and night, always maintaining the appropriate temperature, depending on the season and the nature of the illness.[7]

Needless to say, the walls and floor tiles of light blue porcelain are pleasing to the eye and are cleaned every day, to avoid any infection.

"Before going on to the division of the hygeians," said the Director, "let's take a look at the department in which the traumatic illnesses are treated—that is, wounds, burns, fractures, and all the lesions produced by mechanical accidents or external violence. Unfortunately civilization, no matter how advanced it is, cannot protect us from these misfortunes, and surgery must treat them, as medicine does with illnesses that develop spontaneously."

As they entered the trauma section a doctor was just then medicating a serious wound on an arm that had heavily lost substance.

"Here you have before you a most interesting case. Once this wound, even with the most perfect antiseptic cure, would have left a great deformity with absolute impotence of the wounded organ. Today, however, we can artificially produce protoplasms that, as soon as they are prepared, are applied where a portion of skin or muscle is missing. In this way one makes a true graft of germinative matter that, placed in contact with living tissues, proliferates and reproduces the missing muscle; and thus the arm is restored to a normal state and resumes its functions. The hard part of this operation consists in coming up with the precise quantity needed of protoplasm, which should be neither too little nor too much; but the skilled surgeon manages to achieve the desired goal."

Paolo and Maria saw other cases of fractures and dislocations, which were medicated painlessly and with the greatest ease.

"And now," said the Director, "let us go visit the division of the hygeians."

Maria, who had heard talk of the elimination of babies unfit for life but who knew nothing more about this, was rather anxious and unsure whether she should go into that department, but Paolo said to her:

"We must and want to see everything. Let's go."

They entered a vast room where one heard a confused howling of a hundred babies crying in the arms of their mothers or of other women. It was a very sad scene, because the crying of so many innocent creatures was made even sadder by the distressed look of those women awaiting the doctor's sentence of life or death for their little children.

"Here, you see," said the Director, "all these babies are no more than three days old, and their mothers can accompany them, since now delivery is no longer a sickness that once obliged the women giving birth to take to bed for more than a month.

"Advances in hygiene have made delivery a natural function, accomplished without pain or any sad consequences. Today a woman delivers like any other animal and a few hours after giving birth gets up out of bed to attend to her usual tasks. Here, as you see, almost all the babies are taken away from their own mothers, except for a certain few who are very sensitive and fearful to leave the fruit of their loins here forever and who entrust them to a close relative."

At that moment the baby of number 17 was called.

"Come this way, 17."

A young mother, stout and beautiful, rose from sitting with her baby in her arms. You could see in her face that no fear tormented her and that she was very sure of going home with her little creature.

The hygeian took the baby, who was all but naked, and, stripping it completely, placed it on a sort of perch stool. Immediately a beam of light flooded over it, making it transparent, as though it were made of glass, and the physician, after changing its position and looking at it with a telescope, said clearly:

"Number 17: The child is healthy, sturdy, fit for life."

And then he withdrew, while another doctor, a psychohygeian, leaving the baby on the same perch, directed a more penetrating light over its skull, looking at it for a long time with another telescope that magnified its brain cells hundreds of times.

The examination lasted a full half hour, and then the doctor said:

"Brain normal, no tendency to delinquency."

The two verdicts of the two doctors were transcribed by a secretary, then signed by the hygeian and psychohygeian and handed to the mother, who left happy and proud, thanking the doctors and casting about her, in the crowded circle of mothers, the gaze of a triumphant and happy woman.

She had given the world a healthy, sturdy citizen, incapable of crime.

"Number 18!"

And a new baby was submitted to the same double examination as number 17, eliciting these two verdicts:

"Healthy but not sturdy baby. Fit to live but needs tonic, reconstituent nourishment.

"Brain normal, but with a hypertrophy of the genital center. Lust-prone. Direct its education to weaken this tendency."

Maria hoped that all the visits would have a similar outcome, so that she would not have to witness the destruction of any creature, yet then came number 20, a very frail baby who, in addition, had been born at eight months and who, on being submitted to the examination of the hygeian, brought furrows to the brow of the doctor, who, with a small bell, called over two other consulting physicians waiting to be summoned in a nearby room. One after another they reexamined the poor baby, they too shaking their heads with a sorrowful, regretful air.

The three doctors concurred in this judgment:

"Baby very frail, tubercular, unfit for life."

When the mother heard this dismal sentence she started sobbing, asking the doctors:

"Couldn't some appropriate treatment make my baby healthy?"

"No," answered three voices in unison.

And then the hygeian who had first looked at the baby, turning to the mother, said:

"And so?"

The mother sobbed twice as hard and returning the little child to the doctors, with a barely audible voice, answered:

"Yes."

That *"And so?"* meant:

So, do you allow your baby to be eliminated?

And in fact an attendant took the baby, opened a small black portal in the wall of the room, and put it in there, closing its small door. A spring was released, a cry was heard, accompanied by a little explosion. The baby, enveloped by a flare of hot, 2,000-degree air, had disappeared, and only a bit of ash remained.

Scarcely had she uttered her desperate *yes* than the mother vanished from the room, and the hygeian, his face sad but calm, called out:

"Number 21!"

Maria wept and wanted at all costs to leave this chamber of horrors, but Paolo, who had known in advance how unfit babies were done away with and never wanted to witness such a cruel and pitiful operation, was nonetheless fascinated by the terrible scene, so that he said:

"Maria, one more, just one more, and then we'll go."[8]

Maria took his hand and placed it on her heart and couldn't let go of it, holding onto it very tightly, as though to draw strength from it. She could never manage to say no to Paolo and stayed.

Baby number 21 was even frailer than the baby before it and on top of that was pale, its face blotchy with red spots.

The hygeian, after a very brief examination, pronounced:

"Baby with serious heart weakness, unfit for life."

The mother did not cry but, paler than death, exclaimed:

"No, doctor, it can't be, the delivery was long and hard; that's why my baby is pale. It will get well, surely it will be well. It's the only one I have. I can't have others; my husband has died."

The doctor was visibly dismayed yet said:

"No, no, my dear woman, this baby can live only a few years, but suffering all the while, and its death will be painful, agonizing. We have no way to cure congenital heart weakness."

And then:

"And so?"

The mother had taken her child and clutched it to her bosom, as though trying to cure it with her ardent kisses, her burning love. But it did not respond.

"And so?" repeated the doctor. "You know that the elimination cannot take place without the consent of the mother or, should the mother be dead, the father. Consider that our pity would be cruel, since you would be giving your offspring over to the keenest, most unprecedented suffering, suffering that could last for years. Your baby has no awareness that it exists, and its elimination procedure is neither painful nor lengthy. A minute will reduce it to smoke and a small heap of ashes you can keep. You're young still; you can remarry and bear other children. Think carefully of what you're about to say."

But the mother did not answer and from a stony silence started up a violent weeping interspersed with cruel sobs.

Maria, who all this time had Paolo's hand on her heart, wept too and gave him a look that urged their departure.

"*And so? And so?*" the hygeian repeated for the third time with a slight tone of impatience.

They could see the mother raise her head, as if in an act at once of defiance and desperation, and then exclaim:

"*And so? And so? So, no!!*"

And as though fleeing from a pursuer she left the room with her baby clutched tightly in her arms.

The hygeian looked at Paolo and Maria and said:

"Poor woman! Poor woman! How often she will regret that *no*. She thinks she's being a good mother, and instead she's merely being a cruel one. Eliminating babies destined for suffering and premature death is the true act of pity."

—•—

Deeply moved, Maria and Paolo wanted to see nothing more and left Hygeia, with an urgent need to be outside, to seek out the blue sky and green plants and regain their strength in admiration of Nature—a Nature that, however, crueler and more pitiful than the hygeians, every day eliminates thousands upon thousands of creatures, simply because they're ill-born!

9

THE CITY OF THE DEAD AT

Andropolis. Dissolution of corpses.
Cremation. The siderophiles and
embalmings. Sepulchers.
The Pantheon.

PAOLO AND MARIA, DURING THEIR STAY
in Andropolis, also wanted to pay a visit to the city of the dead.

It is located in a pleasant valley three kilometers from Andropolis.
You arrive there by a broad road entirely flanked by extremely tall
cypresses. Amid those centuries-old trees are flower beds, and the roses
clamber up the cypresses, turning them into flowering garlands.

Where the cypresses end there opens a vast square, in the midst of
which stands a temple, copied from the ancient Parthenon. Facing the
main gate a colossal marble statue, an angel with its wings spread, as
if it wanted to soar heavenward. It holds a torch that burns day and
night, and its other hand rests on a bronze anchor. On the pedestal
that supports the statue is carved this imperative: *Hope.*

On entering the temple they felt seized with a sacred terror. The most solemn silence reigned in that immense hall, barely illuminated by large windows of azure glass that cast a strange light over people and things: melancholy, though not sad.

This was the house of the dead.

In the year 3000 every form of destroying and preserving human corpses is allowed, as long as it harms no one's health. Every dying person states his desire to be buried, cremated, dissolved, embalmed, and the great cemetery of Andropolis comprises all the oddities human ingenuity can devise for the dead.

If the death is sudden or the deceased has expressed no preference for how his or her corpse should be handled, the closest relatives, or in their absence the State, see to those arrangements.

The method most commonly used is to dissolve the corpse in nitric acid. The human body is reduced to a compact nitrate solution the relatives preserve in special crystal globes. Should the relatives upon their own deaths abandon these globes, they are then preserved in the necropolis.

Some of the dying, in their last will and testament, request that the solution of their body be saturated with clay and thus reduced to fertilizer to be buried at the foot of some favorite tree in their orchard or garden. Many, however, favor cremation, and our travelers visited the crematory furnace.

It is a very simple affair. The corpse is placed naked into a sort of platinum urn in the shape of a human body. When the urn is sealed at both ends, corresponding to the head and feet of the dead person, two wires are applied, and a current of very high heat bakes the urn in such a way that in just five or six minutes it is reduced to ash. When the urn has cooled, the ashes are gathered and turned over to the family or kept in the house of the dead, depending on whatever wish the deceased has expressed in a will.

Some wish that, as in ancient Hindu custom, their ashes be cast upon a river or the sea.

Others, however, express their desire to be placed in flower beds, orchards, or fields, thereby fecundating the earth.

For those who have stated a desire only to be cremated without further ado, the ashes are placed in small porcelain urns, kept in the necropolis with the name of the deceased and the date of death.

From the crematory oven our travelers went on to the necrophorous laboratory of the *Siderophiles*.

This is the name given to those singular people who, adopting an idea put forward by a French chemist many centuries before them, want all the iron their corpse contains to be extracted, a small medal coined with this iron, bearing their name carved along with mention of their country and the date of their death. In this way the survivors are able to preserve an eternal memory of their dear departed ones, carrying with them, dangling at their neck or on the chain of their watch or elsewhere, the iron that coursed in their blood and formed part of all their tissue.

Paolo and Maria were able to witness directly all the complicated operations through which one extracts from a human body the iron it contains and then fashions a small medal out of it. The work is difficult and costly, and for that reason this method of destroying human corpses has been adopted only by very wealthy people and is thus aristocratic.

One of the chemists of this singular laboratory was explaining to the visitors the processes by which a person is converted into a small medal, no bigger than an ancient *centesimo* coin, amusing them with certain curious anecdotes.[1]

In Andropolis he knew a very elderly lady, who in a long life amply devoted to dalliance had had many lovers, whom she always asked to be siderophiles. Fate willed it that many of these lovers died at a young age, so that she came into possession of some twenty small medals, from which she had had made a most remarkable necklace. Each small medal was joined to the other with a gold ring and a diamond, and in this piece of jewelry she had gathered the whole history of her life. They tell me that this good woman, as the ancient Christians did with their rosaries, spent all her hours clutching her love rosary, fingering each little medal one by one, kissing one after the other, remembering the poor dead men she had loved.

Our chemist also told how siderophilia flourished especially in the twenty-seventh and twenty-eighth centuries, an age during which it was virtually the only method the wealthy used to do away with corpses. And here in our temple we have a veritable museum of small medals, either found after going astray or assembled by the State through the disappearance of the families to whom they belonged.

Today siderophilia is a rather rare practice, because in the year 2858 it was discovered that a chemist of the day who specialized in removing iron from human corpses to make necrophorous medals was being handsomely paid for the chemical operation but, to spare himself the lengthy ordeal, instead of extracting the iron from the dead person's body, would take a nail or some other piece of ordinary iron and with it simply forge his little medal. Indeed, this sly fellow had invented a highly lucrative industry, since he was converting a small piece of iron worth perhaps a soldo into a medal that paid him up to five hundred lire.

He grew immensely rich, but after him for many years the public of the dead became extremely wary; medals made of human iron, now objects of ridicule, had had their day.

It is only some years ago that an organization of siderophiles formed in Andropolis, and a laboratory they started here can offer all the necessary guarantees, as certain advisors in this Society take turns watching over our operations.

The siderophile engineer, before taking leave of his visitors, showed them a special laboratory where they were carrying out studies to indulge the desires of a millionaire, who wanted not only the iron to be extracted from his body after his death but all its elements isolated one by one: oxygen, hydrogen, carbon, nitrogen, sulphur, phosphorus, and so on.

"This gentleman, who is an Englishman, placed more than a million at our disposal and has himself designed a monument all in semiprecious stone that resembles an ancient pharmacy, where the whole corpus of elements that made up his body is to be arranged.

"No other inscription is to be carved on this monument but this:

"Corpus of elements that formed the body of N.N."

Bidding goodbye to the engineer, Paolo and Maria went on into the Embalmers' Division, which prepares the corpses of those who wish to endure for a time even after death, their bodies preserved in their entirety.

The visit was long and quite odd, since the embalmed in their wills were not content to say they wanted their body to be spared from rotting; they also stated how they wished to be embalmed. And in the year 3000 the methods of preservation of corpses are many and highly varied.

The embalmed bodies are then withdrawn from the families or preserved in the necropolis, depending on the desire expressed by the deceased or by the family.

Our travelers, traversing the long museum of the embalmed, could see with their own eyes that whole populace of proud dead who had wished to survive themselves.

A few had been embalmed like the ancient Egyptians, enclosed in their tarred bandages and shut in sarcophagi of inlaid, painted wood.

Others had simply been dried in an oven, after being immersed in corrosive sublimate. They were revolting to behold, resembling great beanpoles or dried cods.

Further on, enclosed in large vitrines, were petrified corpses, hard and rigid as stone. They looked like statues modeled by a very bad sculptor.

Less awful are those embalmed with the most perfect process known in the year 3000. They are dressed in their habitual clothing and keep their customary features and coloring, but their glassy, immobile eyes seem to be staring always at a single spot. One can admire the art with which they have been prepared, but they are terrifying and seem to protest against the person who wanted, by some strange marriage, to link life and death.

Maria was looking at all these mummies with obvious disgust and could not help but say to Paolo:

"Paolo dear, if I die before you, I want you neither to dissolve me in nitric acid, nor to cremate me, nor least of all to embalm me. Have me buried in the soft, fragrant earth, without any casing whatsoever, so that even in death I can feel surrounded and embraced by our eternal mother from whose womb we have issued. I wish to be dissolved into her and, with my blood and my viscera, nourish the flowers that you will plant over my grave. You'll promise me that, won't you, my dear Paolo?"

"Yes, I promise," answered Paolo, his voice choked by a sob. "But it is you who will lay me in the soft, fragrant earth, since I am several years older than you and before you will have to make the long journey: the one-way journey."

"But let's not speak of such sad things."

"And how are we not to speak of such things here, where we are surrounded by the dead, who reawaken in us the eternal thought of the world beyond, whose secret our civilization has not managed to reveal to us? But let's go to the last point in this sad pilgrimage of ours. Let's go visit the cemetery."

And our travelers reentered the temple and, after crossing it through a small gate, found themselves in a huge garden, entirely populated by evergreen bushes and flowers. In the middle stands a giant bronze column, crowned with an eternal flame.

At the base of the column is inscribed the beautiful imperative: *Hope*.

From the column issue, like so many rays, a hundred small paths that end at the edge of the field of the dead; on both sides of these paths are erected the tombs.

Each tomb is a small garden in miniature, and in their midst stands a boundary stone of black marble, on which is inscribed only the deceased person's name, birth date, and death date. Nothing else.

"You see, Maria, here no distinction is made between rich and poor, geniuses and common folk. Whoever can pay for the stone does so himself, and the State provides for the poor. It is absolutely forbidden to write any word of praise on the tomb or to erect statues or opulent mausoleums. Once, many centuries ago, the inequalities and vanities of humankind were shouted aloud even in cemeteries, and any visitor to them was led to believe that all those dead had in life been men of genius: heroes of the heart or of thought. Whereas the person who had dictated those epigraphs had often tortured the poor dead person, slandered him, perhaps even hastened his death."

Maria then said to Paolo:

"I have always found this equality of all people in cemeteries to be quite fair, yet it strikes me that an exception should be made for men of genius or those who by their charity or heroism have performed a great service for humankind."

"And right you are, but these great people have their apotheosis in a Pantheon that lies a bit farther beyond this necropolis, which we will visit. Here lie the bodies of the great; there we shall find gathered the memories of their works."

"Let me make another observation, Paolo. It has always seemed to me that in our civilization the State plays an excessive, almost invasive part. Why can't the survivors not erect to their departed loved ones a statue, a monument—even a mausoleum, if they so desire? Our time is distinguished above all by the triumph of individualism, and it seems to me that here, where all rights should be on the side of affection and grief, the State intercedes too tyrannically."

"No, my dear Maria, the State is not invasive. Here it simply guides and issues orders because the necropolises are public monuments, but everyone in his own house, in his own garden, in his own homeland is master enough to erect even a temple to some dear departed person, if he so desires. But let's go into the Pantheon: there you won't find any corpses, only dead people who are more alive than when they were in this world."

An avenue completely flanked by giant trees led them into a veritable city, since every region of the globe has there its own temples erected to the memory of great men. And each temple has the architecture characteristic of the country to which these geniuses belonged. There is the architecture of China; of Japan, India, Australia, America, Africa, and Europe.

In every temple stand infinite monuments in the most beautiful style, where the bones of departed geniuses are not laid, but where one finds the epitome, the summation, of their entire life.

In all of them one finds either a bust or a statue that reproduces the outlines of the great departed one, and then, as in some enclosed little church, one finds on the walls all the portraits of him at the various ages of life.

A family tree marks out his genealogy, and a bookshop offers all his works, in their various editions, and his biographies.

Often one also finds the objects that have been most dear to him, his dog or cat embalmed, the flowers he preferred, his walking stick, the armchair in which he sat, and many other objects.

If the dead man was an artist, one sees photographic reproductions of his paintings, his statues, or the buildings he created.

If he was a mechanic or engineer, one finds in the monument erected to him the roads or bridges he built.

In a word, each monument is a speaking biography of the great man to whom it has been erected.

"You see, Maria, that, by eliminating vain mausoleums in the cemetery, the great men are no less honored by us than they were by our ancient forefathers, who, leaving to the survivors the task of remembering their deaths, measured in money and not in merit the height of the statue and the luxury of the marbles—so that often some thoroughly vulgar man had a splendid mausoleum in those cemeteries, while a genius was remembered by nothing more than a very modest headstone."

Paolo, like all visitors to this Pantheon, on entering the various monuments, would remove his hat and genuflect before the image of the great man.

"These are our saints, and they should take the place of our ancient ones, often manufactured by the simoniacal industry of cunning and ignorant priests, their only merit to have fasted or gone against the most sacred laws of nature. These command us to love and rekindle the torch of life in our children."

Stirred but not saddened, our two companions strolled long through the Pantheon of Andropolis, summoning to their memories the great works and deeds of these great figures.

Maria, profoundly moved by the long walk, asked Paolo one last question.

"Tell me, Paolo, here I no longer find the equality I have seen in the field of the dead. Here I find small, or medium-sized, or vast monuments: who is the judge and executor of these large inequalities?"

"The great men, my dear, are all worthy of glory; but they are very unequal among one another. We have the geniuses who with the light of their thought have raised a beacon that lights the whole planet—who, with their works, mark a new era in the history of humankind. And then we have others who, with their talent and their undefended work, perfect the discoveries of those giants; so it would not be fair for them to receive equal glory. It is the majority consensus, the vote of the members of the great Academy of Andropolis, that decides what monument should be raised to the memory of the great departed. And judgment is pronounced only after deep and lengthy discussion."

10

THE THEATERS OF ANDROPOLIS AND
the Panopticon. A listing of shows
in the capital on April 26, 3000. A
gala evening at the Panopticon.

THE CITY OF ANDROPOLIS BOASTS OVER
fifty large theaters, which offer the widest range of shows to delight
the eyes and ears—to delight the imagination and the heart.

Almost all of these theaters are the property of speculators or
industrial companies, though there are also some private ones belonging to wealthy gentlemen who put up the money for them to amuse
themselves and their friends—lovers of music or dramatic art who
entertain themselves as both actors and spectators.

Only the *Panopticon*, the largest and wealthiest of Andropolis's
theaters, is the property of the State; its purpose in presenting its
spectacles is to educate the people to appreciate beauty and the finer

emotions—uniting in its programs all the cleverest discoveries of science and art.[1]

All the theaters of the great cosmic capital are covered only in the cold season, at which time the most perfect ventilation is combined with appropriate heating.

All have more or less comfortable seats at different prices, but high up in the amphitheaters, where in olden times the gallery used to be, ample space is reserved for the poor, who take turns receiving free passes either in reward for good deeds or in payment for services rendered.

In the theaters of the year 3000 every second seat has two metal buttons by which, by pressing with your finger or foot, you can applaud or disapprove the authors, without making your hands sore or having to whistle.

If one presses the applause button, a voice lets out a Cosmic word equivalent to our *Bravo*; the other button emits a long hissing sound, like the sound one makes to tell someone to be quiet.

Performances are held day and night, but more commonly are afternoon affairs, because the inhabitants of the year 3000 have long since found that staying up far into the night is fairly harmful to their health and shortens life. They all go to bed very early and always get up with the sun.

For several centuries night shifts in workshops have become a thing of the past, and laborers have never put in more than six hours a day, since all the mechanical arts have been perfected, and machines have largely replaced manual labor.

The shows of the thirty-first century are much more varied than those known in ancient times, as you will surely agree on perusing the theater listings I have found for a single day in an Andropolis newspaper:[2]

—•—

PERFORMANCES

in the Theaters of Andropolis.

for April 26, 3000

PANOPTICON.—Gala evening, to be attended by the Pancrat. The cycle of cosmic pleasure, from Homer to the year 3000.

PANGLOSSE.*—*Oedipus* by Sophocles, in ancient Greek. *A small sketch of the nineteenth century*, in French.

THEATER OF LIGHT COMEDY.—*Jealousies of a Podestà and Two Mayors*. Comedy in four acts.

THEATER OF CLASSICAL TRAGEDY.—*Hamlet* by Shakespeare, in Cosmic translation from the English.

THEATER OF MODERN TRAGEDY.—*Poor Lisa*. Tragedy in five acts of the famous English writer John Trembley.

THEATER OF THE TARANTELLA.—*La Capricciosa.*—Comedy "just for laughs," with ancient Spanish and Neapolitan songs and dancing.

THEATER OF HARMONY.—Grand *opera seria* by the Andropolitan master Soavi.—*The Last Pope-King*.

THEATER OF ANCIENT MUSIC.—Act of *The Barber of Seville.*—Act of Bellini's *Norma.*—Act of Wagner's *Lohengrin*.

THEATER OF BEAUTY.—Pantomime and *tableaux vivants* featuring a hundred of the most beautiful girls of all races from Asia, Europe, and Africa.

THEATER OF WONDERS.—*Variety Show* with live reproduction of all the cataclysms on earth.—Tonight's performance will be of a volcanic eruption and an earthquake. In preparation for next week: *Flooding of the Mississippi*.

THEATER OF LIGHT.—*The Magical Rainbow*. Fantastic lighting spectacle depicting an aurora borealis at the North Pole and a sunrise as seen from the moon.

THEATER OF PHANTASMAGORIA.—*A Love Scene on the Planet Mars*. A poet's vision.

* The Panglosse is a theater reserved for the highly cultured, where works are performed in their original, now dead, languages, from Greek to Italian, from Latin and Sanskrit to English, Turkish, and Chinese.

THEATER OF TERPSYCHORE.—*Cleopatra.*—*A Dance of Ancient Egypt*, with 500 ballerinas, 200 of them black and 300 white, all young and beautiful.

INSTRUCTIONAL THEATER.—*The History of Locomotion*. All the inventions of land and air transportation represented in various tableaux, from the ox-drawn two-wheel cart to the locomotive, velocipede, electric tram, and aerostat. The background music to the spectacle will match the era of each invention.

ZOOLOGICAL THEATER.—*Noah's Ark*. The actors are all animals masterfully trained by the renowned Parmesan trainer Faimali. On stage will be creatures that vanished from the face of the earth many centuries ago, on loan through the generosity of the Academy of Sciences.

BOTANICAL THEATER.—*The Great Battle of the Plants.*—The only performers here are speaking flowers, walking plants, and whispering meadows. The show, a premier for Andropolis, depicts the struggle of monocotyledonous of coal-bearing soil against plants of the modern era.

THEATER OF INSECTS.—*The Metamorphoses of a Caterpillar*. Humans amazingly disguised as insects act out the history of a caterpillar that, secretly escaping from a cocoon in the form of a butterfly, reaches an island where it invites all the insects to throw off the yoke and the cruelty of humankind, founding an entomological republic.—The spectacle will end with a fantastic dance of the most beautiful tropical butterflies and dragonflies.

MARITIME THEATER.—*The Last Shark*. The story of a plot of saltwater fish to kill the last shark sheltering in a Madreporian grotto of the Marquesas Islands. The entire spectacle takes place underwater and features ancient whales and many other now-extinct animals.

CLOWN THEATER.[†]—*The Misfortunes of an Old-Time Clown*.

THEATER OF WEEPING.[‡]—*The Tears of a Woman Betrayed in This World*.

[†] The aim of the Clown Theater of Andropolis is to provoke laughter at any expense and to cheer up hypochondriacs, the bored, and all the depressed.

[‡] The Theater of Weeping offers only melancholy, not agonizing, presentations, to inject a voluntary note of sadness into the lives of those who are too happy.

THEATER OF MIRACLES.—*Metamorphoses of a Stone*. A very curious and instructive piece, depicting the fusing of a rock, its transformation into all known metals, and its fusing anew, volatilizing, becoming invisible, then returning to its ancient stone form.

THEATER OF PERFUMES.—*Dances of the Scents*. Various symphonies of flowers' most delicate perfumes are presented with musical accompaniment and invisible choirs of women's voices.

THEATER OF AGILITY.—*Ancient Acrobatics*. A varied program that will reproduce the bizarre exercises of the ancient world: the trapeze, the tightrope, and horizontal bars.

ATHLETIC THEATER.—*The Wonders of the Famous Athlete Hercules X*. Hercules X will challenge any wrestler in the world, offering a prize of 10,000 lire to anyone who can defeat him.

SUBTERRANEAN THEATER.—*The Center of the Earth*. Scenes of gnomes and giants contending for dominance of the underworld. Varied geological and paleontological scenes.

THEATER OF SATIRE.—*The Adventures of an Ancient Commander*. A laugh-out-loud comedy. Use of restraining brake strongly advised.

THEATER OF DECLAMATION.—*The Summits of the Ideal World*. Six renowned reciters, three men and three women, declaim Cosmic versions of the most sublime poetry of Byron, Shelley, and Victor Hugo, transporting listeners to the loftiest pleasures of the ideal world.

VOLUPTUARY THEATER.—*The Symphony of Pleasure*. Spectators will enjoy the harmonies of music, perfume, artificial flavors, and hedonistic vibrations, while their sight continuously gorges on the most varied kaleidoscope of images ceaselessly passing over the stage.[3]

—•—

Paolo and Maria had already taken in some performances at theaters in Andropolis, but on the evening of April 26 they wanted to enjoy the evening gala to be attended by the Pancrat with the General Staff of his ministers and all the city's most distinguished figures.

This was also a good way to see the president of the Academy of Sciences, the president of the Academy of Fine Arts, and many great men, well known throughout the world.

The theater's placard announced:

The cycle of cosmic pleasure, from Homer to the year 3000.

The material promised many joyful emotions.

The theater stands apart in a large plaza, which one enters by climbing a wide marble staircase. The architecture is Greek, the style severe.

In the foyer at the top of the stairs are various cafes, to which the spectators can repair for refreshments between acts. A huge crowd filled the stairwell and foyer. Entering the theater our two travelers stood for a moment, enraptured.

The hall is an amphitheatre with tiers of seats, and no boxes, and every seat is different from the next. Only high up do you see a large "paradise" in the form of a gallery, into which the crowd of poor spectators had already been pouring for a couple of hours.

Paolo and Maria had taken two front-row seats, to be near the stage.

Scarcely had they sat down than Maria noticed that in front of them, on a board, was a sort of cap of very thick raw silk, with six wires at the top. For her it was something new and curious that she had never seen in any other theater, prompting her immediately to ask her companion:

"What on earth is that?"

Paolo started laughing and said:

"I won't keep you in suspense. Look at the other spectators. As soon as they've sat down they take off their hat and put on that cap, which is called an *aesthesiometer*. Then they adjust the thickest wire on the board in front of them and take hold of the other threads.

"It is a device invented quite recently by a famous English physicist; up to now it has been used only in this theater and some other big theaters in Europe.

"The wire at the top of the board is connected to a large condenser of electronervous force, which is the same for all the members of the audience, while the other five smaller wires are applied at various points on our body, one for each sense, and we can raise or reduce sensitivity at will."

As Paolo was speaking, he was holding the wires and explaining to his companion how the device works.

"You see, this is the wire for general sensitivity, and it can be applied at any point of our body. Usually just by holding onto it you can sharpen or modulate all your sensations. You get higher and lower sensitivity by pressing with your foot on one or another of these pedals you see below here in front our seats.

"When a spectator wants to raise the intensity of pleasure he feels in any of the theater scenes, he presses 'more,' and his sensitivity mounts with the pressure.

"If, on the other hand, he is feeling too much, he presses 'less,' thus reducing the intensity of pleasure, which occurs at different degrees of tension according to the conditions at the moment and each person's mode of feeling.

"As you've probably noticed, some of the audience members aren't using this new tool, which is a veritable regulator of sensitivity, either because they still find it too complicated or because they're content with the normal state of their feeling.

"When you apply the thinnest wire to your forehead or ear or nose, it acts more directly on the sense of sight, hearing, or smell—making the corresponding sensations more delicate and more exquisite.

"In the ancient theaters pleasure came only through the two senses of sight and sound. But in our spectacles today the note of fragrance has entered in as well, and thus the pleasures of smell can also be moderated or intensified with the use of this aesthesiometer."[4]

Maria shook her head, half admiringly, half ironically, and said:

"This all seems too complicated to me, too contrived. You can put on the magic cap: as for me, tonight I want to be content with my own natural senses, as the Good Lord has made them for me."

Meanwhile the hall, illumined by a light whose source remained invisible and lit people and things like the sun, was filling up, and a very quiet music, whose players were also invisible, was spreading its divine harmonies all about.

All at once the music stopped, the curtains parted that separated the viewers from the stage, and the first scene appeared before everyone's eyes:

It was a prehistoric family preparing to have its meal in a troglodyte grotto.

Naked and hirsute men and women. Stone axes with handles hanging on the walls of the grotto. At the center a fire blazing, and cooking over it half of a huge reindeer, ready to be eaten.

The father of the family distributed to his three wives and his children, forming a circle around him, stone knives of various sizes, according to the age of their user.

And all of them stared longingly at the savory smoking roast, waiting for the father to put out the fire and order the assault.

The prehistoric scene could not have been more faithfully depicted, and its historical precision was all more eloquent because the sense of sight was linked with those of hearing and smell.

While these troglodytes were tearing their prehistoric roast to pieces, pulling apart the long bones with stone hammers and greedily sucking at the marrow, one heard an invisible, crude, barbaric, tumultuous music, and throughout the theater's vast hall one could smell a wild aroma of roasting meat.

Outside the grotto one seemed to hear the far-off roaring of beasts, while the dark sky flashed as if a storm were imminent.

Everything joined in unison and harmony to transport the spectators into the world of hundreds of centuries past, and everyone in the audience seemed to relive that creaturely joy of a Neolithic family sating its Homeric hunger with a wild but savory meal.

"You see, Maria," said Paolo, "I've immediately used my aesthesiometer, because I'm rather enjoying this scene, but I don't like this scent of roasting meat quite as much. I put the aesthesiometer's wire on my nose, press the moderating pedal and almost stop smelling the odor of charred flesh. In fact, the smell has almost become the fragrance of steak, which pleasantly appeals to my palate and rouses my appetite."

Whereupon Maria in her new curiosity decided to put on the magic cap too—indeed, to her great satisfaction.

The first scene ended, the curtains came down, then parted soon after to reveal a second scene.

It was a scene of Homeric war from the days of ancient Greece, as anyone who has read the *Iliad* or the *Odyssey* can easily picture.

While the first scene depicted the animallike joy of eating, this one directly showed the terrible voluptuousness of strife. The horses carrying the warriors into combat neighed, and the heroes with their plumed helmets raised formidable shouts to the heavens, and lances and javelins clashed horrendously. The savage cry of victory filled the air with horror, while the chariots passed over the slain, and their screams were heard in the din and tumult of battle.

When the combat ended there appeared up above, in the high heavens, beauteous Venus, shedding flowers over the victors.

In this second scene as well the music harmonized with the horror of the battle and the sufferings of death, and an odor of blood and clashing iron spread through the air to heighten the colors of the Homeric scene.

I shan't recount all the scenes that followed one after another that evening, representing, in great leaps, the joys of humanity across the progressive evolutions of civilization.

There was a fight scene between gladiators and beasts in the Roman Coliseum, and there too the music was awful and grand in the Roman way, and the smell circulating through the theater was of sweating flesh and rank wild animals.

There was a scene in a Court of Love in a castle in Provence, with the most beautiful ladies and festooned knights.

There was a carnivalesque popular festival in the days of the Medici.

And then a ball in the Tuileries in the era of Napoleon III of France.

And more and still more scenes, all of them gay and festive, from later ages.

During the spectacle there was no lack of applause, and only once a scene was hissed, namely the one depicting a Pantagruelian dinner in a Franciscan monastery.

The memory of monkish times was in itself fairly disagreeable, and the scene was depicted too accurately in the brutal aesthetic disharmony of its notes.

While some of the friars were noisily emitting belches from their obese, bloated bellies, another one was reading aloud from a book of prayers, sneering under his whiskers and secretly munching on a wing of capon a colleague had slipped him.

This scene, though it was one among the representations of joys throughout history, seemed vulgar and unseemly and for that reason was hissed.

—•—

Between acts in the show Maria and Paolo were able to stroll in the corridors and ample conversation rooms with which the theater was furnished—all of them ornate gardens of pretty plants in flower.

Even into the intermissions the music never stopped spreading its delightful harmonies all about.

At the same time invisible currents of varied and extremely delicate perfumes accompanied the music of the ear with another music of scents that alternated and commingled—making true harmonic and melodic concerts that delighted the spectators with an olfactory bliss totally unknown to the people of ancient times.

11

THE MUSEUM OF ANDROPOLIS.
The Arcade and the peripatetics.
The natural science wing.
Possible humans. Analysis
paired with synthesis. The
museum wing dedicated to
human labor. Concentric circles
and centrifugal radii. The blot
on the art-history map.

PAOLO AND MARIA ALSO WANTED TO SEE
the Museum of Andropolis, which is somewhat far from the capital and
visible from a distance, since it is set over the plateau of a vast hill.

It is a huge circular building, and around it winds a columned
portico, an arcade where, especially on rainy days, the citizens of
Andropolis often like to walk.

This is also the favorite walk of the scholarly, who are sure to
find literary and scientific company, people who spend hours there,
resting from the toils of thought while enjoying the splendid panorama of the city that spreads out below it and the gardens scattered
here and there, among the countless neighborhoods of the immense
planetary metropolis.

This is not the haunt of amorous ladies of leisure or the idle rich, and only scientific and literary debate is heard there: so that in Andropolis, with an irony that seems praise, they say to a pedant or know-it-all: *You're such a peripatetic*, or *such a Museum Arcade type*.

The satire, though, is not aimed at the gallery's arcade itself, where the city's most cultivated people instruct one another, amicably conversing and arguing.

And the actual arcade structure is also beautiful, adorned with wandering plants in perpetual bloom, which nicely set off the gleaming white statues that stand among them and are erected to the great men of all time, the illustrious figures in the sciences, literature, and the arts.

This admirable walkway generated the idea of founding a weekly review, *The Museum Arcade*, which publishes, in the form of conversations, the literary and scientific controversies of the day, which actually take place on that site or are fictionally set there.

A person with little time or money to read many periodicals, just by reading *The Museum Arcade*, can claim to follow the movement of thought throughout the world, keeping abreast of all the new discoveries, all the new inventions.

From this arcade you enter through various doorways into the actual museum, which gathers into a single center all the products of nature and of man.

The Museum of Natural History is also circular, curving into the interior of the arcade, and anyone who takes the whole tour can rightly claim to have made a voyage around the world.

Indeed, at one end you start by traversing the world of minerals and rocks, all represented by splendid, large specimens that bear the name of the mineral and its provenance.

In that museum analysis continually alternates with synthesis, so that in the section devoted to minerals, after having seen them grouped together by kind, you find them grouped instead by the country that has produced them.[1]

Thus, for example, where mineral and geological Italy is represented, you see a sampling of all its minerals and then extremely beautiful vertical sections of the Alps, the Apennines, and the stratified rocks of lesser chains.

From the minerals one moves on to the plant kingdom, and here too analysis and synthesis join hands.

Fungi, algae, lichens, the simplest organisms of the vegetable world start the lineup, microscopic beings reproduced in large scale, so that you can take in their structure at a glance.

This is for the common run of the learned; for those who study botany every little creature is preserved in antiseptic fluid, so that it can be studied with the microscope.

Grasses, plants, the most colossal trees are reproduced life-size with their flowers and fruits, and these copies, made of quite varied, imperishable materials, give the perfect illusion of reality. Meanwhile, on a special shelf the real plants are preserved, dried or, in specific instances, preserved in antiseptic liquids, for the purpose of scholarly investigation.[2]

Each plant is displayed in the history of its evolution. In other words, one sees the fossil plant that was, or is assumed to have been, the distant ancestor of the living species and then, one by one, the forms that are linked with them by kinship and descent—like viewing the genealogical tree of a human family. For many centuries now paleontology has no longer been a science unto itself, separate from its sister and daughter sciences. The botanist who studies a family of plants necessarily has to know its lineage and thus the fossil species from which this family derives. This is what the zoologist does with animals; in all the museums alongside the still-living animals we have always seen their fossilized antecedents, and thus at a single glance can admire the wondrous evolution of forms over an uninterrupted continuum of progress.

Paolo and Maria, going through the section of the museum devoted to plants, paused for a long time before the synthetic displays reproducing the flora of a given region.

In these displays the plants are no longer distributed according to their morphological kinship, but rather according to their country. They immediately looked for Italy and saw it admirably represented by an alpine flora, a sea flora, and other lesser floras—from marshland, from islands, and several other sources.

Where alpine flora are represented, not pictorially but by wonderfully embalmed actual plants, you see a small spruce tree placed over a beech tree, which in turn has a chestnut tree at its feet.

And the spruce has its lichens, its moss, and about it the ferns, fungi, saxifrages, and all the tiny, wondrous microflora of the highest regions.

Our travelers paused for a long time in front of one of the displays representing the fertile, magical flora of a tropical forest, where the branches of the largest trees are wound with lianas, arboreal ferns, carrying on their backs the prettiest orchids and the other hundred parasitic plants that superimpose life on life, colors on colors, forming bunches no gardener will ever manage to reproduce in his flower beds and hothouses.

Wherever the flora of a given region are reproduced from nature in that museum, photography is placed in a stereoscope of real-life scenes showing the field, the forest, the swamp; so that, between the plastic reproduction and the pictorial reproduction, everyone can admire with full clarity the vegetal life of a given country.[3]

Even vegetal scenes of the ancient geological world are reproduced in the museum, whether in sculpture or in drawings. The visitor who earlier could easily take a trip into space can now take one into time—condensing in a few short instances the emotions of the voyager and of the historian.

—•—

From plants one enters into the animal kingdom, and here too they are distributed first by family, genus, species, and variety, then grouped together into the fauna of all the regions of the globe.

Every animal has alongside it its geological forebears—not all, however, since ancient paleontology has not yet managed to find the prehistoric ancestors of every species, nor has the rind, the cortex of our planet, been entirely split open and laid bare.

Every animal, beyond its own history over the centuries, has also represented evolution through the periods of its own life.

And thus you see, for example, the eagle's egg and its nest and then the newborn eaglet, and the young, the adult, and the decrepit old eagle. And every species presents its variation owing to sex, climate, and even its pathological forms.

And something else is found here that the ancient museums of the nineteenth century never even dreamed of.

Namely, each animal has alongside it its own parasites, which are reproduced in sculpture and greatly magnified. Thus, beside the rooster you see its mites, its tapeworms, and all the germs that live on his skin and in his innards.

For the animals too every region of our planet has represented its own fauna, from the highest to the lowest forms. And where you are shown the rich fauna of India you see grazing at the feet of the tiger, the panther, and the *cuon* the highly poisonous cobra, while the small parrots and the vultures, in their arched hovering, represent with an infinite number of other birds the ornithological fauna of that fertile land.[4]

The animals, like the plants, form a sequence according to their morphological hierarchy, so that from the worms and mollusks you move on to the insects, from the invertebrates you move on to the vertebrates, following their ascending scale, until you see before your eyes the king of the planet: man in all his prehistoric, proto-historic, and modern forms, finding yourself in a veritable museum of anthropology.

In the year 3000 it has been several centuries since they discovered tertiary man and the anthropomorph who generated him by neogenesis.

And immediately after him you see before your eyes the wild, hirsute Adam of the quaternary age, the caveman, Neolithic man, and finally the whole long array of more modern races that have however already disappeared from the face of the earth—such as the Australians, the Maori, the Hottentots, the bushmen, many blacks, the Guarani, and so many other races, some of whom, however, remain, albeit only in traces, in the thirty-first century.

Thus in Africa there is no longer a single pure black person, but many races of mulattoes recall that ancient origin. And in Malaya there are no longer pure Malayans, but several Malaysoid races into which a rich wave of Aryan blood has entered. In China too there are no longer true Mongols, but a hybrid race of Aryan, Semites, Malaysians, and Mongols.

The rapid and easy communications between one country and another and the profound changes in climate that have come about through human intervention tend in each generation to fuse the races indefinitely, creating a new type, indefinitely cosmopolitan, the fruit of the deep and intimate cross-breeding of ever so many races that had over long centuries remained separate and isolated, creating continual mutual fear and destroying each other with sword, with fire, and even more with the transportation of terrible infectious diseases, which later, with advances in civilization, have almost entirely disappeared from the face of the earth.

From the many prehistoric races the museum has only a few skulls and bones, but with scientific induction they have figured out the external forms, admirably replicated in sculpture in such a way that men extinct for hundreds of centuries appear lifelike.

As for the Australians, the Hottentots, and so many other modern races that have vanished, they are represented by splendidly embalmed young and adult individuals of both sexes. And at their side you see their stone weapons, their primitive crockery—all the poor products of their infantile brains.

Yet the most curious part of the anthropological section of the great zoological museum of Andropolis is that devoted to depictions of the planet's *possible people*.

In the year 3000 physicists and astronomers are utterly intent on perfecting the telescope and hope from one day to the next to be able to see the inhabitants of Venus, Mars, Mercury, and the other planets closest to Earth.

But for several centuries already astronomers' tools have been improved enough to sight the seas, mountains, rivers, and forests of those distant worlds, and with these data some naturalists, richer in imagination than in science, imagined how the planetary inhabitants might appear and rendered them in drawings or sculpture.

These daring depictions, exhibited in the museum with the name of the naturalist who dreamed them up, are truly odd and extremely interesting.

Maria was wide-eyed as she beheld these imaginary beings, whereas Paolo, though also seeing them for the first time, smiled and every so often couldn't help but break out in laughter.

"Oh, my dear Maria, how comical these planetary angels are, how grotesque, above all, how impossible! It seems to me that the naturalists who have discovered them must have known very little comparative anatomy and even less biology. We can imagine only anthropomorphic forms, and so, just as the ancient founders of theogonies could fashion their gods only by clothing them in human skin, so these odd creators of *supermen* were unable to go beyond the human and the animal world.[5]

"Look here, at this 'Venusian'! How funny it is! They've stuck two wings on it—which is the oldest dream we have—and created the angels of theogonies of the Christian, Islamic, and a good many other religions. Man has always longed to fly, and by tacking on two big goose or swan or eagle wings has created his angels. But at least this inhabitant of Venus also has a third eye in its occipit, to see behind it, without needing to turn around. The only really brilliant thing I see depicted in this superman is the clean separation of the urinary and reproductive organs—a fusion that has always, in every age, made men blush and that seems to everyone to be a great mistake on nature's part, destined to disappear with the morphological progress of the higher animals."

Maria blushed without replying and immediately moved on to look at the inhabitants of Mars, Mercury, and Jupiter.

The wildest fantasy had created monstrous, strange, impossible beings that otherwise only the pen of the ancient Doré could have depicted.[6]

In all these monsters, however, one could not find a single organ that did not already exist in man or in other animals, so that the new planetary creature was merely a mosaic of different body parts taken now from birds, now from fish or from insects and mollusks.

You see a superman covered in multicolored feathers, so that he could do without clothing.

You see another fitted with an electrical device that can unleash currents so powerful they would kill any worm or animal it might wish to injure.

Other planetary supermen are endowed here or there with special organs for electric or magnetic sensitivity, but if the fanciful naturalist had managed to guess the function, he had not, however, been able to create the organ itself, and in its place one can read nothing but *organ of electricity* or *magnetic organ*.

Leaving the museum of planetary monsters created by the bizarre imagination of certain naturalists of the year 3000, Paolo, laughing his last and heartiest laugh, had to say:

"Oh, how disappointed these dreamers will be when the telescope has shown them the real inhabitants of the other planets!"

And they headed on to the central section of the museum, no longer devoted to products of Nature but of man.

—•—

Everywhere, in fact, over the many doors leading to that area, you read the same words:

Human labor.

The layout of this department is truly quite ingenious, so devised that you can study at one moment a single industry or form of work across time and space, at another moment all the industry of a single people.

Anyone who crosses the rooms that open one after another in concentric circles studies a single industry, whereas anyone who crosses from the edge to the center can admire all the forms of labor of a single people.

The circular walk is the study of a single industry over time, whereas the centrifugal walk is the psychic examination of a whole people.

In that first visit to the Museum of Andropolis our travelers made only a rapid tour, to get a general sense of it, to admire the outlines, the profile, if I may put it that way, of that giant treasury that brings together the fruit of all human travail over time and space. And I assure you that, on returning home, they were worn out not only in their legs but even more by their excessively long-sustained concentration and the ordeal of so many surprises and emotions.

On that first day, after a tour through all the industries and among the many radii that branch off from that synthetic circle of human labor, they entered only into the section devoted to Italy, which gave them no cause for shame, because even in the year 3000 this country, gently extending between two azure seas as if set between West and East, has still kept front rank in the arts of the beautiful, heir to the great Greek civilization, having had many flourishings, one after another, like so many springtimes.[7]

And just as in the first room that opens the door to the hundred that follow, one sees admirably represented over a large wall map the line, now ascending, now descending, of the main forms of human labor. Maria paused over a black spot, a blot drawn over the last period of the nineteenth century.

"Paolo dear, what's that blot doing there?"

"It is a mark of shame on ancient Italian art, but one that fortunately lasted very briefly. At the end of the nineteenth century there came a period of great decadence, particularly in architecture and painting. At that time mediocre artists, too proud to copy antiquity and not knowing how to create any new form of beauty, lapsed into grotesquery. Forgetful of being the sons of Raffaello, Michelangelo, Brunelleschi, Correggio, and a whole pleiad of divine creators, they made the ugly and the strange a new god or, to be more precise, a new monster of aesthetics, founding the school of *Impressionists*, of *Pointillists*, of *Decadents*, and numerous other monstrosities that inspire only our laughter.

"And just think that in that sickly artistic period even the literati came down with the same illness and wrote in a jargon so baroque, so clumsy and monstrous, that the most aesthetic people to inhabit our planet after the Greeks lost all sense of aesthetics. It was a true epidemic of Preraphaelitism, of the superhuman, that afflicted even very high and powerful minds, such as that of an Abruzzese, one Gabriele d'Annunzio, who, had he lived in other times, would have managed to be one of the great masters of art.

"And instead he was merely a great neurasthenic of Italian literature."[8]

12

THE CITY OF GOD IN ANDROPOLIS.
The Temple of Hope. The church of
the Evangelists. The Temple of the
Unknown God.

IN THE YEAR 3000 IT IS CENTURIES SINCE
a single state religion has existed. Rome has no pope, and the Buddhist
temples and the mosques have all crumbled away, having neither
clerics nor worshipers.

The most cultivated sector of every country professes no faith,
though the vast majority of men and almost all women believe in
the immortality of the soul and in God.

The need for the ideal, rather than vanishing from the face of the
earth, has steadily increased, entrusting itself and uplifting itself
with each forward step civilization takes, making the struggle for
existence less painful and leaving considerable time for the satisfac-
tions of higher needs.

Everyone is free to believe or not to believe in God or in eternal life, but all those who do have a common faith feel the need to join forces and cleave together, to raise a temple and found a form of worship that may unite them beneath the vaults of a single church in prayer, in hope, in adoration.

In Andropolis, a few kilometers from the capital city, a whole wide, verdant valley of forests has been allotted to the dominant religions, and accordingly this valley is called the City of God.

The most beautiful, largest, and most widely attended temple is that of *Hope*, erected by the believers of the whole world to an *imaginary* God—that is to say, to a symbol that contains in itself all our fear of death and all our aspirations to an eternal life and a better earthly life for ourselves.

Our travelers, visiting the City of God, entered into this church, particularly because the cult of Hope was Maria's religion. As for Paolo, he had never felt the need for any form of worship, and whenever his companion sought to convert him to her faith, he would fend her off with a joke and a noncommittal smile.[1]

The Temple of Hope is of immense proportions, magnificent in its marbles, golds, and bronzes, built in an architecture reminiscent of ancient Gothic, though less jumbled and complicated.

On the temple's pronaos is written the same commandment that Paolo and Maria had read in the great cemetery of Andropolis: *Have hope.*[2] This message is reproduced a hundred, a thousand times, painted, carved, sculpted everywhere.

In the center of the church stands a statue of solid gold, with diamonds for eyes—representing Hope. It is a replica, much richer and much more gigantic, of the one our travelers saw in the City of the Dead.

On the statue's pedestal appear these words, the daily prayer of all believers in the religion of hope:

> *O haughty man, how and why would you dare to deny life beyond the tomb?*
> *O ignorant man, how would you profess a second life?*

Suspended forever between the two abysses of ignorance and
arrogance, heal your thought and feeling in the religion of hope.
To believe what your ancient forefathers believed is nonsense.
To deny God and the second life is pride.
The wise man must neither believe nor deny. He must hope.

Around that statue are spread many rugs, and the faithful are seen crouching or kneeling. Some pray with joined hands, some appear to meditate, and some read a prayer book.

Still others are seen laying crowns of flowers at the feet of the Goddess, while others using censers burn delicate scents that waft through the air their azure cloudlets, which seem to enwrap the statue in a cloud of perfume.

The large windows of the temple are all made of a deep blue glass, shedding a fantastical, solemn light over the church.

In that hour, then, the subterranean music of a huge organ was spreading its melancholy notes through the air. Everything in this space seemed appointed to reawaken in the faithful images of an infinite and mysterious future, and the hieratic eloquence of the setting was so powerful that even Paolo felt the need to kneel beside Maria, hiding his face in his joined hands and letting himself be transported far, far away by a vague emotion.

Maria had already been praying for some minutes when, raising her eyes, she saw her Paolo beside her prostrate in the act of prayer. She could not help but smile and say to him:

"O incredulous one, what are you doing? Are you also praying to our Goddess?"

"No, I am not praying, my adored Maria, but I am thinking that all the knowledge and science in this world will never be able to stifle the human need to look beyond the grave, hoping and believing."

They rose, taking a tour around the church and pausing at the altars, which stand in their varied architecture all about the temple.

The altars, I am tempted to say, are so many little churches erected to different forms of the ideal, like the minor altars in ancient Christian churches arrayed around the main altar. In every religion the major gods have always had, like the kings, a general staff of lesser gods or saints to crown them.

And in the Temple of Hope as well, around the great Goddess are seen the minor altars, consecrated to the Beautiful, the Good, the True, to Sacrifice, to Health, to Strength, to Grace, to Courtesy, and almost all the human virtues.

And each altar has its own worshipers who prefer them to all others and bring them flowers and perfumes, the two oldest forms of any cult, once it has abolished blood and burnt offerings.

The cult of this new Goddess of Hope is utterly simple, since its only priests are a few preachers who every day from high in a temple pulpit offer orations on morals or aesthetics but above all on comfort for moral sufferings that unfortunately, even in the thirty-first century, embitter human existence.

Various sermons are delivered at different hours of the day and also in the evening. Every morning, on a roll placed on the door of the temple, one can read the program of the day's sermons, with the hour and the name of the preacher.

For the day of Paolo and Maria's visit to the City of God the program was as follows:

9th hour: Preacher Angelo Feneloni.—
The ignorance and arrogance of deniers of the supersensible world.
11th hour: Preacher Marco Marchi.—
The unhappiness of disbelievers.
13th hour: Preacher Roberto Fedi.—
The future of the religion of hope.
15th hour: Preacher Anselmo Cristiani.—
Charity in religion.
17th hour: Preacher Roberto Speri.—
Critique of religion founded on the cult of suffering.
19th hour: Preacher Alessandro Cesari.—
The struggle against doubt and skepticism.
21st hour: Preacher Dario Devi.—
The poetry of faith and the poetry of hope.

23rd hour: Preacher Paolo Santi.—
On the best ways to convert disbelievers to the religion of hope.

The cult's expenses are paid with the spontaneous offerings of the faithful; the government contributes nothing.

Every year in the calendar of these believers there occur three great festivals.

The most solemn is that of January 1, in which vows are made so that the new year will be happy.

A second festival is observed on April 1, to celebrate the dawn of spring.

And a third, that of October 1, is dedicated to commemorating the founder of the religion of Hope and its greatest preachers, who were that founder's most eloquent and effective apostles.

Since this religion now has the greatest number of followers, a great crowd takes part in these festivals.

The temple is then completely decked out with flowers, and the music of a hundred and a thousand instruments sets the temple vaults vibrating to the most divine harmonies, while clouds of perfumes waft delightful fragrances through the air. By day it is the festival of perfume and harmony, but by night it is the festival of light, and millions of small multicolored flames adorn the temple and the believers' houses.

—•—

Not far from the Temple of Hope, which not only in Andropolis but in all the world's great cities unites the largest number of the faithful, stands the *Christian church*.

Three thousand years of history have passed since the cradle of Bethlehem, which transformed the world, yet still Christ has churches and believers. The Catholic religion vanished over five centuries ago, destroyed by the simony and stubborn ignorance of the last popes, and all the other Christian churches have merged into a single one that rather closely resembles that of the ancient Waldensians.[3]

Christ's religion has been freed of metaphysical dogmas and many ridiculous rituals and has become almost thoroughly just a very lofty form of charity.

Believing or not believing in the divinity of Jesus is left to the faith of each person, but the Evangelicals (as the followers of the Christian Church are called) are baptized at birth with a fairly odd ritual, which consists of wetting the forehead of the newborn with a drop of blood taken from the arm of the father and a drop of blood from its mother.

The priest performs this ritual in the church and upon wetting the forehead says:

You, child of love and suffering, will live loving and suffering.

Your suffering will always come after that of others, and with your love you will heal the suffering of men, who are all your brethren.

In the name of love, in the name of suffering, in the name of Christ, who died for us, I baptize you and call you, etc. etc.

This is the baptism of Evangelicals in the year 3000.

The only sacraments are *confirmation*, *marriage*, and *extreme unction*.

Confirmation is merely a second baptism, administered by the priest at the first sign of puberty.

The neophyte must swear to devote his life to charity, to being a faithful husband and perfect father.

Marriage is strictly religious and is consecrated in the church with a solemn and very poetic ritual centering around flowers and music.

Divorce is granted to all, though hedged with the most serious guarantees, proof against the whims of vice.

Extreme unction has remained as a memento of the analogous Catholic sacrament and is like a farewell that the survivors give to the person who is about to leave this world to enter into eternal life, in which all Evangelicals believe.

Beyond these sacraments, with which they give a religious stamp to the most important acts in life, they have nothing else but prayer and preaching.

They gather in the church on Sunday, and on other solemn days, to listen to the word of the priest (who is always married, indeed must always be married) or else to pray.

They pray alone or all together, singing in chorus, accompanied by organ music.

The Evangelical religion is prevalent above all in northern Europe, where it can truly be said to be the dominant one. But it also has other lesser centers in North America, Tibet, and Siberia.

In Andropolis it has only one temple in the City of God, but this one may well be the largest and most beautiful in the world.

Paolo and Maria visited it and were amazed to find quite faithfully reproduced the ancient cathedral of Florence, Santa Maria del Fiore, which no longer exists, but whose design they had seen in many works of history and architecture.

It is a severe, melancholy church, without paintings or statues, and it inspires respect and encourages silence and meditation.

Walking in that temple one feels the need to slow one's pace and take it in almost mutely, any noise seeming a profanation. To everyone it seems that in that silence the only voice entitled to be heard is that of the priest from high upon a pulpit and the sound of the organ from the crypt of the temple.

In the Evangelical Church, at its two ends, one finds only two facing altars.

In one of them stands a bronze Christ crucified, giant and solemn—the work of one of the greatest Italian artists, who lived in the twenty-fifth century and was called the *New Michelangelo*. Surrounding that bronze thousands upon thousands of small flames are lit day and night.

It is the altar of suffering and sacrifice.

Facing it, the second altar is dedicated to the Virgin Mary. She is depicted in a giant statue of white marble, in the act of opening her arms to the whole world holding crowns of flowers—the work of a famous English sculptor who also lived in the twenty-fifth century and was gloriously baptized the *Second Donatello*.[4]

It is the altar of love and charity.

Our travelers paused some moments before these two altars, observing that before the second many women were prostrate, whereas before the first the faithful kneeling were almost all men.

"You know, Maria my darling, if ever I did feel the need for a religion, I would turn Evangelical, because in this Church, before these two altars, which seem to me to have been erected on the highest summits of human ideality, I feel uplifted. There where reason grows silent, the base instincts disappear, and man feels himself completely transported above daily life to breathe in the purest air and bless himself with a fantastic light not of this world. Before the crucified Christ, who gives his life to redeem the world from Adam's great sin, before the man who proclaims the greatness of the humble, I see the highest aim to which we can aspire, that of sacrificing the individual to the good of all.

"And there, before that Madonna-Goddess who opens her arms to press all humanity to her heart, I see sanctified charity in its tenderest, warmest form—in the maternal and divine love that makes all people its children.

"In the two altars standing in this temple of Evangelicals I see the two poles between which the whole human family moves, *Love* and *Suffering*; I see the fount from which rose and will rise again all the religions that are not fetishisms or idolatries, but aspirations toward the high, toward the infinite; toward something that is less transient, less frail than our poor earthly life."

—•—

With much emotion Paolo and Maria left the Evangelical Church and made their way to a third temple, entirely surrounded by a forest so thick with centuries-old trees that you can barely make out the vast edifice that seems to be hiding amid all that green.

It is the Church of the Deists.

They copied the ancient Pantheon of Rome, and on the door of the temple one reads: *To the Unknown God.*[5]

Bare, the inner walls: neither paintings nor statues nor pulpits nor altars. Only in the middle of the circular edifice stands a great bronze stele on which, night and day, an azure flame is always lit.

Here and there you see the odd worshiper, standing, looking at the flame that noiselessly casts about it its sad and livid light. Not a single woman in this Church of Deists.

Maria frowned, with a sorrowful emotion on her face, and said: "Paolo, dear, I feel a great chill in this temple."

"I feel it too, Maria. I can very well comprehend the worshipers of Hope, I understand the Evangelical religion, but I have never understood what the Deists want with their religion.

"The Unknown God has existed at all the times and for all thinkers without excessive pride. Man knows so little of the world around him and the forces that move him: he is born, he lives and dies between two impenetrable abysses of ignorance, the very small and the very large, and is forced to place at the end of every perplexity, every item of curiosity he has, a great question mark.

"All this is logical, it is natural, it is inevitable, but are we always to remain in the field of thought? How can one worship a perhaps, a question mark? The *Unknown God* is a pure and simple confession of ignorance, but it cannot provide material for a form of devotion, a religion.

"Religion is made of feeling and not thought, and I can't understand it without an altar, without a priest, without a cult. And here I see only bare walls, and I breathe in a freezing air, *senza tempo tinta*, as a great poet said many centuries ago.[6] Nothing speaks to my heart; that pale blue flame eternally lit on that bronze stele says nothing to me.

"No, no, and no! I might well convert one day to your religion, that of Hope; if I were very unhappy I might become an Evangelical, but a deist, never."

"Neither could I," added Maria, accompanying her words with a shiver that ran through her whole body, as if she felt great cold.

And our travelers, homeward bound, left the Temple of the Unknown God.

13

MARIA'S BAD MOOD AND PAOLO'S secret. A session of the Andropolis Academy and the awarding of the cosmic prize. Fertile marriage.

FOR DAYS NOW MARIA HAD BEEN IN THE foulest mood. The wonders of Andropolis, which she was seeing now for the first time, would distract her for a few hours, after which she would plunge back into her usual sadness.

But I'm expressing myself poorly: she wasn't sad, she couldn't be. She loved Paolo with all her heart and mind, and now she was fulfilling the loftiest dream in her life, that of visiting the planet's capital during a trip around the world.

No, she was not sad. She was cross, irritated, upset.

Paolo, who was accustomed to seeing her always placid, dividing her days between one smile and another, had already asked her a few times:

"What's wrong, darling? Aren't you feeling well? Are you tired? Do you want to rest, perhaps, take a few days off from all this constant sightseeing?"

And she would answer irritably, with that look that almost always puts a halt to any further questioning:

"Nothing's wrong, I feel perfectly fine."

One day, though, Paolo added caresses and so much force to the question that she could no longer hold out.

"All right, then, here's why I'm in such a bad mood. You've always told me that the first proof of loving and of two people living one life together was that they no longer kept the slightest secret from one another. And you've repeated to me I don't know how many times that the first lie out of the mouth of a lover to her beloved shatters the harmony between them and jeopardizes their love.

"You know that I, from the day I told you 'I'm yours,' have never thought anything that you didn't know an hour later, nor have I even once felt a joy or sorrow that was not yours immediately after.

"And you too, my dear Paolo, have opened your whole soul to me, and yet you've also said to me that you're keeping a little secret that wasn't wrong or sinful, but that you'd reveal it only at Andropolis.

"I never took offense at this mystery and thought it was nothing but a clever ploy to make me desire something new, since living with you I've had nothing, nothing at all left to desire. Only now we've been in Andropolis for two months, and you haven't unveiled your secret.

"And I have been steadily waiting and still wait; but by now my curiosity has turned into impatience, and the impatience has turned into pain. I torment and lash at myself, suspecting that the secret isn't a mystery but a wrong, some wrong you have not had the courage to confide in me, fearing perhaps that my respect for you would diminish, that respect that is as great as my love. Or if it isn't a wrong, it is at least a weakness, and you, who are the strongest of the strong, are afraid that in the mirror of your soul, that mirror as polished and dazzling as steel, I might see a stain . . ."

Paolo was listening to her and smiling, kissing her hands and fondling her hair . . .

"You dear mad creature, you dear little clown! Little did I know how suspicious and touchy you could be. I promised to unveil my great secret, the only one I have kept from you, at Andropolis, but I never said what day I would reveal it, or if that day would come sooner or later, or perhaps be the last day, the day we leave. So you see, I haven't broken my word yet nor forgotten my promise.

"Well then, the day of revelation has come, and I declare to you, aloud, and most solemnly:

"Tomorrow you will know my secret, on proclamation day for the cosmic prize."

"What time, and where?"

"At the hour of the proclamation, in the great hall of the Academy."

Maria leapt to Paolo's neck and, happy as a frolicking foal, kissed him again and again.

Her bad mood, her displeasure had vanished, dissipating like morning fog at the first ray of sun.

All day long her happiness, accumulated and for so many days unspent, came unleashed, flooding Paolo too with a mad joy. They danced, they leapt, they went chasing each other like children.

Joy is always young, and in its loveliest forms it is even infantile. And all that day and the morning after Paolo and Maria were both no older than sixteen.

—•—

The Andropolis Academy is the world's oldest scientific institute. Its hundred members are culled from the farthest regions and make up, I would say, a true Senate of knowledge.

Chosen by the free vote of all the world's thinkers, they represent all the branches of science, literature, and the arts and have no other obligation than to appear in Andropolis once a year, to be precise on December 31, when the secretaries of the different regions present a summation of the year's scientific, literary and artistic year, each in the discipline assigned to him.

On their return to their country they correspond with the Academy, to address the various questions they have been entrusted with in their study. Thirty of them, chosen by lot, live for the whole year in the capital, where they are splendidly housed. Their honorarium is 500,000 lire a year.

Every ten years they all come together to give the cosmic prize to the person who has made the greatest discovery of that decade. The prize is for a million lire, and the winner then has the right to sit on the government's Supreme Council and takes the title of Sopho, the world's highest term of honor, equal only to that of Pancrat.

In the year 3000, it has been a decade since the last prize, and there are 150 contenders.

It was the very next day after Paolo and Maria had the discussion I have referred to, that the cosmic prize was to be awarded; and our travelers went to the Academy, which they found thronged with hundreds upon hundreds of the curious, come from every part of the world to attend this great festival of knowledge.

The city was entirely festooned, the shops were all closed, and in the plaza music of all sorts filled the air with delicious harmony.

On entering into the great assembly hall Maria saw, to her great amazement, that Paolo led her straight to two large gilded chairs among those reserved for the Pancrat and his ministers.

"But Paolo, dear, why ever are we sitting here? Wouldn't it be better to join the general public and sit over there, where we could view and observe everything at out ease?"

"No, my dear Mariuccia, because this is the seat I've been assigned, and the president has given me permission for you too to sit here beside me. And today it is here that you will have revealed to you my secret, my one and only secret."

Maria was silent, immersed in the ecstasy of a great wonder, in the greatest amazement.

Meanwhile the hall was getting more and more crowded, and a delightful music was soothing everyone's impatient waiting.

All at once the music stopped, a solemn silence spread, and the Academy chairmen took their places, sitting down among the hundred senators of science.

Amid them in a higher armchair sat the president, who wore dangling from a palladium chain at his neck a great gold medal, suggesting that at other times too he had presented the cosmic prize he was about to give out.

The president rose and after declaring the session opened invited the secretary general to read the report on the cosmic prize, which I shall cite only in its main points.

"The competitors for the cosmic prize of the year 3000 are 150. A preliminary analysis of the submissions immediately narrowed the choice down to 50.

"The second stage of selection was harder, because among those fifty discoveries and inventions were many of real value; but gradually the fifty became three, and out of the three it was not difficult to choose the one and assign second and third prize to the others.

"The English engineer John Newton has invented a giant drill moved by a new electrical machine that allows us to bore through our entire planet, reaching the center of the earth. Thus we can know the true structure of the globe, up to now only guessed at but never known—who knows, then, how many new powers we can tap into in the future. The invention is extraordinarily important, and thus we have awarded the engineer John Newton third prize.

"I invite him to come up to the Board, to receive the prize."

The engineer Newton was seated next to Paolo. He stood up and went to the bench of the Sopho, receiving a diploma and a medal.

The music intoned its harmonies, and all those present stood up to applaud the prize winner.

And the secretary continued to read his report:

"The famous astronomer Carlo Copernic has so perfected the telescope that we can see the inhabitants of the nearest planets. This invention marks a new era in the history of civilization, allowing us to broaden the frontiers of the known world. It will infinitely increase the treasury of our thought, also giving us cause to hope that in the not too distant future we can enter into relations with our planetary brothers.

"And so it seems reasonable and just to grant second prize to the astronomer Copernic."

And again new applause and new harmonies.

After Copernic had received the prize there was a long pause of silence and expectation. That silence expressed the boundless curiosity to know who could possibly have made an even greater discovery. To drill through the earth from one end to the other and communicate directly with the antipodals!

And to spy out the life of the inhabitants of Venus, Mercury, Mars! What could be greater?

And the secretary resumed his speech.

—•—

"The third discovery, ladies and gentlemen, is surely the greatest. It is that of the *psychoscope*, a device that allows us to easily read the thoughts of others to whom it is directed.[1]

"I call on Mr. Paolo Fortunati of Rome to step forward now to the bench of the prize committee to demonstrate how the psychoscope actually works."

With these words Maria felt her heart start to pound and looked at Paolo, who after squeezing her hand tight whispered into her ear:

"That was my secret!"

He got up and, making his way to the Academy president's side, took from his pocket a little instrument resembling pocket binoculars and turned it toward the audience.

The silence had been very great, once the secretary had spoken, but now a great noise of chairs shuffling and of people rising upset the peace and serenity of that sacred place of science.

It was the noise of many who suddenly were leaving the hall out of fear of having the thoughts read that were passing through their mind at that moment.

Paolo, despite being extremely moved at that moment, could not help but laugh at this tumultuous flight.

Scarcely had the silence of expectancy returned, with no one stirring, than Paolo trained the psychoscope on a boy of perhaps ten, who was sitting beside his mother, and he said:

"This lad you see here is thinking with great pain of how bored he is to be stuck in this hall hearing speeches he doesn't understand while at home his brothers are playing ball in the garden. His mind is hurling curses at us all . . ."

All the assembly broke out in Homeric laughter.

Paolo now turned his instrument here and there, as though searching for someone or something and unsure where to stop it.

"I won't point out anyone in particular, but in more than ten of the people convened here I read a consummate disdain for the grave injustice committed toward them by our members of the academy. They were competing for the cosmic prize and did not make the finals . . . In one of them I also read horrible thoughts of hatred and revenge . . ."

With these words the earlier tumult swelled up again, only more violently. Added to the noise of chairs shifting and falling as people left the hall were angry shouts:

"It's an outrage! An outrage! Down with the psychoscope! . . ."

Paolo remained undaunted, and the president rang the bell several times, calling for calm and quiet.

Meanwhile more than half the hall had emptied out, and the secretary could resume speaking:

"The Academy decided unanimously to grant the first prize to Mr. Fortunati because, if the other two discoveries enlarge the boundaries of the knowable, the psychoscope allows us a new era of morality and sincerity among humans.

"When we all know that anyone can read into our brain, we will have to overcome contradictions between our thoughts and our actions; we will be as good in our thoughts as we will try to be in our actions. It is to be hoped that with the psychoscope lying will be banished from the world or at least become a very rare phenomenon, something on the wane everywhere, like all functions and organs that no longer have a necessary or useful purpose.

"Not to mention all the advantages that the new tool can bring us in the diagnosis of mental illnesses, in education, in psychology. The science of thought will very soon enter a new world, and surely it is more useful for humankind to know itself than to know the center of the earth or the inhabitants of the other planets.

"Ever since man has appeared on the earth he has made immense progress in the sciences, the arts, literature—in all that concerns the life of thought; but progress in morality still lags far behind and far out of harmony with that of the mind. The psychoscope promises us to achieve this dream of all the ages, namely that moral progress should parallel intellectual progress; and since we all believe that the former is much more important than the latter for human happiness, the Academy has therefore thought it should award the first prize to Mr. Paolo Fortunati, inventor of the psychoscope."[2]

Everyone who still remained in the hall, because they were not afraid that the terrible optic device would read some wicked thought in their head, rose to their feet, thunderously applauding the fortunate winner of the cosmic prize and the fact that his name almost foretold his glory . . .

The only person who did not rise was the happiest and most moved.

It was Maria, who buried her face in her handkerchief to hide the tears of boundless joy flooding into her from head to toe . . .

Paolo meanwhile had risen from the committee members' stand, returning to his seat; and there the tears of the happy couple mingled together, joining them in the ecstasy of a single elation.

And all those present gazed at this sight of a happy couple, persuaded that the embrace of that woman in that moment, in that place, was the first and highest prize for Paolo's immortal discovery . . .

A few days later Paolo and Maria, granted the high consent of the Health Tribunal of Andropolis to join together in fertile marriage, received the solemn sacrament in the Temple of Hope. From being lovers for several years they now became husband and wife, having won, by consent of science, the highest of rights, which once in barbaric times had been granted to all—that is, the right to transmit life to future generations.

Editor's Notes on the Text

Chapter 1

1. The projected speed of 150 kilometers per hour (which, curiously, Emilio Salgari also chooses for his flying vessels in *Le Meraviglie del Duemila*) is actually not so exceptional for the fourth millennium. The average speed of passenger trains in Europe around 1900 was 15 to 25 miles (24 to 40 kilometers) per hour. However, already between 1901 and 1903 two Siemens and AEG electric test cars, on a five-mile-long railway near Berlin, had reached 135 miles (217 kilometers) per hour, and in 1938 the steam locomotive *Mallard* would set a world speed record on the U.S. East Coast main line of 126 miles (202 kilometers) per hour. See Patrick Ransome-Wallis, *Illustrated Encyclopedia of World Railway Locomotives* (New York: Dover Publications, 2001); Don Hale, *Mallard: How the World Steam Speed Record Was Broken* (London: Aurum P, 2005).

2. Cohobated aethers are highly concentrated aromatic substances resulting from repeated distillation of the same matter. Just as Mantegazza introduces these synthetic foods in the diet of the fourth millennium, Antonio Ghislanzoni in *Abrakadabra* had described highly energetic lion's marrow pills, and Agostino Della Sala Spada in *Nel 2073! Sogni di uno stravagante* had introduced food tablets. See Antonio Ghislanzoni, *Abrakadabra. La Contessa di Karolystria*, ed. Edoardo Villa (Milan: Marzorati, 1969), 89–90; Agostino Della Sala Spada, *Nel 2073! Sogno di uno stravagante*, ed. and intro. Simonetta Satragni Petruzzi (Alessandria: Edizioni dell'Orso, 1998), 29, 48. Beyond mere satisfaction of hunger, however, Mantegazza here extends the power of these synthetic foods to emotional stimulation as well.

3. By not qualifying the "Cosmic" language as any known past or surviving idiom, Mantegazza proves more radical than other utopian authors who also imagined a universal language. For instance, the language in Émile Souvestre's year 3000 is "a mixture of French, English, and German" (*The World as It Shall Be*, trans. Margaret Clarke, ed. and intro. I. F. Clarke [Middletown CT: Wesleyan UP, 2004), 13]), while Agostino Della Sala Spada chose Latin in *Nel 2073!* and Antonio Ghislanzoni French in *Abrakadabra*. The "one and indivisible language" in H. G. Wells's *A Modern Utopia* would be "a coalesced language, a synthesis of many," more inclusive than the fusion of Anglo-

Saxon, Norman French, and scholar's Latin in the English tongue. Like Mantegazza, then, Wells does not identify the roots of his "utopian tongue." However, Wells does not seem to aim at his predecessor's absolute novelty, still retaining a link with linguistic tradition by hypothesizing a "wedding and survival of several [languages] in a common offspring," rather than a radical break from the past, as in Mantegazza's futuristic world. See H. G. Wells, *A Modern Utopia*, intro. Mark R. Hillegas (Lincoln: U of Nebraska P, 1967), 21–22.

4. By making his characters undertake an eastward journey, Mantegazza breaks from the myth of the West as the virgin land of the unknown and the future. The choice of Darjeeling as the location for the new capital of the United Planetary States reflects Mantegazza's attraction to India as the cradle of Indo-European civilization, which in *The Year 3000* seems to have acquired global proportions. In his travelogue *India*, written in 1884 after his journey to that land, Mantegazza extols India as "the country that gave us the blood, the language, the religion, and the bread of daily life, and that other, golden bread, as necessary, nay, more necessary perhaps, than the first, which is the ideal." See Paolo Mantegazza, *The Physiology of Love and Other Writings*, ed., intro., and notes Nicoletta Pireddu, trans. David Jacobson (Toronto: U of Toronto P, 2007), 424. At the same time, however, as the novel eloquently shows, the capital city is anything but archaic. It hence combines the aura of its foundational past with the technological power of the new civilization.

5. Ettore Regalia, an Italian anthropologist, psychologist, and paleontologist from Parma, in the 1870s repeatedly explored the "Grotta dei Colombi" on the island of Palmaria, off LaSpezia. There he found evidence supporting ethnic and psychic studies of local prehistoric populations and their flora and fauna.

6. Before Emilio Salgari, who in *Le Meraviglie del Duemila* foresees a catastrophic war around the 1940s that would put an end to conflicts and armies, Mantegazza here gives us a forecast of World War I. Even more specifically Mantegazza's references to two conflicts, one at sea and one in France, might be retrospectively connected with the Jutland battle and the disastrous French battle at Verdun, both of which took place in 1916.

7. Similarly Agostino Della Sala Spada in *Nel 2073!* foresaw the downfall of communism, as Emilio Salgari would do in *Le Meraviglie del Duemila*.

8. These are the first of numerous eugenic concerns in the novel. However, considering Mantegazza's background in medicine and his astonishing foresight, it is surprising to find only a sixty-year average life expectancy in his

fourth millennium. In chapter 5, though, we will find evidence of slightly higher longevity.

9. Carlo Porta (1775–1821) was an Italian poet from Mantegazza's region, the author of numerous works in the Milanese dialect, including the colorful descriptions of popular life in Milan in *Desgrazzi de Giovannin Bongee* (1814).

Chapter 2

1. Curiously the Sahara desert had already become a sea in Della Sala Spada's *Nel 2073!*

2. Some hints of Souvestre's *The World as It Shall Be* resonate here. Mantegazza's *Cosmos* arriving in Egypt to disembark passengers while heading to more remote areas of the world sounds like a more subdued equivalent of Souvestre's *Cosmopolitan*, an "extraordinary ship . . . several kilometers in length" (71), a "'great floating village . . . arriving back from its world tour' and now allowing passengers to disembark at Cairo" (71). Curiously Jules Verne seems to elaborate on Souvestre's floating village in his 1895 adventure novel *Propeller Island*, which describes an even bulkier artificial island-ship, *Standard Island*. However, while Souvestre and Verne aim at impressing readers with the extraordinary dimensions of their machines, Mantegazza, with a significant change in sensitivity, prefers to emphasize the leanness and efficiency of the vessel, just as the modest size of his aerotach goes hand in hand with greater manageability and performance.

3. This detail about the difficulties of managing coal reflects actual changes already taking place in the Italian energy system at the end of the 1880s. A country poor in coal but rich in hydric resources, Italy understood both the economic and the environmental advantages of shifting to electricity and, in particular, from thermoelectric to hydroelectric plants.

4. Souvestre provides similar details for the homes in Sans-Pair, "quadrangular buildings that looked so much alike that they could only be distinguished by their house numbers" (*World* 69).

5. King Bomba was Ferdinand II (1810–59), King of the Two Sicilies, the first monarch against whom the Italian liberal movement revolted in 1848. When he bombarded the city of Messina to subdue the insurrection, his democratic adversaries labeled him "Re Bomba."

6. As the chapter will soon explain the city is named after Filippo Turati (1857–1932), an Italian journalist and politician, and—together with his companion Anna Kulischov—an intellectual pivotal to the creation of the Italian Socialist Party (1892).

7. This may be a reference to Alberto Bianchini, the protagonist of the 1893 novel *Primo Maggio*, written by Edmondo De Amicis (mentioned later in this chapter) after his conversion to socialism. A schoolteacher from Turin, Angelo Bianchini writes a book denouncing child labor and is killed by the military police on May 1 during a political demonstration.

8. Edmondo De Amicis (1846–1908) was an Italian novelist and journalist best known for his 1886 masterpiece, *Cuore* (*Heart*). This children's novel, set at the time of Italy's unification, deals with important patriotic and social issues and emphasizes emotions. One year later Mantegazza would write a literary response to *Cuore* with his novel *Testa* (*Head*), where he highlights the importance of instilling ideas in young minds. De Amicis's nationalist perspective merged with socialist sympathies, leading to his adhesion to the Italian Socialist Party in 1896.

Chapter 3

1. Here we begin to perceive Mantegazza's penchant for asserting the combination of science and art, rather than their incompatibility.

2. Legend has it that when the Italian scientist Galileo Galilei (1564–1742) was still a teenager he watched a bronze incense burner swing in the Cathedral of Pisa and realized that it oscillated back and forth in the same amount of time regardless of each swing's amplitude. Upon this observation Galileo theorized the isochronism of the pendulum, which led to the most accurate technique for timekeeping.

3. A "gymnotus" is an electric eel.

4. Maria's questions and comments, here as throughout the novel, offer a more nuanced and complex perspective on the situations and values being introduced during their visits. But the conversations between the two protagonists or with other characters also reinforce gender stereotypes. The woman emerges as the spokesperson for more moderate and ethical standpoints, in part because of the greater innocence and lack of experience of her young age (emblematic of this is her underestimating self-definition as "an ignorant little woman" [104] who, already struggling with the management of the household, cannot even imagine how a few individuals—men of course—can govern an entire world from the capital). The man acts mainly as a paternalistic figure who embodies the rationality conventionally associated with masculinity, as Paolo's reassuring response to Maria's own self-belittlement well shows. The etymology of *Andropolis* seems to be yet another sign of the preeminence of virility in the United Planetary States. At the same time, however, Mantegazza also upgrades the status of women

in the fourth millennium, granting them political and educational emancipation, as subsequent chapters will show.

Chapter 4

1. In a similar move Jules Verne's novella *In the Year 2889* (1889; subsequently published in French in 1890 as *Au XXIXème siècle: La journée d'un journaliste Américain en* 2889) mentioned the transfer of the political center of the United States from Washington to Centropolis.

2. Once again Souvestre's *The World as It Shall Be* comes to mind: "The city square" of the capital Sans-Pair "where all the roads . . . converged . . . was embellished with fifty drinking fountains and two hundred gas lamps. The museum, the library, the national theater, and the chamber of deputies surrounded it" (69). However, as Mantegazza's description continues, the reader also perceives the crucial difference between the "regularity" of Souvestre's city, which "would have done credit to a chessboard" (*World* 69), and the lack of symmetry, the absence of restrictions, the vagaries of the terrain, and the variety of styles and materials on which Andropolis prides itself.

3. The *scudo* was a gold or silver coin issued in various Italian states from the late sixteenth through the early nineteenth century.

4. Despite the introduction of synthetic foods Mantegazza's fourth millennium does not seem ready to abandon more traditional (and healthier) pleasures of the palate and the eye. Anticipating the current burgeoning of food biotechnology, as Souvestre had already done with the giant fruits and vegetables of his own fourth millennium, Mantegazza perceives the benefits of technological applications to the improvement of food's nutritional power, of its variety and taste. Likewise, despite the high-tech profile of this futuristic society, aesthetics seems to be equally crucial, and flowers are the paramount embodiment of disinterested beauty. Incidentally Mantegazza here reproduces not only the content but also the ornate prose of other works of his where the charm of flowers is central—such as several passages in *Dizionario delle cose belle* and *The Legends of Flowers*.

5. Inserting details on his pioneering discoveries during his fieldwork in South America, Mantegazza here does not miss the opportunity to stage himself.

6. Selective breeding had already inspired projects for the improvement of the human race in the year 3000. In Souvestre's *The World as It Shall Be*, thanks to the techniques adopted by the English for domestic animals, the owner of a factory proudly presents their manufactured races of blacksmiths, porters, runners, and town criers, each manipulated so as to maximize their

ability to perform their selected task (106). H. G. Wells, more serious than Souvestre and as sensitive as Mantegazza to the problem of transmissible diseases, in *A Modern Utopia* would support preventative measures to avoid procreation in at-risk unions or, in case such measures were not implemented, the elimination of the diseased child, the imprisonment of the transgressive parents, and even sterilization if affected by a physical or mental illness.

Chapter 5

1. The *soldo* was a copper coin of Italy, one twentieth of a lira. Here we can see Mantegazza's polemical attitude toward the Italian administration and its excessively complicated mechanism. The simplification of the political organization and administrative management of his fourth millennium can be taken as a reaction against the reality of Mantegazza's homeland.

2. This is an interesting echo and revision of the "Universal Association of Civilization" in Félix Bodin's *Novel of the Future*, whose parliament convenes annually in different towns of the world.

3. In addition to reinstating the importance of nature as the model for culture (although in other passages of the novel it is the power of artificiality that can overcome a savage and barbarous nature), this physiological metaphor to explain connections among local political components and global institutions recalls similar images in other works by Mantegazza that adopt the principles of natural sciences as the framework for analyses of social behavior. Anthropology itself, for Mantegazza, was born as "a natural history of man," a man to be studied with the same "experimental criterion" adopted for "plants, animals and stones." See Paolo Mantegazza, "Trent'anni di storia della Società Italiana di Antropologia, Etnologia e Psicologia Comparata," *Archivio per l'antropologia e l'etnologia* 31 (1901); *In memoria del XXXo anno della Società Italiana d'Antropologia* (Florence: Salvatore Landi, 1910), 4. At times Mantegazza even put scientific taxonomies in the service of political ordering, as in the case of his memoirs about his experiences as a deputy and senator in the Italian parliament. Faithful to his main profession as "a naturalist and physiologist," Mantegazza here invokes the "natural method" and parodically classifies and subsequently analyzes his fellow politicians according to colorful typologies: "*Walk-on deputies*, including the variety of the *telegraphics*. *Profiteer deputies*, or *industrialists of politics*. *Forensic deputies*. *Conscientious deputies*. *Political deputies*." See Paolo Mantegazza, *Political Memoirs of a Foot-Soldier in the Italian Parliament*, in *Physiology of Love*, 509. Mantegazza hence offers interesting examples of the "systematic knowledge" at the foundation of what Robert Scholes has

defined as the "structural fabulation" of the science-fiction genre. See the introduction to this volume (34).

4. Corrosive sublimate, namely mercury chloride, is a very soluble and toxic form of mercury that was used in medicine in Mantegazza's time. It was utilized, for instance, in the cure of syphilis until the introduction of antibiotics.

5. The high rank of the Director reflects the importance that education held for Mantegazza, who believed it improved life in general and, in particular, could develop an Italian consciousness at a moment when Italy, having attained its much awaited unification, was facing the challenge of creating Italian citizenship and had, incidentally, an extremely elevated rate of illiteracy. It is hence probably not accidental that the Director here is Italian. In a sort of wish fulfillment Mantegazza seems to sublimate in the narrative his hope for capable people able to manage schools as a sign of the nation's commitment to such a crucial institution. Mantegazza had also discussed the Italian school system, without sparing it harsh criticism, in earlier fiction and nonfiction works like *Head* and *The Neurosic Century*. Other utopian writers also devoted attention to the school system in their futuristic works, portraying institutions that endorsed or challenged crucial social values. The high school of Sans-Pair in Souvestre's *The World as It Shall Be* pokes fun at the gap between a totally impractical, notion-based, and arid education (instruction in the by-then-dead language Tibetan; the study of hieroglyphs of doubtful authenticity; the mechanical testing of students; the compulsive production of "*forced* scholars, just as gardeners used to obtain melons of the best quality" [65]) and the need for professional skills in everyday life (the school allegedly prepares future engineers, doctors, and businessmen). At different points in chapter 21 of Edward Bellamy's *Looking Backward* Dr. Leete highlights the importance of the universality of education at the higher and lower levels, which in the year 2000 considerably improved the preparation of more disadvantaged classes while not erasing the intellectual differences created by nature. See Edward Bellamy, *Looking Backward. 2000–1887*, ed. Alex MacDonald (Peterborough CA: Broadview Literary Texts, 2003).

6. With respect to the social and political situation at Mantegazza's time, the United Planetary States grants important concessions to women, from universal suffrage (Italy would grant women unrestricted suffrage only in 1945) to coeducational schools (127–28) and equal opportunities for employment in education. (Until the Italian scholastic reform enacted by Giovanni Gentile in 1923, women in fact had fewer and far less varied school options, even though the teaching profession became one of the first dignified and

empowering professions for nineteenth-century Italian women. Here, significantly, the Director's comments displace to the year 3000 the perplexities of Mantegazza's time regarding the acceptable degree of female emancipation. Relying on the temporal shift to avoid any definitive pronouncement on an issue that was perceived as particularly problematic, Mantegazza seems to admit the need for better opportunities for women, yet he is equally worried about excesses that could blemish the essential features of the female gender so ingrained in the collective mentality of his century. Of this unnatural female being (according to male standards) we already have an example in Souvestre's Mlle. Spartacus, who incites women precisely to revolt against condemnation "to the abject cares of housekeeping and motherhood" (*World* 202) and, by proclaiming the "rights of liberated woman" (204), decrees the need to overturn the male-dominated gender hierarchy and rule over men in all sectors of life. Bellamy also upholds women's rights in *Looking Backward*. No longer economically dependent on men, women are granted full participation in society and politics, with freedom of choice in their personal and public lives and without being turned into men or set against men "in an unnatural rivalry" (197). Some years after Bellamy H. G. Wells, in *A Modern Utopia*, reiterates the problem of the economic disadvantage of women that turns difference into impairment, yet he ultimately shows the pitfalls of generalizations about "natural equality or inferiority of women to men" (200) and ascribes to his modern utopia the synthetic power "to reduce and simplify the compulsory canon, to admit alternatives and freedoms" (213) in the relation between the two sexes. Ultimately, however, motherhood seems to remain the main female occupation, although a mother or a mother-to-be has the right to remuneration above the minimum wage, as well as to freedom and respect. Furthermore childbearing itself is in some cases subject to rigorous restrictions. See note 7 below.

7. We can perceive the oscillations in the novel's overall message about freedom and imposition. Whereas, for instance, individual tastes and religious choices are encouraged, other sectors of life are strictly managed by planetary institutions, as in the consent to procreation and the disposal of unfit babies. H. G. Wells would present a similar tension in *A Modern Utopia* between, on the one hand, the need for a minimal state interference in the individual's private lives and, on the other, the urgent regulation of childbearing unions through licensing and profiling to be accomplished by public offices, for the protection of children (192–93).

8. The celebration of universal brotherhood through liberalizing economic measures seems to dissipate doubts that Mantegazza expressed earlier in his

Fisiologia dell'odio precisely about the methods to accomplish this supranational dimension. While several ethnicities are being destroyed (a phenomenon that Mantegazza also highlights in chapter 11), the advent of the United States of Europe is being announced as the first internationalist step toward the creation of one big human family. However, Mantegazza fears that behind the optimism for this future brotherhood of all individuals there might hide methods that are anything but fraternal, such as, for instance, the imposition of this union on the weakest individuals through harsh economic and military measures (oil and dynamite, as he claims), exactly like those democrats who want to attain an ideal and universal freedom through dictatorship. See *Fisiologia dell'odio*, 3rd ed. (Milan: Treves 1896): 51–52.

Chapter 6

1. In the framework of Mantegazza's concern with public health and well-being, gymnastics is a crucial topic in his imaginary fourth millennium, as much as in the Italian way of life he strove to promote during his lifetime. His pioneering campaigns for physical well-being deserve as much attention as do those of the two figures who are currently remembered as the fathers of the Italian sports and gymnastic movement, Angelo Mosso and Emilio Baumann.

2. "To feed the flame."

Chapter 7

1. Ubaldino Peruzzi (1822–91) was a moderate Tuscan politician who supported the cause of Italy's unification and became one of the first ministers of the Kingdom of Italy. As the mayor of Florence from 1870 to 1875, and in several other capacities, he played a pivotal role in the life of the city and is still remembered with a statue in the Florentine Piazza dell'Indipendenza. Peruzzi's wife turned their home into an important salon that brought together leading writers and intellectuals.

Chapter 8

1. Baron Joseph Lister (1827–1912) was a British surgeon who introduced phenol for the sterilization of surgical instruments and the cleaning of wounds, hence successfully promoting safer surgery and reducing postoperative infections.

2. "Röntgen light" refers to X-ray technology, deriving its name from the German physicist Wilhelm Röntgen, who discovered this new form of radiation in 1895.

3. From its attempt to act not only upon physical pain but also upon moral suffering, the *algophobus* seems to be a precursor of what at the end of the novel will be Paolo's prize-winning psychoscope, which, more radically, will even *prevent* moral illness.

4. Mantegazza here seems conscious of one of the main features of the cognitive approach of his own time, namely, the lack of specialization. His own eclecticism can be seen as a corollary of the absence of boundaries between disciplines that characterizes the epoch of positivism. Interestingly, however, Mantegazza understands the inevitability of and even the need for paradigm shifts, hence foreseeing different tendencies that will characterize future intellectual panoramas.

5. This is another instance where, curiously, Mantegazza's predictions go in the direction opposite the actual course of events in the medical and pharmacological sectors, despite his expertise in the field.

6. In Bellamy's *Looking Backward* too money is replaced by cards. However, while in Mantegazza's United Planetary States the value of the new currency is assigned by a selected committee case by case, in Bellamy's work the government issues a yearly "credit card" (Bellamy was the first to use the term) to each citizen, for an amount "corresponding to his share of the annual product of the nation" (94), following a principle of wealth distribution that values all labor equally. H. G. Wells would soon invert this trend with his reconceptualization of "utopian economics." After reminding us of the recurring absence of money in traditional ideal worlds from Plato to Bellamy, Wells reinstates the importance of money, coin symbolism, and gold currency, hence reopening the question of a standard of value (*Modern* 74) beyond what Wells dismisses as the failure of previous credit measures (with a clear allusion to Bellamy).

7. In the footsteps of Souvestre, Mantegazza is here imagining proto-air-conditioning systems.

8. The different and unreconciled reactions to the elimination of unfit babies staged in this chapter well epitomize the novel's open questioning of this crucial crossroads of scientific and ethical concerns. With terms ranging from "horrors" to "fascinated," from "terrible scene" to "pitiful operation" and later "true act of pity," Maria, Paolo, the narrator, and the Hygeian create a poignant plurality of visions inviting readers to take sides according to their individual sensitivity.

Chapter 9
1. This is equal to one hundredth of an Italian lira.

Chapter 10

1. Echoing the famous prison conceived by the English philosopher Jeremy Bentham in 1785, Mantegazza's "Panopticon" applies the rationale of Bentham's original building to a quite different context. Whereas Bentham's prison was conceived in such a way that all prisoners could be observed without being aware, the idea of the panopticon applied to the theater of Andropolis instead brings to the foreground the audience's opportunity to watch virtually any kind of spectacle, thanks to the surprising richness of the offerings.

2. This unidentified "I" does not belong to any of the characters in the novel, but rather to the narrator, who now intervenes in the first person, hence erasing the distance between the year 3000 (Paolo's and Maria's present, which is also the reader's) and the nineteenth-century temporal context within which Mantegazza's act of writing occurred. Furthermore, this authorial interference (whether intentional or involuntary) breaks the realistic framework within which the protagonists are acting, bringing to the foreground the subjective component at which the title hints with its reference to a dream. It hence reinforces the notion that all these adventures should be considered, after all, the author's own dream. Other instances of the narrator's "I" can be found on pages 98, 140, 163, 173, 177, 186, and 187.

3. Souvestre too devoted an entire chapter of *The World as It Shall Be* to the theater performances of his futuristic world, but his main intent was to parody the styles, themes, and effects of the genres of his time and of the melodrama in particular (169–90; nn. 2, 4, 7, p. 244). The short descriptions of the plays at Mantegazza's Panopticon offer a synthetic survey of the main spectacles and theatrical forms across centuries, but with no evident satiric intent. The main effect seems intended, rather, to highlight the variety and abundance of options, appealing to an audience with quite diverse interests.

4. As also substantiated by the contextual explanations about the purpose of the instrument, the Italian term created by Mantegazza—*estesiometro*—emphasizes precisely the ability to measure and regulate sensations. In the recent French edition of the novel, however, the term is incorrectly translated as *extasiomètre*, which takes *ecstasis* rather than *aisthesis* as its root, hence missing the main purpose of the instrument. See Paolo Mantegazza, *L'an 3000*, trans. and intro. Raymond Trousson (Paris: L'Harmattan, 2003), 138. The variable intensities of different sensations made possible by the interactive technology of Mantegazza's "aesthesiometer" create special effects that recall the virtual reality of IMAX theaters, which, however, act only on hearing and vision, not yet on the sense of smell. In the late nineteenth century the theater as a means of entertainment and of communication inspired

rather creative devices, especially in connection with the invention of the telephone (first patented by Graham Bell in 1876 but previously introduced between 1849 and 1854 by Antonio Meucci, who intended to patent it in 1871). For instance, in 1881 France offered a subscription to the "theatrophone," which allowed people to listen to plays, operas, or concerts in their homes or from public booths, thanks to telephone connections with theaters. See Robert Chesnais, "Introduction," *Au XIXème siècle; la journée d'un journaliste américain en 2889. Suivi par Le Humbug. Mœurs américains*, by Jules Verne (Paris: Nautilus, 2001), 19–20.

Chapter 11

1. The ordering principle of Andropolis's museum seems the opposite of what Mantegazza described for his ideal and never completed "Psychological Museum," where he intended to collect material that would represent variations of psychic attitudes across nations, cultures, and races, instead of creating compartmentalized units. For details on the museum's collection see Edoardo Pardini and Sandra Mainardi, "Il Museo Psicologico di Paolo Mantegazza," and Sara Ciruzzi, "Le collezioni del Museo Psicologico di Paolo Mantegazza a cento anni dalla sua inaugurazione," both in *Archivio per l'antropologia e l'etnologia* 121 (1991): 137–84, 185–202.

2. Maurice and Marthe in Souvestre's *The World as It Shall Be* also visit a natural science museum. However, the narrator expresses a different standpoint on the relation between the laws of nature and the intervention of science. In Souvestre's world, due to the progress of crossbreeding and the law of utility, species are no longer connected with the original divine creation: "Most of the creatures made by him no longer existed except in the form science had given them. His work of creation had been put in a flask with alcohol and handed over to the taxidermist" (126). Although both writers adopt similar terms, Souvestre's criticism of the manipulation of sacred nature by the advancement of knowledge becomes, in Mantegazza, support of the noble service that science provides to cognitive progress.

3. Behind the narrator's description of photography applied to the scholarly and educational purposes of science and the museum lies Mantegazza's own pioneering work in the domain of photography. The first president of the Italian Photographic Society, Mantegazza was one of the very first to introduce this new representative and documentary technique into the field of anthropology.

4. The *Cuon Alpinus*, or dhole, is a kind of wild dog to be found in Southern Asia, currently threatened with extinction.

5. These references to angel-like beings recall the two winged creatures at the end of Ghislanzoni's *Abrakadabra*, "Rondine" and "Lucarino" (215), who, after the catastrophic flood that sweeps away the earth's civilization, mark the beginning of a new era. This may also owe a debt to Souvestre's "three avenging angels" (*World* 231), who accompany the destruction of the earth and the human race at the end of the novel before a new world rises from the ruins. Paolo's prosaic scientific explanation, which ridicules these grotesque "planetary supermen" (172), is also an implicit parody of his predecessors, who closed their novels with equally bizarre images. Likewise the overall realistic tone of Mantegazza's scientific imagination and its rather optimistic outlook on humankind in the fourth millennium set up an intriguing contrast between *The Year* 3000 and the more recent *Battlefield Earth: A Saga of the Year* 3000 (1982), by L. Ron Hubbard, who depicts endangered human beings desperately fighting against gas-breathing, nine-foot-tall brutal conquerors from the planet Psychlos.

6. Paul Gustave Doré (1832–83), a French engraver, sculptor, and illustrator, was famous for his illustrations of major masterpieces including the English Bible, Dante's *Divine Comedy*, Milton's *Paradise Lost*, Cervantes's *Don Quixote*, Edgar Allan Poe's *The Raven*, Coleridge's *The Rime of the Ancient Mariner*, and Tennyson's *The Idylls of the King*.

7. These patriotic observations about the endurance of Italy's cultural and aesthetic primacy in the fourth millennium project into the future Mantegazza's frequent claims about his country's unrivalled artistic patrimony and taste for the beautiful. See his many earlier works discussing his "ethnography of the beautiful," including *Epicuro*, *Dizionario delle cose belle*, and *Lezioni di antropologia*.

8. Here Mantegazza vents against the art of his time and in particular against Gabriele D'Annunzio, the most outstanding Italian exponent of aestheticism and of the literary decadent movement, reinforcing negative evaluations he had already expressed in other writings. In fact, however, all this hostility does not eclipse the many elements that Mantegazza and D'Annunzio share, starting precisely from their common attraction to the beautiful and their lofty and flowery prose. For a discussion of the ambivalent relationship between Mantegazza and D'Annunzio see Nicoletta Pireddu, "Ethnos / Hedonē / Ethos: Paolo Mantegazza, antropologo delle passioni," *Antropologi alla corte della bellezza: Decadenza ed economia simbolica nell'Europa fin de siècle* (Verona: Fiorini, 2002), 131–84.

Chapter 12

1. This is yet another example of the dialogical technique that Mantegazza adopts to convey his message about a crucial situation or principle at stake. While Maria shows an unflinching belief in the cult of hope, Paolo declares his absolute indifference to it. The narrator's remarks provide a compromise between these two extremes. He shows, rather than tells, his endorsement of hope by lingering on the description of the temple and the values it represents and highlights the importance of individual feelings. Significantly Paolo himself will soon admit being emotionally taken by the ambiance, and after reaching the conclusion that science and rational knowledge cannot stop the drive to believe and to hope, he will recognize the influence of the infinite, which, like Mantegazza himself, he interprets as "the highest summits of human ideality" (182) and hence not necessarily religious but rather expressing a broader attraction to idealism and spirituality.

2. The pronaos is the open vestibule in front of a Greek or Roman temple.

3. This is a reflection of Mantegazza's anticlerical vision, aimed above all against what for him is the hypocrisy and the corruption of the clergy. Yet this does not invalidate the possibility of or need for belief in nonmaterialist and spiritual ideals. Once again Souvestre comes to mind, with his "National Church" significantly situated in "an old auction room" (*World* 226) and represented by a priest who concludes his sermon "with a national directive on the advantages of growing rutabagas and cultivating the silkworm" (226).

4. Just as the "second Michelangelo" refers to a replica of the world-famous artist Michelangelo Buonarroti, here the "second Donatello" is supposed to emulate the noted early Renaissance Italian sculptor Donato di Niccolò di Betto Bardi (c. 1386–1466). These figures are both worldwide icons of Italian art, and Mantegazza here keeps them alive, although Italy's past is buried in the fourth millennium.

5. Interestingly *Il Dio ignoto* (The Unknown God) is also the title of one of Mantegazza's novels, where this deity, however, refers not to the vague divine figure of the Deists but rather to the doctrine of epicureanism.

6. In Dante Alighieri's *Inferno* (III: 28–29) "un tumulto, il qual s'aggira / sempre in quell'aura sanza tempo tinta"—"a tumult that will whirl / forever through that turbid, timeless air" (trans. Allen Mandelbaum)—recalls Dante's first sight of the Gate of Hell, with its famous injunction to all who enter to abandon hope—in obvious contrast to the imperative *Sperate* (Hope) carved over the Temple of Hope earlier in this chapter.

Chapter 13

1. The complex, mysterious, and urgent questions of the end of Mante-gazza's nineteenth century and fourth millennium are not so much scientific issues connected to the physical forces of our planet (here represented by John Newton, an obvious evocation of Isaac Newton) or the astronomical discoveries of other planets (of which Carlo Copernic—recalling Nicolaus Copernicus—is here the spokesperson), but rather, the secrets of the psyche. Freud's theories would gain ground in a few years, but already in Mante-gazza's "science of thought," which Paolo Fortunati promises to aid with his psychoscope, we find the premises of what will become the analysis of the least perceptible and most disturbing parts of our self.

2. This avowed priority of moral over intellectual progress for the pro-motion of human happiness is also effective to grasp the difference between Mantegazza's and Verne's scientific priorities. For instance, unlike the jury's motivation in awarding Paolo's cosmic prize in *The Year 3000*, Ruhmkorff in *Journey to the Center of the Earth* is remembered as the awardee of a prize for the invention of the induction coil, a device extolled for its purely scientific merits. See Jules Verne, *Journey to the Centre of the Earth*, intro. David Brin (New York: Random House 2003), 54–55.

To order or obtain more information
on these or other University
of Nebraska Press titles, visit
www.nebraskapress.unl.edu.

PROPERTY OF
SENECA COLLEGE
LIBRARIES
KING CAMPUS